The SECRETS of the Montebellis

The Secrets of the Montebellis Series
Book One
Second Edition

CHERYL COLWELL

INSPIRED FICTION BOOKS

The Secrets of the Montebellis

PUBLISHED BY INSPIRED FICTION BOOKS
www.inspiredfictionbooks.com

ISBN: 978-0-9892371-1-6
Printed in the United States of America

Category: Fiction/Suspense

Dedications

To my mother and number one fan,
for your love and faith in me.
To my children for cheering me on
to pursue my dream.
I love you all.

Chapter 1

Heart pounding, Lisa Richards forced herself to ignore the familiar warning signs. Her voice trembled, "Thomas, I *need* this."

He backhanded the air, just missing her face. "I provide all of this, and this is how you repay me?"

She flinched. "Repay you?" She wanted to scream the words, but his glare withered her courage. Dropping her tearing eyes to the plush carpet, she pretended acquiescence. *Why did he behave like this*? More importantly, how much longer could she live like this? He seemed to grow worse by the month.

A quick glance upward caught a smug smile tugging at his lips. *He was enjoying this*? Heat advanced up her neck and something snapped. *Enough*. Her hands clenched. With our without his permission, she would build her dreams.

"Are you coming? I don't want to be late." He pushed through the door to the garage into the pre-dawn, his bicycle secured in the back of their truck.

Without answering, she grabbed her purse and the notebook sandwiched inside a fashion magazine and followed him. On the trip to the bike race at Mont Castello, electricity filled the cab of their truck. Her fingers massaged the tightness behind her breastbone. Their time in the beautiful mountain town should be enjoyable, but her heart harbored twenty-nine years of resentment.

While Thomas rode the hills, she set aside the magazine and made sketches in the notebook, delighted to have this quiet time to herself. After hours, she watched him wheel his bike toward her.

"Great ride! Beat Denny this year."

"Good for you," she said. They walked in silence toward the restaurant for dinner. As they approached, she studied the architecture. A thin smile of appreciation softened her lips, relaxing the relentless tension. Hand-chiseled stonework gave the building the authentic look of old Italy. She climbed the stairs and touched one of the rough timbers that had supported the structure for a century of winters. Embedded in the earth, it claimed as much permanence as the surrounding fir trees, their roots stretched deep into the rich, dark soil.

A crowd hovered on the porch. Thomas grabbed her hand, pushed in past the waiting customers, and jerked the heavy wooden door open. Avoiding the sea of indignant frowns, Lisa focused on the massive tapestries of Italian street scenes that adorned the amber-toned plaster of the walls.

"I'm *Dr.* Richards," Thomas announced, loud enough to turn heads. "I have a reservation. Now." The distracted young hostess recoiled from his expression, checked her list, and rushed them through the dining room. She seated them at a table situated three feet from the booth of an attractive man with silver-streaked hair and intelligent eyes. Thomas sat down in the chair on the far side, leaving her with the intriguing stranger to her left.

"Would you like to order a drink while you decide?" A lazy southern drawl tinged the woman's voice.

Lisa opened her mouth to decline, but Thomas cut in. "Sweetheart, bring us a bottle of your best Merlot."

Watching her husband's attention follow the curvy waitress, Lisa's lips tightened, and she fixated on the menu. The last time she'd expressed her anger at his wandering eyes, he'd twisted her words, leaving her feeling humiliated. But she was not the fool he assumed her to be.

***

Steven Taylor waited in a comfortable booth when a loud voice jerked his attention toward the front door of Varano's restaurant. A pompous man announced himself as Dr. Richards and demanded his table. A lovely woman followed him, head bowed, avoiding the resentful faces staring at them. Her striking blue eyes caught Taylor's and darted away.

He studied her. The summer sun had darkened her olive skin, creating a contrast to the white and orange flowers of her sleeveless blouse. Soft black hair, cut short, accentuated the brightness of her lips. The hostess led them to a nearby table. After years of covering news stories and writing investigative reports, Taylor possessed an uncanny insight into reading people. These two seemed at opposite ends of the happiness spectrum.

Their waitress asked for a drink order. The woman was about to reply, but the doctor interrupted. Her lips closed without protest, and she worked to cover a frown as he gawked at the waitress.

Was this her husband? They appeared to be of similar age—fiftyish. His salt and pepper hair was clean-cut, while his angular jaw jutted out slightly. His small stature and muscled thighs resembled the European riders in the *Tour de France.*

The doctor downed his first glass of wine and became talkative. He refilled his glass and raised it, "To a great day, Lisa." She gave him a thin smile, clinked his glass, and sat hers down. Untouched.

So, her name is Lisa, and she doesn't like Merlot. He shook his head. Relationships were trouble. Taking another drink, Taylor lowered his glass. Sports writing for *USA Cycle Magazine* was his dream job. Since the fiasco with his ex-wife, his job had afforded the diversion he needed, providing great backdrops of cities and towns from which to compose his articles.

His first assignment had been to the northwest for the Portland Bridge Ride in Oregon. He always took a photographer from the magazine to capture the zest of the events. The portraits of the colorful cyclists crossing the bridges in Portland were extraordinary.

He bit into a piece of garlic bread and glimpsed the pine trees through the front window. Holed up here for the last two days had given him time to explore Mont Castello. He knew that the photographs taken of this area would be even more dramatic.

"No, no, no!" A stern female voice caught Taylor's attention. By the front door, two red-faced cyclists worked to remove their clipped shoes. Holding onto each other's shoulders for support, they laughed and swayed precariously until they accomplished their task and walked in socks through the restaurant on the oak floor.

"Hope you have better balance in the saddle," an obnoxious competitor smirked. Though not a race, the Summit Challenge was fiercely competitive.

Taylor ignored the squabble and began a draft of his article while he waited at his table:

The Summit Challenge comprises three steep ascents, climbing a total of 22,000 feet. The cyclists will reach heights packed with snow, even in August.

He thumped his pen and recounted the day's ride, then scribbled:

On day one, riders streaked down, reaching speeds above 40 miles per hour as they navigated the curving road on their descent to the verdant valley below. The sharp, majestic crags rising above the trees were breathtaking, while wide spans of concrete bridges lunged out over whitewater rapids in the giant rivers. The green of the pine forest and red bark of the madrone trees hung behind the circus of colors emblazoned on the rider's jerseys.

Rereading his notes, he nodded. *Not bad.*

Varano's Italian Restaurant was packed. Taylor watched the hungry cyclists devouring pasta, salad, bread—anything to help replace the 3,000 or so calories burned since 5:30 this morning.

His eyes followed Signora Varano, the owner of the restaurant. She stood like an anchor amid the teaming bustle and clanging of heavy china and glass. A frown on her lips deepened while her ebony eyes watched the youthful hostess ignoring new customers and rushing others in an attempt to get her job done.

"Maria," the signora whispered at the frantic girl. "Slow down. Smile. Be courteous."

The young woman halted and exhaled. "Thank you, Grand Anna." She invited the new arrivals to follow her past Taylor's table.

"Taylor." An auburn-haired beauty waved a hand in front of his face.

He spun his head around and focused on the young woman's perfectly formed features. A broad grin covered his face and he stood to embrace his most precious treasure. "Asia, you look beautiful." He held her hand as she sat opposite him in the red leather booth.

She leaned over the table and kissed him on the cheek. "It's so good to see you." She sat back, tucking a strand of her long, dark hair behind her ear.

Taylor gazed at her. Asia was 26, beautiful and brilliant. She had achieved her master's degree and worked for a major architectural firm in Portland. "Who would have thought our careers would land us in the same area," he said.

"I know. You are usually on the other side of the world. Now we get to spend a few days together." She grinned with pleasure.

"What are you working on?"

"An urban renewal program. It's a great career boost."

***

Lisa followed Thomas' stare to the attractive young woman who had just arrived and now spoke with the equally arresting man who stood to greet her. She called him *Taylor.* Dark lashes highlighted his deep brown eyes. A quick glance upward revealed that he was a massive man, nearing 6'4.

Glimpsing his vibrant grin and their affectionate embrace, Lisa's throat thickened. Life was a constant reminder that Thomas' interest had faded years ago, along with any tenderness he might have had.

Stifling a sigh, she grasped for assurance. Her dreams were coming true, her vision taking shape. Yet, every inch of forward movement had cost her. Only Thomas' vanity allowed her to succeed in taking a part-time job. After a colleague remarked about his *control* problem, Thomas began to flaunt her, "freedom do whatever she pleases."

While working as a receptionist at the Verina Fields Real Estate Agency, an opportunity had presented itself, allowing her to participate in a much grander scheme than she could have imagined. However, it was a high-risk proposition and the businessman she dealt with caused her stomach to twist in knots. Staying optimistic, she continued to ignore the red flags.

She gulped her water, eyes darting toward Thomas. Like a mother bear hiding her cub from its murderous father, she remained vigilant in keeping her activities concealed. He monitored her time, scrutinized her comments. Across the table, his eyes studied her. She hid a nervous swallow and focused on the waitress heading their way.

Their server placed a plate of pasta in front of her, creating the diversion she needed from his scrutiny. She dipped into the lasagna, bringing the hot, stringy cheese to her mouth. The scent of warm garlic butter wafted up from the breadbasket and filled the air.

While Thomas recapped his day, Lisa caught glimpses of Taylor holding the hand of the beautiful woman. Envy gripped Lisa's heart as she listened to *Asia* talk about the work she was doing. Taylor lavished her with praise. Frustration tugged at her lips Through the years, Thomas had painted a demeaning portrait of her with their friends. His comments chipped at her self-confidence, but she was proving her worth, week by week.

The blond waitress refilled their water glasses while Thomas related the vivid details of a crash. "We were streaking down the mountain, hit a hairpin turn and, bang, right in front of us lay a downed rider. The guy must have skidded on the gravel. He was in a world of hurt. Our whole group braked, slid our tails back and dodged any way we could."

Lisa's head jerked upward as Taylor stepped to their table. "Please excuse my interruption. I'm Steven Taylor from *USA Cycle Magazine*." He held out his hand to Thomas.

Lisa studied the face of the stranger. He was attractive—not pretty like a *GQ* guy, but strong and solid. His manner suggested sophistication, yet he was casual and disarming.

He smiled at her and continued. "I overheard your reference to the crash today and would like to interview you. Can we set up a time to talk?"

Thomas' exuberance was apparent as he shook the big man's hand. "I am Dr. Thomas Richard. I'll be riding during the day but will be back here tomorrow night for dinner. Will that work?"

"Tomorrow night would be great, if it's not too imposing on your company." Taylor's eyes focused on Lisa.

Her mouth opened to respond, but Thomas cut in. "Not at all. This is my wife, she'll be fine with it."

Taylor didn't acknowledge him. Realizing he was waiting for her response, Lisa answered with a hasty smile, "I'd be pleased to have you and your guest join us." She glanced over at Asia.

"I'm sorry," Asia spoke to the group, "but tomorrow I have business to manage, so he's on his own."

Thomas looked back at Taylor, "Well then, does 6:00 suit you, Steven?"

"I'll be here and, please, call me *Taylor*." He sat back down with Asia and continued their conversation.

Thomas finished his meal and headed outside to recount the day's events with his friends.

She kept her eyes on her food, ignoring the friendly banter around her, and finished eating alone. When the server brought the check to the table, Lisa glanced out the front window, took out her credit card, and paid the bill. Catching Taylor's stare, her face reddened. His eyes searched her face, threatening to expose the mixture of emotions lodged there.

She bristled at the intrusion into the complexities of her life. Jerking her eyes downward, she left the restaurant, but could feel his gaze follow her. Instantly, she regretted tomorrow's dinner arrangements.

She drove their tan truck the twenty miles down to the valley with Thomas' expensive road bike anchored in the back. His animated talk died down as the effects of an eighty-mile ride at altitude drained his body of its last bit of energy.

The curving mountain road soothed her tension. In the distance beyond Bella Vista, she recognized the small cluster of lights that belonged to the town of Tangle Grove and her mood lifted. Her thoughts were her own now and she reflected on how far her dream had come.

Her family had played a major part in the history of Tangle Grove, and she wanted to be a part of the town's development. It was becoming a charming place that befitted its heritage. Thanks to the involvement of the Montebelli Corporation, she could participate in an important way—if the corporation lived up to its promises.

Thomas snorted in his sleep, and she jumped. He hated anything to do with her family heritage or Tangle Grove. But this was her business. Tomorrow would be a landmark day in her career. Through careful plotting, secrecy, and, unfortunately, lies, she had succeeded in concealing her involvement from Thomas.

She gripped the wheel tighter. Even thinking about her ventures this close to him felt precarious. This project was all she had. At any moment, his discovery could lead to her emotional, and financial, ruin.

Chapter 2

A knot of excitement sat stubbornly in Lisa's stomach as she calculated the day's plans and attempted to eat breakfast.

"I *expect* you to be on time for dinner tonight," Thomas scowled.

His curt remark infuriated her—even more so because he had a reason to complain. Lately, everything seemed to be speeding up, screaming for her attention. Grabbing his jacket, he stomped out the door and headed for the second day of his ride in Mont Castello. As soon as he'd gone, she raced to put the house in order before her meeting, slamming the door as she left.

In no time, she arrived at the humble courthouse in Tangle Grove. The building, used for civic meetings, measured barely twenty by thirty feet and had a worn wooden floor that creaked under the weight of even the slightest visitor. Mold grew silently in the corners, under the wood trim, and especially in the dark closets. It grew, invisible to the eye, but there was no mistaking the odor.

This structure was one of the first problems the Priority Committee had decided to address. Though the building was small and old, it anchored the town, stating its importance, if not its squatters' rights. Long before any of the current residents, it had cloistered outlaws and witnesses beneath its sagging roofline. And listened to generations of gossip.

From the front of the courthouse, Lisa glanced back down Maple Street, the main road that entered Tangle Grove from the Strada del Vino, the *Wine Road.* The lynchpin in her design was the two-story commercial building that sat across the street on the right. It housed a café and insurance company, with two apartments on the second story. She grinned and imagined the other new buildings that would flank the rest of the main commercial street.

Taking a deep breath, she turned the door handle to go inside and found the room already occupied. She halted. Jim Cook, the mayor of Tangle Grove, was moving chairs to help ready the room for Asia, the young woman from the restaurant last night.

Lisa's temporary confusion surged back to envy. It was Lisa's project Asia had described to Steven Taylor. Angst tensed her lips, but she forced a smile and reached out her hand. "Hello, I'm Lisa Richards."

Asia returned her smile and extended her delicate hand. "Asia Taylor. I'm pleased to formally meet you. What a coincidence meeting at the restaurant."

"It's a small world here," Lisa answered. A warning voice whispered, *too small to keep secrets.*

At that moment, three of the four other Design Team members bolted through the door with noisy chatter. Mari Harris, an artist, had a gift for visualizing and communicating ideas. Mari had owned her own home in Tangle Grove for years. Though presently exhibiting her work at a gallery in Bella Vista, she held visions of making Tangle Grove a thriving art town.

Gale Wallace was born in this small town seventy-nine years earlier. Her appearance brought visions of a pioneer woman—stocky and weathered, with wiry hair like the proverbial old grey mare. She and her husband, John, worked the farm his family had homesteaded on Old Mine Road.

It was Gale's expressed concern that the area must retain its country flavor and not end up like Bella Vista. Though convinced of the need for a stable economy and dependable jobs for the townspeople, she made it clear she would stand against any attempts to transform the community into a place, "...where people can't afford to own their own homes and the taxes are so high, young families can't afford to live."

Lisa's son, Jesse, the last member of the Design Team and the only other man, followed them in. Gale was lecturing him. "I just don't see why a smart young man like yerself can't find anything better to do than bartend for all them tourists in Bella Vista."

Jesse cast a patient grin. "Hey, it gives me time to get out on the river during the day."

At twenty-seven, Jesse's lack of direction worried Lisa. Growing up and working in Bella Vista, and now financially limited to a small studio in an old building in Tangle Grove, Jesse seemed excited to be involved in the transformation of his new home.

She caught his eyes and smiled. He was handsome like Thomas, but stockier like his grandfather, Jess, from whom he had inherited his blue eyes that sparkled with humor. When he reached her, a smile flashed across his face. *He is irresistible*, she thought as they hugged.

Her arms released him when she noticed his attention extend beyond her to the rear of the room. She knew he had spotted Asia. "Don't even bother. She's got an older man waiting for her back up in Mont Castello." The information didn't seem to faze him, and he left to introduce himself to the auburn-haired *goddess.*

"Hello, I'm Jesse Richards."

Asia stuttered. Lisa couldn't blame her. Jesse's blue eyes, combined with the charm he exuded, caught her off-guard. Asia grasped his outstretched hand. "I'm Asia Taylor," she smiled and held his gaze.

In Lisa's opinion, the eye contact lasted longer than necessary. "May I help you finish setting up?"

Asia and Jesse started. Asia withdrew her hand, turned toward her briefcase, and pulled out her computer. Jesse cast his mother a quizzical look. She indicated with her eyes that they would have a conversation later.

After that shaky start, Asia appeared determined to win them over with the professionalism of her graphics. During the meeting, she used a 3-D model and a computerized slide show for her presentation, narrating each frame with finesse.

In spite of the internal turmoil Lisa was experiencing, she couldn't help but be impressed and forced her focus onto the reason they were all here.

With her first presentation, Asia captured the heart of what Lisa had envisioned. Tangle Grove had been a pioneering town. It boasted an authentic opal mine, waterfalls, farms, vineyards, and a local farmer's market. The *feel* of the area was different from Bella Vista.

Lisa hoped they could capture just as much charm, but in their own way.

What Asia proposed was a two-story downtown area in an *old town* style. Not the old western type, but more like a Main Street, USA. The sketches illustrated charming settings that made you want to visit or live in Tangle Grove.

The excitement stirring in the room let Asia know she had nailed it. Beaming as hearty praises of agreement flew her way, she continued to answer questions, many from Lisa on behalf of the Montebelli Corporation.

Gale Wallace had tears in her old eyes as she walked around to shake Asia's hand. "I just want ya to know how much this means to me and many of us who grew up here." She choked with emotion. "We all consider this a special place, but never had the know-how or the money to build it the way we knew it should'a been done. This is really gonna be somethin'."

She turned to Lisa. "Thank ya fer all yer hard work. And fer gettin' that corporation to take yer advice and pour the money into Tangle Grove." She squinted. "Yer sure we can trust these outsiders?"

Lisa nodded, flitting her eyes away. "Thank you, Gale. I'm sure they'll do well by us."

***

The rest of the day was a breeze. Lisa left the meeting with her heart soaring and drove down Maple Street to Siebert's farm and stopped. If all went according to the plan the corporation's attorney laid out, she could end up owning the farm outright. She yearned to trust his word more than anything she had ever desired.

She'd first contacted the Sieberts on behalf of the Montebelli Corporation. Their house was little more than twelve hundred square feet. Located on ten acres, the property was in dismal shape when she found it. Three or four generations of the family had lived there at intervals or all at once. They had been anxious to sell it.

The first day she'd inspected the property, she saw why. Garage sale finds lived among the overgrown weeds and untamed old roses that imposed themselves at will. Remnants of a vineyard struggled to produce grapes on untended vines that rambled along the ground.

Near the corner of the property, a formidable barn stood with boards missing here and there. One large barn door hung precariously by its corner, a gust of wind causing it to bang against the siding. She touched the old square foundation stones that had borne the weight of this forty-foot structure for ninety or a hundred years, maybe more.

Gazing upward, she felt awed by the large center beam still supported by massive crossbeams, set on even more massive vertical posts. The whole feel was that of an upside-down ship. She knew the story of the architect, her great-great-grandfather, the Dutch ship builder.

Grandma Klara had loved telling the stories about him to Lisa and her cousins over and over. "When Jochum Van Buren, emigrated from Holland, the only work he could find was building barns, which he saw as ships rolled upside down." Lisa smiled with pride. While other designs had broken down over time, the Dutchman's continued standing strong.

Restarting the car, she drove toward her home in Bella Vista. The small town rested at the south end of a narrow valley created by large mountains on one side and smaller peaks on the other. Views of three and four mountain ranges rose in all directions. Overtaken by affluent residents, the gently sloping hills in between were sprinkled with expensive villas surrounded by vineyards.

Arriving in town, she passed the shops and restaurants that catered to the tastes of their discriminating customers. Creativity abounded, making her glad all over again that her dad had encouraged her to move back after college.

She checked her watch and her stomach knotted. There was barely enough time to change and meet Thomas for dinner in Mont Castello. He would love it if she were late.

Racing home and up to her room, she pulled off her work clothes and raised the lid to the laundry basket. Before she could drop her slacks in, however, she spied a piece of paper protruding from the jersey Thomas had worn yesterday. The name, *Christie,* and a phone number were written in delicate handwriting on a napkin.

Her hand flew to her breastbone and massaged the new pain that stabbed her chest. "Just great." Her eyes watered as she tugged on a soft blue blouse and zipped up cool summer slacks. She wasn't looking forward to keeping up a pretense while Steven Taylor scrutinized her failing marriage. Tonight, it would be harder than ever to put on a *happy face*. Just a little longer.

The trip from Bella Vista to Mont Castello helped to settle her. Always beautiful, the winding road curved its way up the mountain range, the terrain changing as it gained elevation. Fresh air blew in through the window, laced with the smell of pine trees.

Her new sedan slid into a parking space on a side street near Varano's Restaurant. She planned to sit in the background while the men talked about cycling. Thomas said the ride would end around 5:30 and he would meet her here a half hour later. The clock read six o'clock when she entered through the front door of the restaurant. Lips tight, she checked out the full lobby, hoping not to run into the woman who might be *Christie*.

The owner, Signora Varano, greeted her with her heavy Italian accent. "Welcome to Varano's. One for dinner?"

"No, actually I'm meeting my husband." Sweeping the room behind the rounded figure of the owner, her eyes met Steven Taylor's. He sat in a booth with one arm draped over the back cushion, watching her. Her stomach pitched. *Blast.* She turned toward the owner and smiled to gain time to compose herself. "Thank you. I see my party." She lifted her chin and walked over to the booth.

Hello, Mr. Taylor." She reached out to shake his hand.

"Taylor, please." He stood and returned the gesture. Turning toward the booth, he motioned for her to sit down.

"Have you been waiting long?" she asked.

"Not at all. My first interview finished a few minutes ago."

***

Taylor was glad things had worked out like this. Watching Lisa interact with her husband the night before had raised his curiosity. Her non-reaction to Thomas' rudeness seemed to contradict the strength he sensed. "Would you like to order something to drink while we wait?".

"Thank you. I'll have a glass of iced tea."

"What, no Merlot?".

"I don't care for Merlot." She tilted her head. "Sometimes my husband forgets things when he's excited about something—this bike ride, for example."

The waitress took their order, and he decided it was time to find out more. "So, what do you do?"

She paused for a moment. "A little bit of this and that. My son is grown, but I still have a home to take care of in Bella Vista, and I work part time."

"I haven't made it down to Bella Vista yet. What kind of work do you do?" Something flashed across her eyes, but not so fast that he didn't catch it.

"I work at a real estate office in town."

"So, you're a realtor?" That would make sense. She exhibited personal charisma, was attractive and intelligent.

"No. I, um, work in the office."

"Hmm." He saw her more as a broker or owner.

She frowned at his reaction. Resentment tainted her response. "Like I said, a little of this and a little of that."

The waitress brought their drinks and Lisa turned the attention away from her life. "How long have you been a writer?"

"The last dozen years or so. I live in Arizona now, but before that I owned my own corporation in Nevada." He watched her give a small, almost imperceptible start. He followed this lead. "Do you have business in Nevada?"

"No," she answered quickly. "A client at the agency was just talking about Nevada."

Taylor could always spot a lie and now his interest was in uncovering more, but not too fast. He sensed a growing hesitancy on her part, so he continued about himself.

"When my wife *met* someone else, we divorced, and the court ordered half of my holdings to go to her. There was no way I could run a business with half of the equipment. So, I sold out and paid her off. I foundered a bit while I looked for a new career that I could enjoy and didn't tie me down. After a few years, I settled on writing."

***

Lisa appreciated his openness. "I'm sorry about your loss. Did you have any children with her?"

"I have a great daughter," he answered with obvious pride. "You met her here last night."

Lisa had just taken a sip of iced tea when Taylor's remark caused her to inhale and choke. He instinctively smacked her on the back a couple of times until she was able to get control of her coughing. As she did, she began to laugh. Taylor looked baffled until she was able to speak again.

She explained, "She is your daughter?"

"Yes," he answered, still not understanding, until it dawned on him. "Did you think she was my lover?"

"Yes—or your wife," she confessed. "You and Asia both have the same last name, so I made the assumption."

"So you thought, 'Here's this dirty old man with this gorgeous young thing,' huh?" he teased.

She laughed again. "I'm afraid so."

Once again, a perplexed look came across his features and he asked, "How did you know her last name was *Taylor*?"

Lisa realized she was getting into a corner. "Oh, we were in a meeting together in Tangle Grove this morning."

A look of surprise crossed his face as he tried to assimilate this new piece of information. "That's Asia's new project. What were you doing there?"

The inference that it was Asia's project struck a raw chord. Lisa had worked far longer on the Tangle Grove plans than the beautiful newcomer. Coupled with her growing anxiety, she blurted, "Sometimes they let me in on the important meetings."

He back peddled. "Hold on. I didn't mean to infer anything. I was just surprised by the coincidence."

She grew hot with embarrassment. "I'm sorry. I had no right to vent my frustrations on you. I've just been under a lot of pressure lately."

He nodded and studied her for a moment. "I'm always fascinated by people's dreams. Tell me about your ambitions."

She hesitated, considering the question, but a deep voice from over her shoulder interrupted them.

"Lisa's ambitions are taking care of me," Thomas interjected as he joined them. "Good evening," he said, reaching across the table to shake hands with Taylor.

Lisa's head jerked up. *How long had he been standing there?* She quickly reviewed any of the conversation he might have heard and moved farther into the booth so he could sit down. Working to calm her nerves, she put on a smile and tried to dodge Taylor's eyes as they darted back and forth between her and Thomas.

They ate dinner and she vaguely heard the questions Taylor asked. Thomas described the accident he had witnessed. The cyclist was fortunate that his injuries were only a minor broken bone and a lot of skin left on the pavement. It was more than Lisa wanted to imagine. After a few more questions, the conversation finished, and the men were ready to leave.

Early that morning Thomas had driven to Mont Castello with Jeffrey Mills, another cyclist. Jeffrey had finished his dinner and motioned from across the restaurant. Thomas stood and thrust his hand toward Taylor. "This was an enjoyable evening."

With a tight-lipped smile, Taylor nodded, shook Thomas' hand, and thanked Lisa for her patience during the interview.

"Sorry I have to call it a night, but I have another early start tomorrow," Thomas said. He walked out without a word to Lisa, leaving her to pay the bill.

Taylor laid some bills on top of the check before she could get to her credit card. "This is a business expense for my interview," he said.

"Thank you," she murmured. They left the table and emerged through the large wooden door into the cool night air. Thomas, engaged in conversation in the front seat of an SUV, drove off without a backward glance.

"May I walk you to your car?" Taylor offered.

"It's just around the corner," she replied, but he insisted. The streets were almost empty. When they turned onto the side street, a light breeze filtered through the trees. Taylor was silent as he escorted her.

Her heart felt heavy. It was not often that her life was thrown into her face like the last two nights. his perceptiveness proved to be an accurate mirror, reflecting back emotions and tensions that she worked hard to keep locked away. "This is it." She mustered up a tired smile. "Thank you for interviewing Thomas. It will provide him with bragging rights for the next year." She thought he would at least smile, but he didn't.

Instead, he searched her face. "I don't know you very well, but after our conversation, and then watching your interactions with Thomas, I don't understand why you put up with his *manners.*"

The seriousness with which he spoke caused another stab of pain in her chest. "Thank you for your concern." She swallowed against the knot in her throat. "I'm working on it."

His voice was gentle. "Don't take too long."

Without replying, she pulled out her keys, eased into her car, and drove away. Feeling exposed, exhaustion overtook her. She was certain Taylor thought her weak and trapped. She hated it when she sensed people thinking that. She was not trapped. She had discovered her strengths and found a clear path for her life.

Frustrated, she could only estimate how much longer her plan would take. Thomas couldn't demean her abilities once she successfully accomplished her objective. And she was well on her way.

Chapter 3

The phone badgered Lisa from sleep. Pulling it to her ear, she heard an unfamiliar voice. "Hello, Lisa?"

"Yes."

There was a hesitation. "I hope I didn't interrupt you, but this is Asia Taylor, and I think we had an appointment at 9:00."

Lisa's eyes flew open, and her jaw dropped. "I'll be about half an hour."

Asia was a dear. "Take your time. I have a lot of details to work on until you arrive."

When Lisa arrived at the courthouse, laughter floated from an open window. She stepped over the paint-bare threshold to find Asia engaged in playful conversation with Jesse.

"Hey, Mom." Jesse stood to kiss her on the cheek.

She looked from one to the other, but this morning had a completely different reaction. "What kind of mischief are the two of you up to so early?"

"Not as much as you were up to last night," Jesse taunted.

Her mind raced over the events of the night before but could not land on anything.

At her blank look, Asia offered, "Please don't be embarrassed, but my father told me about the case of my mistaken identity."

Lisa felt relieved to find that was all Jesse meant. "Guilty. I seem to be apologizing a lot today."

"No worries, Mom," he said. "It explains why you gave me *the look* yesterday."

She chuckled at Asia and Jesse, two of the truly beautiful people, but not just physically. She could sense the underlying attraction in the room and remembered that feeling from years ago. Thomas had been that way—hadn't he? She exiled her disquieting thoughts. "So, what's on the agenda today?"

"I want to go over the building styles for each of the properties owned by the Montebelli Corporation," Asia answered. "The designs are drawn up, but we're offering some guidelines that will work to highlight each building's design in relation to its neighbors'. I'm assuming you will relay the information for approval?"

"Absolutely," she said. "I'll report all the details and get back to you with any changes."

Asia's expression revealed relief that she would not need to repeat everything to a higher level of decision makers. "So far, the Montebelli Corporation is the largest investor in the Tangle Grove project. Because of their financial commitment for a good deal of the infrastructure, I saved the most artistic of the Baker and Thymes designs for the corporation's buildings."

Lisa picked up her favorite sketch for a small hotel. Her heart swelled with pride. It would occupy the large corner of the Siebert property nearest the town center. The only other three-story building was the courthouse. She traced her finger over the plans for the hotel. A front view showed a fifteen-foot arch that faced Maple Street with shops on either side.

Through the opening, a paved courtyard would be visible. In the center, a bronze fountain would anchor elegant tables and chairs. Guest rooms were slated for the upper two stories, while shops opened from the first floor onto the streets and patio below. She envisioned a flower shop, deli, and clothing stores to interest the hotel's guests. Her enthusiasm was unconstrained as she asked for more details and had Asia write down new ideas and changes.

At one point Jesse asked, "Mom, are you sure the corporate officers will want to do that?"

Her head swung up defensively. "I'll be discussing the details with them, but we've been in lengthy discussions, so I know what they're after."

He changed the subject, anxious to get to his favorite plan—the new condominiums. An hour later, they broke for lunch and headed for the coffee shop in Tangle Grove. Lisa wanted to see Asia's reaction to the building she helped remodel six years earlier. It was just as impressive as the rest of the downtown would be.

"This is cool," Asia remarked, as they entered the coffee shop.

"Gabe and Lilly did a great job decorating it," Lisa said. Her eyes swept over the detail in the tall ceiling.

"That too, but I was speaking of the architecture," Asia continued. "It's as though our company designed it as well. Who owns this?"

Lisa grinned. "The Montebelli Corporation."

"I should have known, but it makes me wonder why they hired us. Who designed the interior?"

Pleasure turned up the corners of Lisa's mouth and she answered, "Actually, I sketched up the design."

Asia and Jesse exchanged looks. "Come on, Mom, how would you know how to create something like this?"

The smile dropped from Lisa's face. "Yes, I suppose the only thing I'm good at is cooking and laundry, right Jesse?"

"Sor-*ry*," his eyebrows wrinkled with distress.

Biting her lip, Lisa tried to undo her sarcasm. "I know you didn't mean anything. Look, we've covered a lot of ground this morning. It's not your fault I'm tired." She excused herself, feigning a headache and the need to lie down. *I have to learn.* Every time she let a little out about her involvement with the town's plans, those close to her couldn't comprehend it. Thankfully, the people she worked with held a far different opinion of her capabilities.

Driving home, she regretted encouraging Jesse to join the Design Team. In addition to his lack of faith in her, his knowledge could unwittingly serve as a threat. An unbidden shudder passed through her as she imagined Thomas' angry surprise at what she had accomplished behind his back. A real headache was throbbing by the time she pulled into her garage. She swallowed two aspirin, grabbed a pillow, and sank down into the welcoming comforter on her king-sized bed.

***

"What are you doing?" Thomas' shout woke Lisa. His narrowed eyes bore into hers. "Is that all you can do—sleep?"

"I had a headache." Panic rose in her chest when she saw the clock. It was almost dinnertime, and she hadn't even thought about what to cook. "Just give me a minute and I'll get your dinner."

He spun around taking off his jersey and glared at her. "I don't know what you do all day, but it's clear your interest isn't here." He threw his clothes against the mirror.

Angry tears stung her eyes, but only served to increase his ranting.

"I left you a message telling you we have company coming for dinner. Steven Taylor was on the mountain, and I invited him and his daughter to join Jesse and us at seven o'clock. It's six-thirty right now. What do you propose to do?"

She sat in shock. She'd gone straight to bed, not thinking to pick up any messages. Her confounded mind worked through a spider web of emotions, striving to grasp images of the stores of food in the freezer and pantry. An idea sent her stumbling with unsteady legs down the stairs into the kitchen.

With her heart racing, she opened the freezer and blessed her housekeeper, Jenny, for organizing it this week. She grabbed two packages of filet of sole and shrimp, turned on the oven, and dumped jasmine rice into the rice maker. After tossing the shrimp with seasoning, she wrapped a filet around each scoop of shrimp, sprinkled the top with lemon juice, breadcrumbs and melted butter and set them in the oven to cook.

A package of creamy French cheese caught her eye, and she placed it on a vine-patterned serving dish and surrounded it with Parmesan flatbread. Dashing to the library, she grabbed the vase of flowers from a table next to her reading chair. With them placed on the bar near the hors d'oeuvres, the picture was complete.

Breathe. She called up to the bedroom, "Thomas, do you think you could greet the guests while I change?"

"I'll be down in a minute." He sounded slightly calmer now that he had showered and changed. The doorbell rang as he descended the stairs. "I'll get it," he said and strode past her without a glance.

She took the last seconds to set candles on the table and then disappeared up the stairs into the bedroom. Rummaging through her closet, she found a long casual gown and threw it over her head. Made of peach-colored gauze, it flowed in soft layers. She exhaled.

With shaking hands, she fastened on a gold necklace that highlighted an immense reddish-orange fire opal. After putting on fresh lipstick, she ran a brush through her hair and paused for the first time in thirty minutes. *Okay, time to play hostess.*

She grasped the rail as she descended the stairs to the living room and saw Jesse speaking to the group. He looked up at her and stopped mid-sentence. "Wow, Mom, you look great."

The rest of the company turned to follow Jesse's eyes. She blanched, eyes darting to Thomas. He hated her stealing the show. He forced a smile and made a small attempt at raising his glass to salute her. She faltered at his annoyed expression but continued down the stairs. "Are you all famished?" she asked.

Jesse answered for everyone. "We are, but the hors d'oeuvres are helping."

"I still have to make the salad, but you're welcome to join me." She enjoyed having guests in the kitchen while she finished the preparations. Thomas preferred to keep his guests in the formal part of the house and frowned at her when Asia asked for a knife to slice the tomatoes. Jesse pulled the lettuce leaves apart. Lisa noticed the two young people chatting and locking eyes.

After pouring the wine, Thomas and Taylor began a conversation about the day's ride. Lisa watched her husband. At some point, he'd blocked her out, built a wall between them. How many bricks she had provided for that barrier? She touched the fire opal that hung over her heart and pressed the aching place beneath it. The mystery was *why*. Why had his passion turned away? Why had he become so cruel? His career and position in the community were all that mattered anymore.

Catching herself, she pushed the muddled thoughts away. Answers to those questions could unravel the flimsy fabric that held their lives together. She was still too vulnerable to delve into the source of their difficulty. She smiled as she worked, hoping it hid her anxious thoughts.

***

Taylor stood on the periphery of the kitchen, absorbing the scene and watching the strain in Lisa's face as she maneuvered under Thomas' scrutiny. He felt like shaking Thomas and telling him to wake up. Lisa deftly handled the mundane and turned it into a celebration for her guests, yet Thomas seemed to hold nothing but disdain for her.

When the food dishes were finished cooking, they carried the serving plates to the dining table and everyone gathered around, standing behind their chairs.

"Let's give thanks," Lisa said and bowed her head. The others followed her lead. Thomas shrugged an apology at Taylor as her voice opened in prayer. "Lord, we thank you for this food, this day and the loving care you've shown us. Please bless our new friends with your grace and peace. Amen." She looked up and smiled. "Please, be seated."

Taylor couldn't remember any of the conversation from the dinner table. He talked, listened, and answered questions, all on autopilot. Lisa was a mystery. He wondered if some distorted religious belief kept her from demanding Thomas' respect. Or leaving. And what did she mean last night when she said, "I'm working on it?" Normally, he could collect a few clues and piece the story together. This time the more clues he uncovered, the muddier the water became.

Chapter 4

Tires exploded. Metal scraped against pavement, sending sparks flying at the next group of riders as they rounded the bend at top speeds. In their path lay the unavoidable obstacles of downed cyclists who had worked every angle to avoid hitting an injured rider.

Taylor added dramatic touches to his article. His comfortable room at the Catania Inn Bed and Breakfast supplied a perfect workspace in which to write his story. The Summit Challenge had lasted Thursday through Saturday, which left Sunday morning open for him to finish typing his manuscript and email it to his office.

Flipping through his notes, he decided to include some of the historical background he garnered from the area.

The Summit Challenge grew from an idea posed by the local cycling organization to give riders a challenge and attract tourists to their tiny mountain town. Mont Castello sits in the shadow of the largest peak, Mt. Thurman, named after the leader of its first known expedition in 1868. Sir Edward Thurman and his English team set up a base camp near the present town.

A sizeable group of Italians also arrived for the climb. After the first ascent and tragic death of their leader, the Italians chose to settle here. Drawing on their heritage, they created an Italian alpine village, christened, 'Mont Castello,' because of the many crags that reminded them of the castles in their homeland region of Valle d'Aosta.

By late morning, Taylor finished his story. Now the day was his and he felt like getting into the mountains for a little exploring. A trail led upward from the side porch off the front lobby. Clothed in khaki walking shorts, T-shirt and hiking boots, he followed the path for over an hour as it traversed up Mt. Thurman.

Two historical markers on the trail recounted events that occurred more than a century before. One weathered sign still carried the carved names of several of the original climbers. Although worn thin from sun, rain, and snow, it was still possible to make out a large portion of it. Scanning the names, the only one he recognized was *Varano*. Signora Varano's relative?

By this time, his appetite was raging, and he began the descent. With so much focus on the climb, he hadn't bothered to turn back and look at the view. Now, however, he swayed from the magnificence before him. At least six mountain ranges were visible until the horizon dipped out of sight. Lakes and meadows filled the spaces between some of the closer slopes. The late morning sun cast a bright golden light on everything it touched. The air was perfectly still and clean. He breathed in and sat down.

He felt humbled by all he saw. *God's creation.* The words came unbidden to him. He hadn't thought about God for a long time. In fact, the last time he could remember was when Asia was born. *What a miracle a child is*, he had concluded and then he had thanked God for her. It was a moment of certainty, when he knew God existed and that God knew him, Steven Taylor.

Lisa's prayer last night had been real, as if God was in the room. The simplicity of that brief conversation struck him. His mother had talked like that. Now here he was on this mountain, overlooking *His* handiwork. "It's beautiful," Taylor ventured. His heart felt full. Seeing Lisa's strained eyes in his mind, he felt the urge to ask, "Please, help her." He lingered in that tranquil state until he couldn't ignore his stomach any longer. He hustled back down, feeling a joy he hadn't felt in a long while.

There was a different crowd in Varano's restaurant today. The colorful jerseys of the bicyclists were gone. Blue jeans and T-shirts clad the travelers, who drove north and south along the highway that ribboned its way through the mountain pass. It was still early for lunch and the young hostess from his first night at the restaurant seated him at a small table.

"Miss, is there any literature on the history of the Varano family?"

The girl beamed as she brought over a brochure. "Right here." She pointed to a few brief paragraphs. "This is all about my family. If you want to know more, you can ask Grand Anna. She will talk for hours about her grandfather and great-grandfather."

"And what's your name?"

"Maria Lucia Varano." She answered with a sense of obvious pride.

After she left, he examined the fascinating account of the story. It told of two brothers, Fabio and Doriano Varano, who had journeyed from Italy with the expedition. Their purpose was to climb a fabled summit that remained unconquered. A British band of climbers also planned to climb, causing a bitter competition.

Taylor raised his eyebrow at the mention of treachery that caused the older brother and leader of the group, Fabio, to fall to his death into a deep crevasse. Sir Edward was able to bypass Fabio's team as they tried in vain to reach their fallen hero. The article made it evident that the mountain should rightly be called *Mt. Varano.*

Skimming over the article, Taylor noted the highlights. Apparently, the surviving brother, Doriano Varano, damaged his leg in the rescue attempt, unable to return to Italy. The others returned in the spring, bringing more provisions. Doriano sold supplies to groups of climbers, mapmakers, and pioneers, while his wife, Maria, cooked hearty meals for the weary souls. Eventually, they enlarged their home to create a public dining room.

Taylor smiled at the promotional tagline in the article. *News traveled and Varano's Italian Restaurant became well known as the place 'of presidents and pioneers.'* It boasted that the current owners were direct descendants of the original proprietors, using the same delectable recipes from the old country.

Anna Varano passed by his table. "Interesting story," Taylor commented, pointing to the family history.

"You don't know the half of it," she said, her ire instantly stirred.

Taylor intervened before she could get started. "I have an appointment with my daughter soon, but when I come back, could you tell me the rest of the story?"

Signora Varano's face lit up. "Of course, Mr. Taylor. We will sit and I'll show you photographs and letters."

***

Thomas placed the call he should have when he first caught wind of Lisa's involvement with the Montebelli Corporation. Years ago, he had hired Larry Spartan of Spartan Investigations to follow Lisa's movements when her actions seemed suspicious. His hunch had been right.

"Spartan Investigations." Abby's nasal greeting always sounded like an old-time switchboard operator.

This is Dr. Thomas Richards. I'd like to speak to Mr. Spartan."

"Oh hi, Dr. Richards. What can we do for you?"

Once again, she struck him as a busybody and hoped Larry managed to keep the degree of confidentiality that he promised. "I would prefer to keep my business between Larry and myself if you don't mind." The words came out sharper than planned. He breathed to relax.

It was rare anymore that he lost his temper with Lisa anymore. In the past, she'd shrunk back, but something was different. She was hiding something. As a psychiatrist, he had honed his ability to sense these things.

"Larry here. What can I do for you this time, Thomas?"

Agitated, Thomas said, "It's Lisa again. I need to find out what she's into."

"Symptoms?"

"Lapses in time where I don't know her location. Defiant eyes. Unaccountable excitability."

"Has she said anything to make you suspicious?"

Thomas nearly shouted, "She doesn't need to say anything. I'm her husband. I know my wife. Wouldn't you know if your wife were acting strange?"

"Not married." Larry coughed. "I'll follow her, but I'm booked until next week."

Opening his mouth to protest, Thomas shut it again. One didn't push Larry Spartan. The guy was tough, ex-military, although he never said which branch. Needless to say, he towered above Thomas. And Thomas was certain he had glimpsed distaste in the man's eyes when they had shut down Lisa's last project. "Fine, get back to me," Thomas mumbled and hung up the phone.

He sat at his desk for a moment, going over the nuances that had triggered his mistrust. Again, it was hard to define. Taylor's seemed taken by the show she put on. It would be good to keep the man close at hand while he was in town.

***

Taylor had not been making excuses with Anna Varano. He had plans to meet Asia in Bella Vista around two o'clock. Jesse was working the Sunday lunch shift at a classy bar and grill and invited Taylor and Asia to meet him when he finished working. It seemed that she and Jesse were enjoying hanging out whenever she was not working in Tangle Grove. He could not deny the two young people suited each other.

The scenic drive down the mountain from Mont Castello only took thirty minutes. He slid his rented SUV into the first empty parking space and could tell he would enjoy walking through this engaging town. Asia said *Zach's* was in the third block on the left as the road entered the downtown area.

Passing an outdoor store, he made a mental note to come back and check it out. A few vests and lightweight jackets in muted greens, rusts, and reds created a visual feast, hinting of autumn that was just around the corner.

Bella Vista Jewels held a prominent spot next door with a dazzling display to attract shoppers of a different mindset. He noticed a small sign that read, "Authentic Dutchman Mine Opals." Below the sign were brilliant opals in artistically designed settings like the one Lisa wore last night. Curiosity got the best of him and since he was still early, he entered the store.

"Could you tell me about the Dutchman Mine Opals?" he asked the elegant saleswoman.

Putting on a winsome smile, she answered, "Do you want the short or long version?"

Being a journalist, Taylor chose the latter. "If it won't go over fifteen minutes, I'd like the whole story.

"Ten minutes will be plenty of time," she assured him and began her tale.

"The Dutchman was Jochem Van Buren, an immigrant who settled in this valley around 1880. He came in search of his younger brother, Lowie, who arrived in Mont Castello twelve years earlier with the Thurman expedition."

Taylor's mind jerked to attention at the connection to the story he had just learned in Mont Castello.

She continued. "Jochem found Lowie living in squalor in a cave outside of Tangle Grove. Shipbuilders by trade, they turned their skills into barn building. By 1890, the Dutchman made enough money to purchase some acreage, which included Lowie's cave. They planted the flatland and Jochem had his hands full keeping Lowie out of fights, building his barns, and overseeing the crops.

Whenever he could, Jochem would climb up to the cave which overlooked the valley and as listed in his journal, 'talk to his God.'" A smirk twisted the corner of her lips.

"On one such evening, a sudden cloudburst covered the area with rain and hail. Rummaging through Lowie's old belongings in the cave, he found a lantern and, never being one to sit still for long, he explored every aspect of the cave. After a couple of hours, he was making his way back to the main entrance when his lamp caught an amazing-colored stone in a crevice." She paused for effect and increased the tempo.

"Fascinated, Jochem took his knife and chipped away at the rock. It exposed a brilliant orange stone with 'fire like hell inside,' as he described it. Not knowing what he had uncovered, he marked the spot with a line of small stones and chipped off a piece of the 'fire stone.'

"Without waiting for breakfast the next day, he rode his fastest horse to Bella Vista. The busy mercantile store housed a small library for the locals. Huddling next to the wood stove, he flipped through a tattered book that told how to identify gold, silver and gemstones. It was worn from the countless hands that had grasped it in the way men had grasped their dreams of becoming wealthy through gold and silver.

"Making his way to the back of the book, he read descriptions of gemstones. None matched his stone until he came across an entry for *fire opals*. They were most common in Mexico but had also been discovered farther north in the United States. Realizing the possible value of his find, Jochem wrote to a jeweler in San Francisco and described his stone, asking for an estimate of its value. Then he went home to await an answer."

The saleswoman had obviously retold the tale hundreds of times, creating more value for the sale of the stones in her store. Taylor noticed the ploy but enjoyed the story anyway. "And did he get an answer?"

"Unfortunately, more than he hoped for. It wasn't long before some men came to *negotiate* the sale of the mine. They shot Lowie dead and threatened Jochem at his house. But Jochem had three sons who were crack marksmen. The instant the men drew their weapons, multiple shots rang out from the windows of his cabin and the five strangers lay dead in front of the Van Buren's home.

"Since Tangle Grove was too small to afford law enforcement, the sheriff from Bella Vista came out and declared Jochem within his rights to defend himself. They searched the men for identification. A slip of paper had the name of the jeweler and *Mr. Van Buren* written on it. Authorities were notified to question the jeweler, but no reply to the sheriff's inquiry was ever received."

"So Jochem was able to mine his opals?"

"Yes, he certainly did," she answered. "He worked it up to the day he died at 55 years of age. The mine continued to operate productively until 1934 when most of the gems ran out. His descendants tried their hand until 1954 but found nothing significant."

She seamlessly directed his eyes toward her wares, her tongue touching her upper lip. "What we have here, are limited pieces of fire opal from our vaults that we purchased *directly* from the Van Buren estate. Each gem is hand-selected and custom fashioned by our goldsmith for a one-of-a kind treasure."

"Lovely," Taylor said.

Her eyebrow raised in a question, expecting to sell one of the fine pieces.

"I notice that the colors range from yellow to light orange, with tinges of blue." Taylor said. "I recently saw a huge piece that was brilliant orange and red, with amazing fire. Do you have one like that?"

The woman's expression altered. Her face tightened and the smile vanished. Forming her words with obvious disdain, she asked, "Would it by any chance have been worn by *Mrs. Richards*?"

Not liking the turn the conversation was taking, and not wanting to discuss Lisa behind her back, he replied, "I saw it on a woman in town. Is it a special piece?"

"I would rather not discuss the piece. If you have no other interests, I really must help my other customers." With that, she picked up the stone, turned her back on him and walked to the back of the store.

He left the store shaking his head. Every direction he turned brought more mystery surrounding Lisa Richards. He grinned. This was turning into an interesting side adventure. Strolling to the next block, he spotted Zach's and wandered in.

"Hi, Daddy," Asia said when she saw him. She swiveled out of her seat to hug him.

"Hi, Honey. Jesse."

"Hello, Taylor," Jesse replied. "Can I get you a cold one before I'm off work?"

"Just a soda. I could use something cold and friendly." Jesse turned his head to one side as if asking for further explanation, but Taylor shook his head, indicating it was nothing.

"What have you been doing today?" Taylor asked Asia as he sat down next to her at the counter.

"I took a wonderful photo tour of Tangle Grove. Lisa did an excellent job feeding my company all the data we needed, but it adds another dimension to actually be here—walking on the canvas we are about to paint in 3-D."

"Interesting way to put it," Taylor commented. Not wanting to sound too interested, he asked, "Just what sort of information did Lisa provide—street maps and such?"

"Are you kidding?" Asia's energy level heightened. "That woman is brilliant."

Jesse's quizzical face popped up above the back of the bar where he was refilling the club soda.

"I don't believe you two," Asia said. "Jesse, you're on the committee with your mom, surely you've seen the reams of papers she provided my employer on everything from the history of the area to the ethnic percentages and styles of houses?" When he still looked blank, she shook her head and continued. "Lisa's taken into account the terrain, weather, and the *flavor* of the community—not just her impressions, but those of dozens of people she personally interviewed to get their visions.

"Plus, she works closely with the Montebelli Corporation that owns many of the downtown commercial structures. They've not only paid my company's retainer but have pledged a good chunk of change for the cost of the new aesthetics like streetlamps, landscaping, benches, and public art." Asia was out of breath just listing a brief description of Lisa's contributions. She looked from one man to the other and laughed. "What do you think she does all day, play house?"

While Taylor's mind poured over this new information, Jesse was the first to speak.

"I'm on one committee with Mom, but I joined late. I guess I assumed the others had done more, well most, of the work. Mom's always been a hard worker and creative. It's just that it was centered on us. Besides that, Dad was grumbling that she was working for a company for a measly $400 a week. He said if she wanted a career, she should go back to school and learn to do something worthwhile that pays more than a pittance. I had no idea she was putting that much effort into this."

"Asia, what do you mean she *works closely* with the Montebelli Corporation?" Taylor asked.

"Well, she studies my plans, makes suggestions for changes, and then relays the information to the corporate officer above her. She's a city council member and a volunteer on two of the main committees—the Design Team and the Priorities Committee. She's one of the central figures moving this project forward."

At this point, a light went on in Taylor's mind. Lisa had said, *I'm working on it.* That was an understatement. It was odd that her family was so clueless at the depth of her involvement in the development of Tangle Grove. "Jesse, don't you talk about your interests as a family—about what's going on in your lives?"

"I've been out of the house for quite a while, but we do sometimes. Dad talks about some of his more interesting clients—without names of course. We talk about biking. I have my job and I'm always doing something outdoors."

"And what about your mother?"

"She's been kind of out of it for a few years. Dad says she's been going through the change. You know, cranky, emotional, distant. She's better than she used to be, but it's like she's smiling, then any little thing sets her off. You remember yesterday, right Asia?" Asia nodded.

"What happened?" Taylor asked.

"We were just admiring an updated building in Tangle Grove that houses the coffee shop, when Mom pops up and says she designed the remodel. I made some lame comment about being surprised at that—I really was surprised. Anyway, she lashed out then apologized. Said something about being tired and having a headache and didn't stay for lunch. It's like sometimes I don't know how to be around her without offending her."

Taylor tilted his head. "Maybe this is something she's doing that's important to her."

"Sure hope Dad doesn't find out."

Taylor raised an eyebrow. "Why would that be an issue?"

"He owns her attention. Plus, he's obsessed with Bella Vista, to the exclusion of any other town. He wants me to live here, but honestly, I'm not going to spend my whole paycheck on an apartment, just so I can flash my address around. There are too many other things I want to do in life."

"Surely he knows Lisa is on the city council?" Taylor said.

"He quizzed me on that. I think she told him it had to do with community volunteering or something. That seems to be acceptable—makes the family look good—just so she doesn't take too much time away from home to do it."

Taylor was silent. As he contemplated Jesse's words, angst began to grow in his gut. None of this was adding up. The two young people seemed to want to change the subject. Jesse announced he was off work and asked where they wanted to explore today.

Taylor knew instantly. "How about the Dutchman's Mine?"

A wide grin spread over Jesse's face. "Who told you about the Dutchman?"

"The saleswoman at the jewelry store."

Jesse smirked. "That would be Angela Basso. She's always got her nose in everyone's business."

"It was odd," Taylor said, "she was offended when I asked her about the pendant your mother was wearing last night."

"I bet that set her off," Jesse laughed. "She is so stinking jealous of Mom's jewels." He continued to chuckle. Asia and Taylor were not following, so he explained. "Mom is a descendant of the Dutchman. The best stones that came from the mine are kept in the family. Angela Basso's family also grew up here. Her great aunt, Katherine, married Daan, one of the Dutchman's sons, but later disappeared with another guy. Daan didn't hear from her for years, then heard rumors she'd died, so he remarried. After he died, Katherine returned and tried to get an inheritance. There was an expensive battle, but the court ruled in favor of the Dutchman, so Katherine was left out in the cold."

"How did Angela come by the *authentic* Dutchman stones she has?" Taylor asked.

"That mine flourished," Jesse answered. "Every member of the family had a stash of the less valuable ones. Over time, estates sold, and Angela's family bought up as many as they could get their hands on. They keep the stock down to keep the value up, like diamonds. The rare stones, like the one my mom had on, have never been out of the family. It drives Angela crazy that she can't get her hands on them."

Taylor and Asia smiled, now that they understood *the rest of the story*.

"So, do you have a secret family passage into the mine?" Taylor asked.

Jesse grinned. "Better than that, I have a key."

Chapter 5

Sweltering wind rushed at them, causing Taylor to close the windows and turn on the air conditioning in his dark green SUV. To get to the famous mine, they made the fifteen-minute drive from Bella Vista to the southern tip of Tangle Grove, past acres of finely cultivated grapevines coursing their undulating lines over gently rolling hills.

Jesse pointed out the sights and the three explorers admired the distant mountain views as they descended into a lower and wider region of the Valle d'Aosta.

Taylor smiled, impressed. Where Bella Vista's residents clustered in a narrow, beautiful tip of the valley, the area that held Tangle Grove spread out with large farms and vineyards and had a mountainous backdrop to the southwest.

The sun was still high and left a soft golden glow over the crops and old buildings that occupied this community. Taylor caught Jesse watching his face and rewarded the young man with his transparent appreciation.

"I prefer Tangle Grove to Bella Vista," Jesse said. "It's one of the reasons I wanted to be on the Design Team. I share Mom's vision for the area." They pulled into the dirt parking lot of an old two-story building. "This place is divided into five cramped apartments."

The structure looked square, and the roof was not too old, but the building was as plain as could be built. One large tree did its best to shade the west side from the afternoon sun, and a few shrubs had been stuck in randomly to hint at landscaping.

Jesse shrugged. "Pretty grim, but we have plans to make her into a *grand old lady*. He got out and entered the central common door that led inside and soon reappeared in shorts and hiking boots. Swinging a large key for the waiting passengers to see, he smiled. "Let's go exploring."

Taylor checked out his loafers and looked down at Asia's tennis shoes from her morning stroll. Jesse followed his line of thinking. "You'll be fine. We can drive to the mouth of the cave and it's pretty level inside.

Taylor backed the car out and continued on the Strada del Vino north toward their destination.

"Dad, turn in here a minute. I want to show you something," Asia directed.

Taylor made a left-hand turn onto a paved road marked *Maple Street*. They hit a pothole and continued to bounce past a run-down farm with a large barn near the corner.

"This is going to be the beginning of the new downtown area of Tangle Grove." The enthusiasm in her voice was evident.

"That's an interesting old barn." Taylor pointed out the window.

"That's the old Siebert place. My mom loves that barn," Jesse said. "When the Montebelli Corporation purchased it, she recruited me and a friend to help her clean it out. You wouldn't believe how much junk we cleared off. The corporation let the Sieberts continue to live in it and pay rent."

"Why was your mom cleaning this up for the corporation?" Taylor asked.

"She mostly just organized, but she carted out her share."

He frowned. What could entice Lisa to put this much effort into an old town? She was married to a doctor, had plenty of money, prestige, family and friends to occupy her time. What was she doing tromping through an old farm cleaning up debris?

Asia pointed to a small building straight ahead of them. "That's the old courthouse." Excited, she pointed, "Pull over here. This is the building Lisa re-designed."

The picture window of the coffee shop huddled in a recessed area under the upstairs apartments that hung out over the patio. Two ancient-looking columns seemed to hold the weight of the second-story protrusion, creating a perfect place for the small tables and chairs to sit protected from the harsh sun or unexpected rain.

Heavy molding surrounded the window and large door. The overflowing flower boxes and wooden shutters attached to the stucco facade gave the place the same sense of being in Italy as did Varano's.

"Very impressive," Taylor said. The more he studied the building, the more there was to see. A Virginia Creeper vined its way toward the second story. In a short time, it would give the building the look of being very old and historic. *She definitely has a gift.*

Asia began an explanation of the project. "Because of the heavy Italian history here, we wanted some of the buildings to keep that flavor but also to intersperse *old town* buildings like those built in Sacramento or even in parts of Portland.

"Settlers came from different places, and we want Tangle Grove to showcase that fact. Lisa identified at least five major cultures that influenced the area. We've worked hard to come up with building designs that incorporate those, but also blend without clashing. It's been tricky, but we did it. Lisa had a few suggestions to add to my model, but she was thrilled."

He noted Asia's deep admiration for Lisa and the way the project was going. He smiled. Heck, he should buy up some property in Tangle Grove. He chuckled at himself for getting caught up in the vision.

"We should get going soon if we want to get up there in the sunshine," Jesse said.

Taylor turned right at the courthouse, following Jesse's directions. After two more turns on bumpy, narrow streets, they made a left onto Old Mine Road.

"This road connects the Strada del Vino, that runs down the center of the valley, with Fire Mountain Road, that follows the creek around the base of Fire Mountain." Jesse pointed off to his left. "Fire Mountain holds the Dutchman's mine. It was named, in part, for the fire opals."

Taylor's head tilted back at the angle of the mountain, which seemed to rise straight up out of the valley. They approached a narrow two-lane bridge with a sign that read, *Wildcat Creek*. Even in late summer, there was a substantial flow.

"This water is what keeps the valley green. The water rights go back over a century." Jesse seemed pleased to offer some local trivia.

Taylor was tentative as he crossed the bridge. It looked ancient, but after he got a feel for it, he realized it was sound and accelerated over the last half to the other side of the creek.

"It's deceiving," Jesse said. "It looks like a small flood could carry it away, but everything the Dutchman built has stood the test of time. The granite blocks they cut and placed will be here forever."

A worn sign on the far side of the bridge read, *Sweet Elke Park*, and had an arrow that pointed to the right. "The park is named after Jochem's daughter, Elke, who died in 1902. She was only ten. Her grave stands near the water, one of her favorite places to play. Jochem had a stonemason inscribe a marble slab and place it there."

"What does it say?" Asia asked.

"It's written in Dutch and says 'Onze kostbare Elke, Onze Edele,'" answered Jesse. "That translates roughly, 'Our precious Elke, Our noble one,' with the dates of her birth and death."

Taylor remarked, "I wonder why they wrote *noble one.*"

"People have speculated about that," Jesse answered. "Some say she had a noble character and there's a song that was passed down within the Dutch community that seems to bear that out. However, one of the early settlers recorded that *Elke* means noble one or noble child. There are lots of other stories, maybe it's a mix of them."

They passed the entrance to the park on their right and took the steep road that wound up the mountain about half a mile. A sharp turn to the left ended in a flat open space. The entrance to the mine was beyond the clearing and enclosed with large stones that created a wall sixteen feet high.

A metal door stood solidly in the stone wall. Dents and scratch marks told the story of the vandals who had attempted to pry open the massive vault. A sign read, *Van Buren Mine—No Trespassing.* A final, *KEEP OUT*, restated the order in bold red letters.

"Even with a key, it looks like you'd need an army to open that door," Taylor said.

"Again, looks can be deceiving," Jesse answered. He thrust the heavy key in the lock and a series of clicks sounded behind the mass of metal. "The Dutchman ordered this door from San Francisco and had it hauled up by wagon. It took months, but he was serious about protecting his mine."

He pointed to his left. "You can make out where the mountain used to extend for another twenty or so feet. He blasted and cut it away to create a smaller entrance. It's still large, but he felt he could better secure this size of an opening."

Taylor examined the remnants of the mountain where it once occupied the ground on which they were standing. "Good idea. In the process he created an area for wagons to turn around and head back down to the valley."

Jesse nodded. "This was a busy place for a lot of years. The old man got rich and had hired guns up here around the clock." The door opened a crack at his firm tug. A musty smell belched out of the cave through the narrow opening and Jesse pulled harder on the door.

Taylor reached around to help pull. It moved easily. "This door must be nine inches thick."

"You're close. The frame and hinges were specially made to withstand the heavy weight and make it possible to open. The Dutchman built the massive timber and stone wall to hold it."

The door creaked as they tugged it open. Jesse pulled a flashlight from his fanny pack, and they ventured inside where the dank smell was even stronger. Closed off from the outside, the air remained cold and damp.

"How do you happen to have the key to this place?" Taylor asked.

"Actually, it's *a* key. There are three in existence. Grandma Rose, my mom's mother, gave this one to me. Jochem had three sons and each of their families has a key. Any of us can work the mine, but the gems are depleted. They pulled the last big stones out of here in 1946, and except for a couple, most displayed poor quality. Family members tried to find new veins that might house the precious opal *eggs*, but finally gave up."

"Look at this," Asia pointed toward an old wooden bunk bed, a table, and two chairs. A rickety cupboard stood to one side.

"The hired guns lived here when they were on duty," Jesse explained. "There were four guards all together and they worked two-on and two-off, around the clock. During the day, there was a lot of activity, but at night, the watchmen complained about the unidentifiable noises coming from the back of the cave. Soon it got out that the ghost of the Dutchman's dead brother, Lowie Van Buren, haunted the mine."

"Did the guards really believe it?" Asia asked.

"I don't know, but it kept most people from disturbing their card games at night."

"Can we see some of the other tunnels?" Taylor's curiosity heightened.

"We can, just let me get the flashlights we keep in here." He shone the light on the cupboard and opened the drawer. There was only one flashlight.

"That's odd." Jesse opened the drawer farther and reached in the back. "We always keep two flashlights in the top drawer. I remember putting them away the last time I was here."

"How long ago was that?" Taylor asked.

"At the beginning of summer. My cousins and I come up here every year on the night of the full moon in June. It's a family tradition. In the old days, it used to be for Jochem's birthday on June 4, but we changed it to the night of the full moon so we could see better. It gets spooky up here," he finished with a laugh.

Shining his light on the table, he found the missing flashlight and handed it to Taylor. He continued to scour the area with a flood of light. "What's going on here?" Walking over to the bunks, he tapped the flashlight on a half-page of newspaper lying on the top bed of the unsteady bunk.

"What's the date on the paper?" Taylor asked.

Focusing his light on the printing, Jesse bent closer. "It's dated June 12th, the week after we were all here. Dan or Pete probably came back and hung out. Okay, let's go exploring."

Taylor paused and shined his light on the piece of newspaper. It was folded around the classified section—*Property for Sale.* Pen markings circled three listings.

"What is it?" Asia asked.

"Nothing, just looking at the headlines." He folded the section of paper and slipped it into his pocket, then turned to join Jesse and Asia who had entered one of the first *rooms.* His flashlight scanned the wall where it rose far above his head. "Why are these walls so high?" he asked.

"The miners followed the cracks and faults as far as they would go, picking out the opals as they went. The opals form in cavities created by disintegrated trees and bushes. It's thought that the super-heated water dissolves some of the silica and deposits it in cracks like these." He pointed to an empty chasm.

"The Dutchman found massive deposits as he followed tree limbs embedded in the tons of rock and clay that make up this mountain. When the miners depleted a surface, they chiseled off a new layer and followed the new deposits. Some of the walls go forty feet high."

They wandered through many more of the rooms. Some of the ceilings rose higher than others, indicating more productive areas.

"How do they *know* the mine is depleted?" Asia asked.

Jesse laughed. "The treasure bug is beginning to bite. The miners never found any deposits over thirty-five feet. Because they were tracing old branching structures, they could tell this was a forest. They followed it throughout these caves until it ended. My family continued to scrape more of the walls away, but after removing tons of clay and rock in all directions, they found nothing. We've all come back now and then hoping to find a new vein, but so far we've come up empty-handed."

Asia touched the wall. "Too bad," she laughed. "It would be fun to dig your own treasure."

"My mom thought that too," Jesse said. "As kids, we came out here on the weekend with our small pickaxes and lunch. Dad wasn't much interested in it, but Mom made it a fun outing with my cousins. It created great memories."

"I've got an opal ring that was given to me as a gift," Asia said. "It's a beautiful light blue with bits of bright orange and yellow fire in it."

"That's what people typically think of when they think of opals," Jesse explained. "The ones that were mined here are called *fire opals* and range from brilliant yellows and oranges to deep reds and even a handful of rare black opals that are highlighted with amazing colors."

"I've never heard of black opals," Taylor commented.

"My grandmother owned the largest one in our family. They call it *The Dutchman*," Jesse said. "Mom has it now and wears it on *very* special occasions."

An image of Lisa flashed through Taylor's mind, the brilliance of the black opal dancing highlights across her dark hair and reflecting sparks into her blue eye. The warmth of the uninvited vision caught him off-guard, as did the sudden chill that struck his body.

A low, windy howl burst from the back of the cave. Chilling cold entered the room and surrounded them, causing the hair on his arms to rise. Asia stifled a small cry and Taylor gasped as fear gripped him.

"That's our *ghost*," Jesse explained, failing to cover up his own trepidation. "People have searched the cave for the source, but no one has been able to identify where it comes from."

Taylor pointed his flashlight all around. *Nothing*. He stepped into the main passage and did the same. "How far back does this cave go?"

"About ninety feet total," Jesse answered. "They didn't find opals in every room, but there was a great deposit that kept going in that direction. However, the last twenty feet produced nothing. After chipping away for years, they finally abandoned that trail.

"The Dutchman was dead by then and the wealth of the family allowed most of the others to move out of the area to larger cities. The few family members who remained, ran out of funds and enthusiasm to keep going. Nothing has happened since the 1950's."

It was 1954 to be exact, Taylor mused, not wanting to bring up the subject of Angela Basso again. "What kind of equipment did they use toward the end? Surely there are better ways to mine now besides picks and shovels."

"There are," Jesse answered, "but it's expensive. And the mine proved relatively unstable, at least in this area. There were a few injuries when a couple of the miners pushed too fast through the clay and rock. After that, Jochem made it a policy to go slow and steady, beefing up the tunnels as necessary when following a fault.

"That reminds me, come back in here." Jesse traveled back toward the main room. Following him, the chill subsided, and Taylor found himself shrugging off what was left of the shakiness in his gut.

Pointing his light over the top of the square boulders at the main entrance, Jesse read an inscription chiseled into the granite. "It reads, *Langzaam en Regelmatig* which means *Slow and Steady* in Dutch. It's our family motto."

Taylor studied the words. "Good motto, but it flies in the face of our modern world. For most of us it's, *fast and furious*, but I guess that wouldn't do in a crumbling cave."

"I think I'm ready to go," Asia's voice quivered. "I didn't dress warmly enough to handle the cold in here." After spending time in the dark and encountering the *ghost*, Taylor guessed she wanted to escape into the sunlight for a different reason.

"I'm sorry I didn't think about that," Jesse apologized, concern evident in his voice. Gesturing toward the opening, he said, "Go on out and I'll put the flashlights away. I'll call Dan later and find out if he's been hanging out in here."

Outside, the light blinded them. Even though the sun was lower in the sky, the contrast to the extreme darkness of the cave left them squinting. Asia stepped to the car and felt in her bag for her sunglasses.

"Well, what do you think?" Jesse seemed happy to share this part of his life with them.

Taylor said, "That was a fascinating experience. Thank you for the personalized tour."

"It was really amazing," Asia added. "What a treasure to have in your family—the cave, I mean." She laughed, partly to rid herself of the lingering uneasiness.

"I know how you feel," Jesse said, his eyes directed at Asia's shaking fingers. "It took me a long time to get used to the sensation in there. In fact, it still unnerves me."

Taylor wandered to the edge of the clearing and took in the view of the valley below, his hand shielding his eyes. With the sun lower in the sky, long shadows stretched over the fields below. When his eyes moved toward Sweet Elke Park, he spotted a gleaming red convertible leaving the area. It crossed the bridge and turned right onto Fire Mountain Road, following the creek toward Bella Vista. A minute later, a tan truck pulled out and drove toward Tangle Grove on Old Mine Road.

"Ready to go?" Jesse asked Taylor. He and Asia were waiting in the SUV.

Taylor took one last look, then settled in the car and began the trip back down to the valley. As they crossed the bridge again, Jesse suggested they take Fire Mountain Road to see if they could catch the sunset. Taylor made a right turn after the bridge onto a paved two-lane road.

Excited, Jessie directed their attention to the fiery display behind them. Taylor adjusted the mirror on his car door, entranced as the sun blasted the clouds with a red-orange infusion. The sky lit up with purple and scarlet—colors so brilliant, they radiated their hues on the ridge of the mountain, making the observers believe the trees had burst into flame.

"Amazing," Asia gasped. "It does look like fire." She continued to comment while they drove the five miles back to the junction where the road ran into the Strada del Vino.

When they came to a stop, a tan truck approached the intersection, traveling from the direction of Tangle Grove. "That's Mom," Jesse pointed.

Taylor recognized the tan truck that had left the park moments before they started down from the cave. He tapped his horn, and they waved when Lisa crossed in front of them.

Her mouth opened in surprise. She hesitated, then braked and pulled onto the shoulder. Taylor swung onto the main road and moved in behind her. She adjusted something on the seat and rushed out the door to meet them near the bed of the truck.

Her yellow summer dress looked as fresh as her hair and makeup. Taylor caught the scent of perfume as she approached.

"What have you three been up to?" she asked with what seemed like forced enthusiasm. Her eyes darted furtively, rousing Taylor's suspicious nature.

Jesse launched into an account of their afternoon, including the fact that someone had moved the flashlight in the cave and left a newspaper on the bunk.

Taylor watched her lips tighten. "It was probably Dan and some of his friends." She tried for lightness. "I seem to remember one of the flashlights lying around last time I was in there."

"When was that?" Taylor asked, focusing on her eyes.

"I don't actually remember," she said and changed the subject. "Asia, are you meeting us at 8:00 or 8:30 tomorrow morning? I didn't write it down."

"At 8:00. There's so much to do this week, I thought we'd better get an early start. Plus, I want to show Dad some of the plans."

"I promise I won't be late," Lisa gave an empty laugh. "I doubt I'll ever live that down."

Taylor raised an eyebrow and Jesse supplied the missing data. "Mom overslept her meeting with us on Saturday morning, and she's right, she won't ever live it down." He gave her an affectionate bear hug and Lisa played at being offended.

"You look pretty. What did you do today?" Jesse asked.

"I had to meet with someone from the corporation."

"Are they paying you for all of your time?"

"Don't I wish?" Lisa dodged her son's impertinent question. "I'm sure I'll get some perks along the way. But right now, I need to get home to make dinner. See you tomorrow." She hastened back inside the cab and drove off.

The encounter lingered in Taylor's mind after she left. Why did she seem so edgy? And deceitful?

***

Jesse asked Taylor to drop him off at his apartment. They said goodnight, then father and daughter headed to Bella Vista for dinner.

They arrived at a casual restaurant that Jesse said had been a favorite of the locals for over a quarter of a century. Sunday evening proved to be a slow night, so they were able to walk in and settle into a booth next to the wide front window. The sun was almost set, leaving just a few pink streaks across the sky. Stars began to glimmer, as did the lights up and down the enchanting streets of Bella Vista.

"Some town, huh?" Asia commented while they watched the pedestrians strolling down the sidewalks, window-shopping.

"Some world."

"What do you mean?" She tilted her head.

Taylor took a deep breath, letting it out slowly. "There's just so much here—it has the best of everything. I've never connected with a place before."

"I know what you're saying. Mont Castello is a perfect getaway mountain town, Bella Vista is the perfect resort town, and Tangle Grove offers so many design possibilities that I could never get bored here." She paused. "Jesse is a major bonus on top of all that."

"It's pretty sudden, don't you think?"

"Right now, it's just a mutual attraction, but so far I can't find any downside. He seems genuine and open about himself and his life; no pretenses like I would expect with a *pretty boy*." Then she laughed. "I think his mama raised him well."

"I think you're right on that account," he agreed.

He imagined Lisa taking her son and his cousins to the mine and digging for buried treasure. Then he thought of Thomas' resistance. How much of her life had he tried to suppress? And did that, or the empty nest syndrome, trigger this all-consuming Tangle Grove project? Whatever it was, it was driving her hard.

He noticed a convertible pull up next to the curb across the street. A man opened the door and stepped out. He was tall and blond and looked like a sports ad model as he strode up to an expensive-looking restaurant. He flashed a wide smile at two women who were on their way out. Recalling his old ways, Taylor was familiar with the blushes and laughter that resulted.

***

His thoughts getting darker by the second, Thomas waited at home for Lisa. Though he wanted to reprimand her tardiness when he heard the garage door open, he didn't want to alert her, so he dropped into his favorite chair instead and opened his book.

Rage was a precarious thing, but Thomas knew the trick to overcoming it. He slowed his breathing, thought of the near future when he would know all about Lisa's little secrets, and forced a smile. By the time she rushed into the kitchen, he was calm again.

"Hi, Thomas," her cheerful voice rang out. "Dinner in a sec."

His eyes traveled over her attractive dress and makeup. He grunted and lifted the book up to cover his rage.

Chapter 6

"Don't trip on that loose board," Asia warned Taylor. She led him up the courthouse steps on Monday. A hum of excited voices already filled the small room when they opened the door.

"Good morning," Lisa welcomed them. She looked confident and in control. He watched joy emanate from her face while she handed out packets and spoke to those in the building. *A big improvement over her demeanor last night.* Their eyes caught and she averted her gaze.

Asia took his hand and led him to a 3-D model of the two main streets proposed for downtown Tangle Grove. Two-dimensional lines and drawings represented the rest of the town. The mock-up of the new courthouse showed the replacement for the one in which they stood. It was not only official looking, but it set the tone for the rest of the town with its white clapboard siding and impressive clock on a central steeple. Granite steps extended the whole length of the building and gave a solid look to the facade, as did the massive double doors. Three stories of shuttered windows lined the front of the building like sentries.

"Asia, this is far and above anything I pictured." Pride filled Taylor's heart. Jesse arrived and waved at them just as Mayor Cook suggested they sit down to start the meeting of the Design Team. The mayor handed it over to Asia, who thanked him and jumped right in.

"The first thing I would like to accomplish is to provide this committee with the final decisions regarding the buildings that are involved in phase one of the new downtown. The Montebelli

Corporation has finalized all of their exterior building renovations." She looked at Lisa, who gave her a quick nod. "Mayor Cook is satisfied with the design of his accounting office, Verina Fields will open a second real estate agency in Tangle Grove, and Denny Chapman will be opening his law office here. The other business owners have also approved their changes.

"The rest of the properties are not up for sale at this time and the owners are not in a place to finance these kinds of improvements, which brings me to our second purpose. This is the time to ask questions, discuss ideas, and debate items on the agenda. I suggest we be as liberal as possible, but still be able to corral in any new project plans that fly in the face of the overall design you have adopted."

Taylor excused himself as the official meeting began. He decided to walk around Tangle Grove and get the *feel* of it, as Asia put it. From the courthouse, he made his way down Maple Street and passed an insurance company on the left-hand corner. He approached the coffee shop that Lisa designed, and the smell of cinnamon rolls and strong coffee drew him in through the open door of Sweet Elke Cafe.

A pleasant young woman stood behind the counter. Taylor gathered she was about Asia's age. "What can I get you?" she asked.

The trays of baked goods were enticing. "I'll have a bear claw and a cup of black coffee." Gesturing toward the display case, he asked, "Do you make all of these?"

"Not me," she laughed. "My husband is the baker and I'm the barista. It comes out about even and we each get to do what we love best."

"And what's your name?"

"Lilly," she answered, just as a toddler came in from the kitchen. "And this is Tina." A cherub-faced little girl waddled over to her mom and played peek-a-boo through her own thick, black curls that tumbled wildly from her head. She gave him a half smile and hid her face behind Lilly's long skirt.

"Hello, Tina, it's nice to meet you."

Tina giggled and made her way around the counter with a piece of bread she had been chewing on. She offered it to him while she jabbered, mimicking the hospitality she had seen her mother offer.

"She's utterly charming," he complimented.

"What brings you to Tangle Grove?" Lilly asked.

"I was in Mont Castello last week, covering the Summit Challenge for *USA Cycle Magazine*. My daughter is in Tangle Grove to go over plans for the town, so I decided to hang around for a while. It looks like a nice town," he added, diplomatically.

"Did I hear something about bikes?" A voice came from the kitchen, followed by its owner—a young man of medium build with the same eyes and dark, curly hair as the child. "Hello," he said and offered his hand. "I'm Joe."

Taylor shook his hand. "Hello. Yes, I was talking about the ride in Mont Castello last week. It was pretty spectacular."

"I know," Joe grinned. "I got to ride it." He looked over at his wife, "Lilly let me off for *three* days. That's my once-a-year exception to the daily grind—pun intended," he laughed.

"Your place is very welcoming, especially the aroma. I hear you're in charge of the tempting fare here."

"Absolutely," Joe said. "This is my first love—besides Lilly," he amended, "and Tina," he added as he grabbed her up and held her high over his head. The child giggled and squealed, then ran away when he set her down, daring her dad to play *chase me*. He let her go and stayed to talk with Taylor at his table for a minute.

Lilly came out and refilled Taylor's coffee.

"Did you do the decorating here?" Taylor asked her.

"Most of it. We had a general idea of what we wanted to do. Joe is Italian, so that was a given as a decorating style for our bakery. We hoped we'd be opening our shop in Bella Vista, but the rent was so high we had to look elsewhere."

Joe added, "People were talking about the changes in Tangle Grove, so we checked it out. That's when we met Lisa Richards. She helped us with some of the ideas and with the name. It's not Italian, but it echoes the history of the town. The construction on this building was almost finished, but when we told her what we wanted to do, she arranged to have the plans altered to create this amazing setting."

"Then she owns this building?" Taylor asked.

"No idea," Joe answered.

Taylor took another bite of his bear claw as an excuse to analyze this new information while Joe discussed the bike ride. When Taylor finished, he smiled. "Great pastry."

The sound of a spoon banging on a metal pan sent Joe jogging back toward the kitchen. He called over his shoulder, "Glad you enjoyed it. Come back anytime," and disappeared through the swinging door.

Taylor paid his bill, thanked Lilly for the coffee, and ventured back outside. The opposite corner of the street would accommodate the remodeled accounting office of Mayor Cook. The existing building consisted of cement block, painted grey with white trim. Sidewalks started and stopped along the street where some citizens had tried to improve things from time to time. Having seen the overall plan and the starting point, the amount of work needed was staggering. So was the willingness of these people to do it. Lisa would have her hands more than full keeping up with the progress.

Continuing down Maple Street, he recalled images of the new storefronts that would replace the existing structures. He stopped at the end of the downtown area where the Siebert property began and the Montebelli Inn would sit. Perfectly situated for a hotel, it offered views of the vineyards and the rest of the Siebert farm.

Farther down, the barn and grounds of the Siebert homestead would host a large weekly farmer's market, plus other activities throughout the year to draw visitors from the surrounding towns and counties to Tangle Grove. While briefing the overview of some promotional ideas for economic development, Taylor noticed Lisa's name was on the bottom of the proposal, again.

The morning heated up while Taylor took in street by street, trying to see it as Asia and Lisa did. Wiping his forehead, he guessed that the meeting would soon be breaking for lunch. He turned up a side street that led back toward the courthouse so he could peruse one more length of the project.

Many dilapidated homes resided here, with fewer commercial buildings. He stepped closer to the street when two dogs barked at him through a sagging chain-link fence that barely contained them. In one place, laundry hung unevenly to dry on a line that stretched from a house to a dying tree. *It's going to take A LOT to turn this town around.*

Crossing Pioneer Road to the courthouse, he spotted the members of the team filing out to his left, Asia and Jesse among them. He was angling toward them when a movement caught his eye on the right side of the building. The handsome blond man from the restaurant last night held Lisa's shoulders. She looked up at him, hands resting on his forearms while he spoke.

Taylor stopped midstride. *What's she up to?* He frowned as his mind raced to decipher the situation. She glanced over and her eyes widened. Breaking free of Taylor's scrutiny and the blond man's arms, she disappeared into the side door of the courthouse.

The man charged to the back parking lot and slipped into the red sedan. Taylor started to piece things together. They were together at Sweet Elke Park yesterday. *She'd just left him when she ran into us—no wonder she was so nervous. Is this what she meant when she said she was working on it?* His reasoning reinforced his motto of staying clear of feminine entanglement.

On a whim, he changed directions and reached the red convertible before the driver backed out. "Hello, I'm Steven Taylor," he said with forced congeniality and extended his hand.

"Yes?" the man snapped.

Taylor grasped for a reason for his intrusion. "I'm with *USA Cycle Magazine* and I'm doing a story on cycling in the area. Would you know where the most popular rides are?"

The man's eyes narrowed with impatience. "I wouldn't know. I'm an attorney from Nevada."

"Oh. What are you doing in a place like this?" Taylor spread his hands in a sympathetic gesture.

"I had to see a client." Following Taylor's hands that encompassed the disrepair around them, he gave a critical glance and said under his breath, "It'll be too bad if it all crashes down around her."

"By *her* you mean...?"

Checking his words, the man interrupted Taylor in mid-sentence. "I need to get going." He backed his car out of the parking area. Gravel sprayed as he sped toward the Strada del Vino.

Taylor's expression darkened. He watched the stylish man drive away. *What did I expect?* What he imagined clearly pulled Lisa off her pedestal. He walked toward the courthouse steps and Asia and Jesse waved him over. When he reached them, he asked, "Well, did you accomplish much?" His eyes flashed back and forth from them to the front door.

"We did but we'll probably need to work until five to finish with this portion of the job," she said with a satisfied smile.

"Five o'clock?" Jesse complained. "Why don't you guys wrap it up and I'll agree to everything you decide—I need a hike."

"Actually, your part of this is handled," she said. "I don't see any reason why you need to hang around." Jesse wrapped her up in a bear hug and planted a sweet kiss on her cheek."

Asia blushed and laughed. Taylor added in a mock threat, "Hey, guy, you just kissed my daughter."

"Don't I know it," Jesse laughed at him and released Asia.

"I'd better get this man out of here," Taylor said. "Jesse, I need to get some exercise myself, may I join you?"

Just then, Lisa walked up. She exchanged an uncomfortable look with him, then turned her attention to Jesse. "That was exhausting, but lunch should pick us up."

Jesse kept a straight face. "Asia said she doesn't want me anywhere around the afternoon meeting. All I do is drag everything out and confuse everybody."

Asia looked horrified and opened her mouth in protest. Lisa looked at her son and said with dry mirth, "Don't worry, dear. I've lived with him for twenty-seven years and I always know when he's lying."

"That would be a helpful power to possess," Taylor said, peering directly at Lisa.

She glared back, ignoring his comment. "I think Asia is right. We'll get much more done without you vying for her attention."

It was Jesse's turn to contend with red cheeks. "Touché. Taylor and I are going for a hike after lunch. I thought I'd show him Elke Falls and hike up the back side of Fire Mountain."

At the mention of Elke Falls, a slight start passed over Lisa's face. Her eyes shot a quick glance at Taylor, who was watching for just such a giveaway. *She's guilty as sin, literally.*

Changing the subject, Lisa said, "Let's get a sandwich at Sweet Elke's. They do a great job." They crossed the street with Jesse and Asia in the lead. That left Lisa to walk with Taylor, who lagged behind, causing a lengthy gap to open between the two pairs.

"So, I met your *friend*," Taylor stated. When she said nothing, he demanded, "What's going on here?"

There was a long pause before she answered, "There is nothing *going on* here. Gary Bristol is a representative of the Montebelli Corporation. He is in town to check on the progress."

"Then why wasn't he at the meeting, and why the clandestine rendezvous in Sweet Elke Park yesterday?" Taylor hissed.

Her head jerked sideways, eyes full of fear and surprise.

Bingo. Let her explain that away.

Taking a breath, she uttered her words with care. "Mr. Bristol is only here to handle *financial* arrangements for the corporation. I oversee the design and planning aspects. There's no need for him to sit in on these meetings. We met at the park yesterday to discuss some things privately regarding this project. You may have noticed there aren't many options for private meeting spaces here in Tangle Grove. You also might have noticed that Gary is quite attractive. It wouldn't do for me to be seen in public with him. It would raise too many questions that I'm not ready to answer yet."

Taylor paused on the sidewalk and turned toward her, "And don't you think it would look suspicious being spotted alone in a little-used park? I think you can do better than that."

Instant fury swept over her countenance. "Anyone who would've come upon us in the park would have seen two people pouring over dull paperwork and boring talk of business. Not that any of this is your business, but I know *exactly* what I'm doing and how to get what I want."

She twisted away from him and caught up to Jesse and Asia. "Hey guys, I left some papers at home that I need for this afternoon. Go ahead and have lunch and I'll see you at two o'clock, Asia." With that, she crossed the street and got in her car without a backward glance.

They looked at Taylor for some explanation for the sudden change. He just shrugged his shoulders as if he had no idea and then walked into the coffee shop they'd reached.

Lisa pulled a U-turn in her black sedan and sped down Maple Street. She passed the coffee shop window, eyes straight ahead.

Inside, Jesse and Asia chatted and ate their sandwiches. Taylor replied to their queries, but only a small portion of his mind was on the conversation. *Why am I involving myself in this? It's none of my business what goes on in this woman's life.* Still, he was surprised at the betrayal he felt, and at how much he hoped that Lisa's answer regarding the attorney was the truth.

He thought back to the night outside of Varano's restaurant. She'd seemed so vulnerable, trying to fight her way out of a life that kept her small. It had pulled at his compassion. Now here she was, being deeply secretive about this unsavory attorney. Her life teamed with contradictions. And what did the guy mean that it could *all come crashing down around her*? Was the corporation she worked for putting her in jeopardy—and Asia's project with it? He was certain Lisa was too naive to know she was in over her head. The man from Nevada seemed menacing.

Wait. A sudden thought occurred to him. With a plan in mind, he entered the conversation with more enthusiasm and took a delicious bite into his mile-high turkey sandwich. His mind was stuck on one word: Nevada.

Chapter 7

After lunch, Asia headed back for the courthouse, which left Jesse and Taylor to make their plans for the afternoon. Soon the tires of Taylor's SUV were crunching on the gravel as they pulled into the parking area of Sweet Elke Park.

Taylor got out, grabbed a water bottle, and leaned against the car to stretch his legs. He took a long look around. Even with the noise of the water flowing through Wildcat Creek, a strong, discernible peace flooded through him as he stood there. He raised an eyebrow at Jesse.

"It's cool, isn't it?" Jesse said in a low voice.

"What's causing this sensation—the water?"

"It's hard to say. Scientists might say it's ozone generated from the crashing water. Others swear it's the spirit of Elke Van Buren. Legend has it she drowned saving a youngster who fell into the water. Apparently, the child was running from a large wildcat when he tripped. Elke is purported to walk the banks of the creek, guarding those who pass here. The feeling of peace, it is said, comes from the sense of being watched over."

He took another deep breath and looked down at the creek. "I'll wager on ozone."

"You're probably right, but don't let my mom hear you say that. She believes wholeheartedly in the story. She was hiking around here when she spotted a wildcat stalking her. Then, for no reason, the cat growled and ran off. A peaceful breeze passed over her and all the fear left. She says she knows God sent a guardian angel, Elke or not."

"What was she doing hiking out here alone?" Again, he was aggravated at Lisa's lack of common sense.

"I told you she used to bring us here as kids. She loves this area and comes up here often—says it gives her a place to clear her mind."

He thought about that for a moment, remembering his own experience on Mt. Thurman. "Does your dad ever hike with her?"

"It gives Dad the creeps. He's a psychiatrist, you know. Wants an answer for everything. Something this tangible without an explanation doesn't work for him." Then he added with a serious note, "He doesn't like Mom coming here, but it seems to be one area he can't control. He has this whole issue of her *family*. It's the only place where she outranks him."

He decided not to follow the line of questioning. He'd gotten the picture. This was the one place Lisa could come be herself. The legend keeps most people away and her guardian angel keeps her safe.

"There's a trail that begins over here," Jesse said, leading the way alongside the creek. Massive trees lined the shallow banks and filtered the afternoon sun. They hiked a short distance and came upon a large, gracefully carved marble grave. The base rose three feet off the ground and the headstone loomed another three feet above that. It sat above the rushing water. Fresh flowers spilled from the permanent vase cut into the white marble. Jesse stopped and stared at the flowers. "I wonder who put these here."

"Maybe your mother came by," he suggested, without revealing what he'd seen. "She was in Tangle Grove yesterday, perhaps she stopped and brought flowers."

"I guess so," Jesse replied and moved past the tomb.

"Hold on," he said and leaned over the grave. He noted the writing on the headstone, and then his eyes wandered over the flat marble and several interesting markings. A beautiful compass embellished the top of the slab. "Why would that be engraved on a tomb?"

"People have speculated that since the Dutchman was a ship builder, he might have had some kind of superstitious belief that the compass would keep Elke's spirit from losing her way."

Continuing to search the stone, Taylor noticed the thinner lines were marked, 'N', 'S', 'E', and 'W'. He traced the thicker, secondary lines down over the edge on the left-hand side of the stone and discovered another engraving. This one was a picture of a door with what looked like rays of light coming out. "This looks like a replica of the cave door. Maybe the rays indicate the brilliance of the fire opals."

"That's what we thought, too. There are other markings at various points. We always hoped they were clues to another treasure, but nothing's ever come of it," Jesse said. "Look, here are more rays on the other side that seem to extend to nothing at all. There's a smaller door with a rounded top and some kind of scrollwork on it, and Elke's birth date, October twenty-first. If they are clues, none of us have ever been able to piece them together."

"Do you mind if I take a couple of photos?" Taylor indicated the camera on his cell phone.

"Be my guest," Jesse grinned. "Treasure piquing your interest?"

"Let's just say I like to solve mysteries." It only took a few minutes to snap all the shots he wanted. He traipsed to the head of the grave near the water and took a photo of the back of the headstone. So far, nothing was coming to him, if there even was a meaning.

They continued on the trail, level with the creek, until the path turned uphill, and they began to hike in earnest. The crashing of the waterfall beckoned them upward. Refreshing spray blew across their faces, as Taylor followed Jesse up the cascading falls. His lungs labored as they pushed off from boulder to boulder, avoiding the rushing water in between.

One more jump and they reached a flat spot where they could rest and watch the path of the water plunging into the creek below. The vistas that opened seemed to go on forever with one mountain range following another, drawing Taylor's eyes to a most distant point that at last became obscure and blended into the atmosphere.

Taking in the scene from one end of the valley to the other, he fell silent. He drank from his water bottle and his breathing slowed. Jesse was equally quiet. Neither man felt the need to carry on a conversation. With few large trees to shade them, the warmth of the afternoon sun intensified. Sweat ran freely down their faces and the softest of breezes cooled them.

"I like how green everything is, even in late summer," Taylor commented. "I grew up in Arizona. Still have a house there. It has a different kind of beauty, but by this time of year, you really don't want to be outside."

"Do you have family there?" Jesse asked, after taking a long drink of water.

"I have an aunt, my mother's younger sister. She was always my favorite, probably because she spoiled me." He smiled at the thought of her. "Aunt Caty. She's still in great health, walks a lot when it's not too hot. Has two kids, my cousins, who live near her. Other than that, my parents have passed on and my younger brother lives in New York with his wife and my two nieces. Neither of us had a son, so it's the end of the *Taylor* line from our end." He laughed. "I guess I didn't need to give you my whole family lineage, did I?"

"No problem. I'd like to have kids someday—maybe three or four." He grinned and Taylor could tell they were both thinking of Asia.

Taylor looked back over the valley. "I imagine this was a great place to grow up." His mind drifted. What would it be like to settle down in a place like this? With a woman like Lisa? He sobered. This was the second time he was stunned at the strong emotions he felt toward her. Years had passed since he'd allowed thoughts like that to enter his mind. The peace of this area must have relaxed him to a point where dreaming seemed natural, safe.

He blocked out the idea. She was married for one *big* thing. And even if she wasn't, he'd been down that dead-end road with deceitful women before. Except for Asia, he hadn't met *one* who wasn't scheming. For now, he enjoyed great friends in places all over the country and had a terrific daughter. That was all he needed.

Jesse had started to climb again. Taylor put the lid on his water bottle and followed him. The trail continued up and over the mountain. By the time they climbed down the other side and doubled back, the sun had started its descent. They came out of one last clump of trees into a clearing. Once again, the sky cast amazing flames onto the ridge.

"Do you recognize where we are?" Jesse asked.

He took a few more strides and looked around. The door to the Dutchman's mine stood on his left. The powerful rays of the sun were striking the metal surface and hardware on the door, causing light to radiate in all directions. Excitement caught in his chest. "That's the picture etched into Elke's grave."

Jesse laughed aloud. "I know. I was hoping to catch the time just right for you to see it. Still, it doesn't answer any questions."

He took photos of the spectacle. "Well, it won't hurt to keep it all documented," he said and caught one more angle. He walked over to the edge of the clearing and looked out toward Sweet Elke Park. "Can you see her grave from here?"

"No. The park is farther around the side of the mountain. What are you thinking?"

"Well, if the Dutchman was as detailed as he seems to have been, then I guess those markings on Elke's grave are exactly where he wanted them. It's hard to judge for certain, but it would seem that the southern tip of the compass marking would just about point to this spot—as the crow flies. It wouldn't take a professional much time to find out."

"That could be," Jesse said, "but it'll never happen."

He studied the imaginary line from the grave to the mine. At Jesse's comment, he glanced at the young man. "Why not?"

"Mom has always resisted publicity that brings attention back to the mine and Elke's grave. She says that stirring up mysteries brings out the rudest kind of fortune hunters who have always trashed and vandalized the area."

He thought about that. Maybe Lisa had other considerations—like keeping the area abandoned for *private* meetings.

Jesse's voice interrupted his thoughts. "Mom is the eldest of Joren Van Buren's descendants. That puts her in charge of the mine, the private land around Elke's grave, and a whole host of other family *heirlooms*, like Fire Mountain." He laughed at his understatement. "There's really not a lot to do unless some problem arises that needs a decision made. She has sole authority."

"Does that ever cause any rift in the family?"

"Not anymore, now that the stones are gone. No one else wants to manage the grounds, or problems. When Grandma Rose was about to pass on, she called Mom in for a private meeting. Mom never spoke much about it, except to say that Grandma passed on the traditions of the family to her, along with the legal documents and titles that her attorney prepared. I once asked her if there were any family secrets involved. She got a funny look in her eye and told me I would just have to wait until she passed on the *secrets* to me."

Taylor took in the new information, contemplating what kind of secrets could be possible. Jesse shifted his daypack and suggested they walk the rest of the way down via the road. The trip back was quiet. They were tired from the exertion of the hike, and it felt good to be going downhill on a smooth road.

They were almost to the car when Jesse's cell phone rang. "It's Mom," he said and turned on the speakerphone so Lisa could hear him tell Taylor, "My mommy wants to know why I'm late getting home." Taylor laughed.

Lisa's dry reply came back, "The only reason I'm calling is because a certain young lady has been waiting for an hour to decide what to do because her father and his young friend have gone off to play John Muir."

"I thought you were meeting until five o'clock," Jessie said.

"We were exhausted and decided to quit early. Now we're sitting around the pool in our bikinis wondering where you are."

Taylor noticed that Jesse's step quickened toward the car, then stopped. "Mom, you don't have a bikini."

Lisa laughed. So did Taylor.

Jesse frowned, "Funny."

"I'm sorry, but you started it."

Taylor could hear the teasing in her voice.

"We really are sitting around the pool, and I imagine it would feel great to dive into this clean, cool water after a long hike. I fixed some enchiladas and there are ice cold drinks in the cooler. Sound good?"

Thomas took the phone from Lisa at this point and added, "Jesse, tell Taylor, that includes him too."

Taylor wondered how Lisa felt about that after this afternoon's clash. There was one way to find out. "I wouldn't miss it," he said, angling his mouth toward Jesse's phone.

"We'll be about twenty-five minutes," Jesse said, and ended the call.

As they drove back over the bridge, Jesse shouted, "Look!" A huge mountain lion crept through the underbrush next to the path they had been on only minutes earlier. Taylor stopped the SUV and watched it leave. He and Jesse looked at each other and Taylor whistled. The hair on the back of his neck tingled.

Chapter 8

At the Richards' residence, Jesse led Taylor through the immaculate house to the backyard. Thomas read the newspaper while Lisa and Asia chatted under a blue and white striped umbrella. Taylor raised an appreciative eyebrow at the contemporary landscape and blue-tiled pool. On the far side, a large, angular waterfall cascaded into a small pond.

Thomas called out, "Taylor! Come on outside." He arose and shook hands. "You guys picked a hot one to take a hike on."

"It was a scorcher. Thank you for the invitation," Taylor said.

"There are extra pairs of trunks laid out in the guest room—I'm sure something will fit," Thomas offered.

Taylor turned to Asia and Lisa. "Hello, ladies."

"Hi, Dad," Asia replied. "Did you have a good time?"

"Great time." He appraised Lisa's cool reaction and wondered at her acting abilities—just a normal, happy housewife.

"Hello, Taylor," she replied. "You look like you could use a dip in the pool."

"You're reading my mind," he taunted. She ignored him and reached for her iced tea. He asked, "Which way to the guest room?"

"I'll show you," Jesse offered. He grinned at Asia. "We'll be right back."

***

Lisa glanced up as they returned in swimming trunks, Taylor with a towel thrown casually over one shoulder. Jesse leaned to give her a kiss on the cheek and grab a handful of nachos from the table. She used the diversion and clipped, "A way to a man's heart." He grinned and stepped sideways to give Asia a quick hug.

"Can I get you a beer, Taylor?" Thomas asked, his face bright. Lisa knew he was elated about entertaining a celebrity of the cycling world.

"After a short swim," Taylor replied and dove into the pool.

"Me, too," Jesse said, jumping in after him.

Taylor struck out with long, powerful stokes and was nearing the end of the pool. Though shorter in stature, Jesse's strokes were quick and efficient. It was impressive to see him catching up to the bigger man. Taylor caught on and increased his speed. By the time they reached the end of the home stretch, Jesse was nearly even with him. The silent competition and playful atmosphere helped Lisa relax. She glanced at Asia, and they chuckled.

"I think I'll have to get in on this." Thomas rose and dove into the pool, giving himself an extra push for the next wave of the competition. Taylor and Jesse followed and pushed off hard. The threesome tore down their *lanes*, turned at the end with powerful flips, and charged back. The excitement mounted. Splashing water rose high in the air as the men neared their goal. They reached the edge, Thomas just a stroke behind. Asia and Lisa were laughing by this time. The men gasped for air as they hauled themselves out of the pool.

"You guys aren't bad for old men," Jesse teased. He grabbed a towel and sat down next to Asia, offering to give her a wet hug.

"No, thank you," she laughed and pushed him away.

"It's a good thing I stay in shape. Of course, you two had a head start," Thomas said.

Taylor's forehead wrinkled, ending in a faint, one-sided smirk. He continued to dry off and found a chair next to Thomas, who handed him a bottle.

"To the conquerors," Thomas offered. The three men clinked their bottles. Lisa and Asia shook their heads.

"I'll be right back," Lisa said. She entered the kitchen, listening through the screen door as the men discussed their swimming histories. Thomas recounted his experience of growing up in California, swimming and surfing at the beach. Taylor was on his college swim team and still swam regularly at the hotels where he stayed and the gym when he was home.

"Where do you call home?" Thomas asked.

"He doesn't," Asia chimed in. "He travels all the time."

Taylor glanced at her and smiled. "That's true, but I still own a home in Arizona."

"Dinner's here," Lisa said and placed a platter in the center of the table. "I'll be right back with the salad."

"Can I help?" Asia offered.

"No, thank you. The salad is all I need, so please dig in." The hungry group heaped their plates with the steaming Mexican fare.

Thomas continued his tale of surfing and seemed delighted to boast about his exploits along the southern California coast. "I grew up in Malibu. My family was wealthy and encouraged me to travel in the summers, so my friends and I explored one beach after another searching for the perfect wave—and great babes," he said in a mock hushed tone.

***

Taylor watched Lisa bring the salad to the table and sit down. There was a temporary lull in the conversation as everyone started in on the meal.

"The flavors in this are amazing," Asia commented between bites.

"My mom's a great cook," Jesse said, his plate nearly empty.

"It helps to be serving starving hikers and swimmers," Lisa smiled. "Did you enjoy yourselves?"

"It was spectacular," Taylor responded. "The views from Fire Mountain go on forever and the folklore around Sweet Elke is...stimulating."

Thomas shook his head. "Did Jesse fill your head with all the legends and *ghosty* lore?"

Taylor noticed Lisa's mouth tighten.

Jesse's eyes shifted between Lisa and Thomas. In an apparent attempt to avert a quarrel, he changed the conversation to a new topic. "We saw a huge mountain lion as we were leaving. It disappeared into the brush just when we crossed the bridge."

Asia's eyes widened. "Did you have a gun or something to protect yourselves?"

"They weren't in any danger," Lisa said. She kept her eyes on her plate.

"What she means," Thomas cut in, "is that wildcats are more afraid of people than we are of them. All you need to do is rattle some sticks and make a lot of noise and they run off."

Taylor noticed that Thomas seemed agitated, and that Lisa avoided the conversation.

Thomas asked, "Would you like another beer?"

He answered, "No, thanks, but water would be great." Lisa had just finished filling her glass and passed the pitcher to Taylor. He gave her a thin, cordial smile and took the handle of the beautiful glass antique. "Thanks."

Thomas opened another beer and guzzled half of it down in one gulp. Taylor noted a stash of empty bottles sitting next to the ice chest. Lisa followed his stare and cringed when their eyes met.

"Well, maybe we should plan a hunting party," Thomas said, a sarcastic expression directed at Lisa. "It's about time we clear out that menace that haunts the park."

She cast him an angry look and left the table. "I'll get more water," she said, and picked up the pitcher. When she passed the ice chest, Taylor saw her grab the empty bottles and carry them inside.

"I think she's got something going with that cougar," Thomas gave a demeaning laugh. "She used to be my party girl 'til God saved her from its jaws. Now she'll hardly drink and has a headache more often than not, if you know what I mean."

"Dad!" Jesse's face reddened.

Thomas acquiesced. "My apologies," he said, unsmiling. "This story has just gotten a little stale—excuse me." He got up with a waver, bumping the table and spilling the water glasses. Scowling, he made his way into the house.

Asia's mouth dropped open. Jesse's color reached the tips of his ears as he explained, "I'm sorry about that. A bad mixture of sun, beer, and a raw nerve. I shouldn't have brought it up."

"You can't walk around everyone's Achilles' heels," Taylor said. From inside the house, they heard a loud crash and Lisa cry out. Taylor jumped and ran to the kitchen, where he found the water pitcher shattered on the floor. Lisa crouched, holding her arm while trying to pick up the glass with her other hand.

"What happened," he demanded, eyes searching the area. Jesse and Asia arrived a moment later.

Lisa attempted to chuckle and tried to brush away her tears without being noticed. When that failed, she worked to calm her voice, "I'm so clumsy. This was my grandmother's pitcher and…now it's gone." She continued to collect the pieces into a pile, trying not to sniffle. "It's all right, just a sentimental piece of glass."

Jesse pulled his mom up and gave her a comforting hug. Taylor grabbed some paper towels and sopped up the water.

"No, please," she begged, "you're company, I can get this."

"Actually," Taylor said, grabbing the broom, "you've served us quite enough. Now, please, go back outside with Asia and let Jesse and me clean this up." When Lisa took Asia's hand to head back to the patio, Taylor noticed angry red marks on her arm. His teeth ground in an effort to maintain his temper.

Thomas came to the kitchen door just as the two men finished cleaning up the mess. Jesse ignored him and headed back outside.

"It's just a very old and ugly pitcher," Thomas said. Then his voice rose, "She's more upset about that pitcher and her precious family secrets than about embarrassing me in front of my company. It's my house—I can break anything in it."

Taylor's head swung around. He glared down into the shorter man's face. "Did you do this?" He pointed to the broken glass but meant so much more.

Thomas stepped back and his bravado crumbled. "It was an accident." He attempted to laugh it off. "What's the big deal? I came around the corner too fast and knocked into her as she was coming out. There's nothing I can do about it now. She can buy a new one tomorrow."

Remembering that he was a guest, and the stash of empty beer bottles, Taylor backed off, but he seethed inside. *Why was Lisa choosing to live this way—and have her secrets on the side?* "Yes, I guess women can get all worked up about the smallest things," he said.

Thomas missed the sarcasm. "All this fuss," he said. "Let's go back outside. Can I get you another beer?"

With all the control he could muster, Taylor said, "You know, I'm exhausted from the hike. I think I'll get back to my room and get a good night's sleep." He heard tentative laughs drifting in through the screen door. "I'll just go say good night." He moved past Thomas.

Jesse finished telling a joke. When Taylor got to the door, Lisa had a smile on her face. It was forced and that made him even angrier.

"Taylor, I'm so sorry about the scene I caused," she said. Please, come sit down and I'll get dessert ready. Her tone sounded dispirited.

He wasn't about to play this game but put on his own false smile and lied anyway. "Please forgive my departure. It has nothing to do with the upset, really. I'm just bushed, and my waistline could do without dessert for a change." He knew Lisa was trying to normalize the situation, whatever that was. Apparently, she also sensed it would be unwise to push Thomas tonight.

She headed for the kitchen and Taylor turned to Asia, "Honey, are you leaving soon?" He didn't want her around this erratic behavior.

Oblivious to the exchange in the kitchen, she replied, "I think I'll hang out for a while."

Jesse must have sensed Taylor's apprehension. He got up and followed him to the front door. "Don't worry about Dad. He's just a jerk when he drinks."

"Still, he seems awfully angry. It might do for you to stay here tonight."

Jesse thought about that for a moment. "I'll make sure Asia gets home, then come back and sleep in my old room. I still do that occasionally, so Dad won't think anything of it."

Taylor put his hand on Jesse's shoulder. "Good man," he said, then turned and left.

***

Jesse took a deep breath and rejoined Asia.

She gazed up at him. "It's too bad about your mom's pitcher, but everything seems fine now. She's just gone in to get dessert."

Jesse looked down at her sweet face and, on impulse, bent down to kiss her softly on the mouth. As she responded, he lingered, enjoying the amazing sensations pulsing through him. He backed away, their eyes still holding each other. "I've wanted to do that ever since we met."

The moment ended when Lisa's footsteps approached the patio door. She opened the screen and set down the dessert tray. "Just strawberry shortcake," she announced with a weary voice.

"It looks wonderful," Asia remarked at the mix of fresh strawberries and blueberries tumbling over the whipped cream.

Jesse studied her sad eyes. "You're tired, Mom. If you want to go to bed, we can clean up."

She gave him a thankful smile. "I think you're right. I'm exhausted from the day." She rose to leave just as Thomas showed up with another beer.

"Where are you going?" he demanded.

"I'm tired and going to bed," she answered, not meeting his eyes. "Dessert is ready, and Jesse will handle the cleanup." With that, she made her way toward the stairs.

Jesse watched as Thomas gave her a scalding look then slumped down in his chair and made an attempt at conversation. He soon excused himself as well.

An hour later, dishes done, Jesse drove Asia back to the room her company had reserved for her in Bella Vista. They pulled up to the curb near the front door of the Raffinato Inn. Its four-story façade conjured up antiquity, but the hotel was less than a dozen years old. Hand-hewn stone made up the arching entry and overhung the oak and beveled glass doors.

Jesse walked around the car and opened Asia's door. He took her hand to help her out.

"My, how gallant," she smiled up at him.

"Not at all, fair maiden," he teased back. The brightest of stars lit the night. In front of the hotel, he pulled her to him, kissing her long and slow. They held hands after the kiss. "It's hard to let go of you," he said, gazing into her exquisite eyes.

She smiled. "Thank you for a wonderful evening. Will I see you tomorrow?"

"Oh, yeah," Jesse nodded and smiled broadly. *And every day for the rest of your life.*

One last hug and he opened the hotel door for her. She walked in and waved through the glass. He got into his car and drove off to his parents' home, seeing Asia's beautiful face in his mind's eye. *Now what are we going to do about this?*

Chapter 9

Clouds gathered overnight and did their best to hold off the oppressive heat that promised to escalate. Taylor sat on the deck off his room in Mont Castello and let his mind wander. *Did I overreact with Thomas?* Some men get sloppy when they drink. Perhaps it was just an accident like he said. But, if he hadn't grabbed Lisa's arm, he wouldn't have hurt her or broken the pitcher.

Was Lisa overly sensitive like Thomas suggested? There were certainly times in the last few days where she riled easily. Taylor decided not to come to any hard conclusions just yet. Inside, however, he knew one thing—he detested Thomas Richards.

Feeling restless, he put on hiking boots and climbed the familiar trail heading up Mt. Thurman. Stopping at the historic marker again, he read the names aloud, now recognizing more of them. "Alberto and Georgio Romano, Adamo Basso, Emilio Moretti, Fabio and Doriano Varano, Filippo Costa, Costantino Montebelli …"

He grabbed the sign and traced the name *Montebelli*. A grin spread over his face. So, they were from around here. Who were these powerful people who wielded money and influence over Tangle Grove? And had Lisa running ragged for them? Desperation for significance could make her vulnerable to anything anyone promised. "Let's go see who's descended from the Montebellis, and if they are friend or foe to Lisa."

Trekking back down the mountain, he pondered why he was so caught up in the intrigue that surrounded Lisa. Because it involved Asia? No. Her company was experienced in working with people and corporations. She wouldn't get hurt. Then there was Asia and Jesse's romance. What kind of upbringing had he experienced? Both Thomas and Lisa exhibited erratic behavior at times. Did it run in the family?

As much as those things bothered him, in truth, he sensed she was in trouble. He could manage the allure he felt easily enough, but he couldn't deny his concern for her as a person. She seemed headstrong, ready to ignore the threat he instantly recognized in that attorney.

Another thought nagged. Certainly, there was no love between her and Thomas, and the man was clearly abusive. So why not just leave the guy honestly and pursue a career or whatever she was after? What kept her there? These questions pressed him to find out the truth.

***

An hour later, Taylor headed to the museum he'd seen in Bella Vista. Entering the old brick building located on a side street, he stuffed a couple of dollars into the wooden donation box and addressed the caretaker who sat behind the counter. "Good morning." He stretched out his hand. "I'm Steven Taylor."

The old guy checked his watch. With a gravelly voice he muttered, "Not quite noon—just made it under the line." He shook Taylor's hand. "I'm Stan Harding. What can I do you for?"

He chuckled. "I saw the name *Montebelli* on a historical sign while I was hiking this morning. Are there any existing relatives around?"

Stan tilted his head and eyed him with his moist bottom lip stuck out. "What are the chances of two people coming in asking that same question in the same week?"

Taylor's eyebrows raised. "Who else was asking?"

"Verina Fields, a realtor in town. She came in looking for any information I had on the Montebellis."

"What did you tell her?"

"Same thing I told Adam and Stephen Basso three years ago. I've searched through all our records and there's no mention of the Montebellis."

Taylor frowned. Why would Lisa's enemies, the Bassos, and her employer, be curious about the Montebelli family? He tapped his fingers on the counter. On the one hand, it would be natural for residents to wonder about such a big force in their community. Lisa's connection to this could just be incidental.

On the other hand, Asia had commented that outside of Lisa, Baker and Thymes' only correspondence with the Montebelli Corporation was with their business office in Lake Tahoe. If the Basso's wanted to hurt Lisa's relationship with her employer, first they'd need to know who it was. That might explain why Lisa maintained their confidentiality. But what would the corporation's reason be for keeping such secrecy?

An impatient frown pinched Stan's wrinkled face as he waited for Taylor's next question.

Taylor cleared his throat. "Sorry, just thinking. I wonder if you have any information on the first settlers in the area—like the Dutchman I've been hearing about, and his descendants."

The aging man curled his gnarled fingers around the brass top of his cane and limped across the uneven timbers to a large desk with a shelf above it. Taking down a much-used leather bound book, he set it on the desk and opened the rugged cover to the first page. Old tintype photos lay under protective plastic covers with handwritten names set at an angle below each person. A typed label repeated the handwriting for clarity.

"They're all here," he said, stubby chin lifted. "We have one of the best kept histories around. I believe in roots, and work to keep the history of the original residents intact."

Taylor turned the pages. "What is this old newspaper article about?" He pointed to a headline that read, "Van Buren's Fortune Defended."

Stan smiled, happy to answer a familiar question. "That's an article regarding the long, drawn-out lawsuit brought against the Van Buren estate by Katherine Basso. It cost Jochem a pretty penny, but he won. Before he died, he set up a family trust. After the problems with Katherine, he wasn't taking any chances that outsiders would get hold of his descendants' property again." He pursed his lips. "Even with all the precautions, they're still having problems with the Bassos."

That caught Taylor's attention. Pretending to study more of the photos, he casually asked, "What kind of problems?"

Eager to talk about the local gossip, Stan leaned closer and lowered his voice for dramatic effect. "Well, the scuttlebutt is that

Angela Basso and her friends are trying to get the state to take Fire Mountain away from the Van Buren's and turn it into historic public land. 'Course the state won't pay a tenth of what it's worth. Jochem would turn over in his grave if that ever happened."

"What good would that do them? The mine is depleted as far as I understand."

"Angela believes differently—anyway she'd like to go look for herself. But the main reason," he looked squarely at Taylor, "is just for spite. She and her mother were irate when Rose Giovanni became the Guardian. Always bad blood between those women. When Rose passed the honor of the *Guardian* to Lisa Richards, she became the target."

"What's that about—the Guardian thing?" Taylor's curiosity heightened.

Stan winked. "Most people think it only exists as a responsibility to manage the family's extensive trust. But there's a lot more than they're telling. Enough has leaked out that we know there are secrets only the Guardian is privy to—and *that* creates no end of envy on the part of the Bassos *and* a lot of others."

"What kind of secrets are you talking about?" Taylor wondered what other information he might be able to gather about Lisa.

"Well, if we knew, they wouldn't be secrets, now would they?" Stan smirked but continued with the details of the conspiracy. "Some say they have to do with the whereabouts of another rich vein of fire opals. Some involve the ghost that haunts the mine, and some explain the clues left on Sweet Elke's grave." Eyes twinkling, his voice became lower and even more dramatic. "That whole area is surrounded with mystery."

Taylor surmised these were just colorful stories brought on by insatiable curiosity. Moving toward his next goal, he asked, "How was Rose Giovanni connected to the Dutchman?"

Stan's head jerked back at the change in subject. He frowned and dropped the conspiratorial tone. Turning the book forward a couple of pages, he pointed to a photograph of a pretty, dark-haired girl holding the hand of an austere woman with fair hair. An equally grave man stood behind them.

"That's little Rose Giovanni with her father, Emilio Giovanni and her mother, Klara Van Buren. Klara was the daughter of Adriana and

Joren Van Buren, the Dutchman's eldest son—here's a photo of them." He pointed to the opposing page.

Taylor studied the photograph. He could see the base of Fire Mountain in the background with the hint of a narrow dirt road winding its way up toward the mine. A portion of a large wooden house was visible behind the family.

Klara stood in front of her beautiful, somber mother, Adriana, both in elegant lace dresses. The blond, haughty-looking husband, Joren, had a black suit and striped vest. They appeared prosperous compared to most of the people in the other photos. Studying each of the names written in longhand underneath the photo, he pointed. "Only Adriana's married name is here."

Stan looked at the photograph. "Hmm. Doesn't look like anyone bothered to put down her maiden name. Maybe she's listed somewhere else." He looked back a few pages. Unsuccessful, he scratched his bald head. "I never noticed that. Well, there's probably a few who got left out here and there." Then he had another idea. "Let's check the legal records. A marriage license should do the trick." He smiled at his own cleverness.

Picking through the keys on his key ring, he took a small brass one and inserted it into the front of an antique file drawer, labeled *Copies of Official Records of Harding County*. Seeing his family name, he smiled. "Not many people stay put these days. They just give up their roots and family foundations."

He found his quarry. "Aha, *Marriage Certificates*." Leafing through the documents, arranged in alphabetical order by the groom's last name, Stan came to the *Van Buren* section. "Daan and Katherine, Joren and Adriana. Here we are!" he exclaimed upon finding the record. Then he said, "Oh," with great disappointment.

Taylor peeked closer. It looked like water had damaged a portion of the original document. A smudge obscured the bride's last name where someone tried to dry it. It had been copied that way.

Stan sighed. "That's disappointing. Well, if she was born around here, the birth record will have her name." He rubbed his chin. "But I wouldn't know where to start, would I?" He turned to Taylor, "I guess we'll just have to chalk it up to another fact lost in history."

Taylor felt disappointed too. "Well, thank you for your expertise. This was an interesting excursion back in time." He shook Stan's hand and left the building, squinting in the bright noonday sunshine.

Asia and Lisa were spending the day in meetings and Jesse was working until dinner, so Taylor decided to eat lunch alone in town. It would give him a chance to piece together some of his thoughts. Finding an inconspicuous restaurant near the museum, he walked in and ordered at the counter. After paying, he chose one of the booths along the wall. They were constructed of golden oak and had high backs for privacy—just what he needed.

He took out his pen and notebook to write down the facts he knew. The small section of folded newspaper he found in the Dutchman's mine fell out. Frowning, he changed his mind and decided it was better to write down the things he didn't know.

Unfolding the newspaper, he started his list. *Newspaper was in the cave. Who put it there? How did they get in?* Then he looked at the circled ads. All three were located in Tangle Grove. *Were Jesse's cousins interested in properties in Tangle Grove?* He made a note to ask him.

After writing down the address for each property, he turned the paper over to see if there were any other markings and noticed smudges where dirty fingers had held the newsprint. He placed one of his fingers over a fingerprint. His dwarfed it. *A woman's? Lisa's?* He imagined her playing in the mine with the kids, dirt covering their hands and faces after digging for buried treasure.

An idea snapped his head up. *What if Lisa went to dig for fire opals?* Perhaps as the Guardian, she knew things, like where to look for the opals. And, researching properties for the Montebelli Corporation, she was the most logical person to be circling Tangle Grove ads, at least as far as he knew. *Whoa.* Perhaps she was selling fire opals to buy stock in the corporation, or to buy her own investment property in Tangle Grove. That would explain her herculean efforts to improve it.

That would also align with her, *I'm working on it,* comment. Just a *tiny* secret to keep from your husband, along with a *private* attorney. The thought of Lisa with that guy still irked him. What was she up to with all her sneaking around? He spent an hour in between bites writing down what he may have discovered.

While deep in thought on the far side of the restaurant, he was barely conscious of two women who came in. They were engaged in conversation as they walked to the back to place their orders. When his ear caught the words, "Fire Mountain," his attention zeroed in.

He glanced around the back of his booth and recognized Angela Basso from the jewelry store. She was dressed in a light silk blouse, unbuttoned provocatively low. The coordinating skirt fit smoothly over the curve of her hips, with a side slit that ended inches above the knee. Very high heels added even more height to the already tall woman.

The woman standing next to Angela was shorter by a foot. They appeared to be about the same age, but this woman was broad, her flat shoes adding a squatty quality. Her clothes added to the impression of stockiness with her plain white cotton shirt ending at the widest portion of her hips. As she listened to her companion, her square jaw seemed to have a constant strain around her lips. Taylor ducked out of sight and listened.

"When have they scheduled the vote?" the woman asked Angela.

"September 26th, but I've asked a *friendly* state representative not to put it on the agenda until the last possible moment. He assured me he's gathered enough support up north to pass it—as long as there aren't enough people around to raise a stink. The vote will be over and done with before Lisa has a hint of what's going on."

The clerk stepped to the counter. "Hi Verina, what are you having today?"

Taylor's head jerked back. What were the chances of there being a second *Verina* connected to Lisa?

"Give me a minute, Jerry," she said. While he delivered an order to another table, Verina turned to Angela and laughed, "How about an order of Fire Mountain on a platter? Let's see how *she* handles disappointment. It's about time that family had to eat humble pie."

"The fun thing will be to see her reaction when it happens on her watch as the Guardian," Angela said. At that point, Jerry came back to the counter.

While they ordered, Taylor felt it best to slip out unnoticed through the door. So, Stan Harding was not just making up stories in his spare time. There really was a push to take Fire Mountain away from the Van Burens.

Sitting in his SUV, he pondered his next move. His first thought was that Lisa was due her just desserts for her deceitfulness, but he couldn't bring himself to side with a group led by Angela Basso. He decided to warn Lisa that she was in a battle. If this Verina was her employer, Lisa needed to know she was not her friend.

The first thing he had to do was verify Verina's identity. Jesse had pointed out the real estate office where Lisa worked when they headed out of town to explore the mine. Taylor made a U-turn in the street and headed north. The office was located in the last block of downtown Bella Vista. Knowing that Lisa was in a meeting with Asia, he pulled up to the curb and parked, hoping to gather some information below the radar.

Pausing at the door of Verina Fields Real Estate Office, he noticed several photos of the same woman he had seen with Angela Basso. She posed next to her many listings, confirming his suspicions. He opened the door, and an eager young man sprang up from his desk and stuck out his hand.

"Hello, I'm Frank. What can I help you with today?" Frank retained the comic look of a hungry car salesman and Taylor struggled to avoid laughing at the man's antics.

"I wanted to check if any of these properties are still for sale." He showed Frank the newspaper ads.

"Well, let me see." Frank took the paper and sat down in front of his computer. He motioned for Taylor to have a seat as well. After a short time, he got his answer and frowned. "Nope, they've all been snatched up. Tangle Grove is really taking off these days—can't keep anything in stock. However, I do have a few exclusive listings that just became available." He handed Taylor a flyer. "They aren't due to go public for another week, but I'll give you first crack at them."

Taylor took the paper politely. "Thanks, but I was really interested in the others. Could you tell me who purchased them?"

Without looking at any other information, Frank said flatly, "The Montebelli Corporation."

Cloaking his knowledge, Taylor asked, "Who are they?"

Frank grimaced. "They're this giant corporation that's buying up commercial properties in Tangle Grove, almost before they hit the market. It's got the residents a bit unnerved; no one knows how their plans will affect the town. They've already pushed the new central business district away from another developing area, frustrating the investors who were trying to get the new downtown going there."

"So, no one knows who they're dealing with? No one's met them?"

Frank shrugged. "We have a part-time receptionist who also works for them, monitoring the best real estate buys. Our broker, Ms. Fields, handles all the commissions—I mean sales," he corrected himself, clearing his throat.

Taylor understood the subtext. "Not a fair shake, if you ask me. Why doesn't the receptionist pass the sales around instead of playing favorites?"

"It's not Lisa's fault. She tried to cut me in once but," he paused and darted his eyes to the two closed doors in the office, "it didn't work out."

The fishing was paying off. "That sounds awfully decent of this Lisa. She sounds like a loyal person to work with." He gave his friendliest smile.

Frank's eyes shifted at the word *loyal.* His lips tightened and all pretended mirth was gone. "She is loyal." Then, almost to himself he said, "Loyal and trusting."

"What was that?"

"Nothing," Frank said. "She's just a really nice person who works for two companies that take advantage of her inexperience."

"Do you mean that corporation?"

Frank nodded. "Verina says she's doing all kinds of work for them for a meager salary. Says it's ridiculous that Lisa fancies herself as some kind of commercial agent, handing all these properties to them, and that she's going to end up with nothing."

"It sounds like Verina's a little protective of Lisa."

Frank snorted. "I wouldn't call it that." Quieting his voice, he confided, "I think she's jealous. I think she'd love to take over Lisa's position with the corporation and get her out of the loop."

Surprised at the revelation, Taylor asked, "Is there anything you could do to help her?"

"There could be." Then, seeming to come to some kind of conclusion, he gave Taylor a half smile. "Sorry to involve you with in-house politics. Is there anything else I can help you with?"

"No, that was it."

Frank flashed his salesman grin again. "Here, take my card, and if you want to see anything else, I'd be happy to show you around."

Taylor took the card and read it aloud, "Frank Harding. Are you related to the Harding's as in *Harding County*?"

Frank brightened. "Yes, we were one of the first families in the area."

"Well, nice to meet you, Frank." Taylor shook his hand and walked outside, closing the door behind him. *Bingo. Many birds with one stone.* He sat in his car before deciding to start another list, this one entitled *Lisa's enemies.*

At the top he wrote *Angela Basso.* Lisa seemed to be aware of her, but maybe not to the extent she should be. Next was *Verina Fields.* Did Lisa know enough not to trust her employer? He scribbled, *Gary Bristol.* Giving Lisa a small benefit of doubt due to her *inexperience*, as Frank called it, Taylor felt certain this guy was more a menace to her than an accomplice.

He thought for a moment and turned the page back to his unanswered questions. It was obvious Lisa was the one who circled the newspaper ads they found in the cave. Now how did the paper get in there? He needed to talk to Jesse.

***

Normally Taylor would have walked down to where Jesse worked, but he wanted to park his car away from the real estate office. He drove back into town and parked in front of an upscale dress shop across from Zach's. A stunning blue dress hung in the window, the color of Lisa's eyes. He shook his head, hard. This had to stop. It was unclear what kind of game she was playing, but his instincts told him she was more naïve than malicious.

The door opened into Zach's Bar and Grill and a man exited past him. Inside, Jesse set a glass in front of a customer and nodded to Taylor, who sat down on an empty stool.

"How's it going?" Jesse asked.

"Interesting day."

Jesse's eyebrow went up. When Taylor offered no information, he asked, "Can I get you anything?"

He asked for a bottle of sparkling water. "When we were in the cave and found that newspaper, you said you were going to ask your cousin if he'd gone back after your gathering. Did you ever find out about that?"

"I talked to Dan, and he said he hadn't been back in there since our overnight. It was bothering me, so I called my other cousin, and he hasn't been back to town either. Both of them have their keys, so no one's used them. Why?"

"There's some information I need to share with you—in private. When do you get off work?"

"At eight, but Asia's meeting me here and we're going out to dinner." At Taylor's frown, Jesse added, "You could join us if you want to."

Even though Taylor had no qualms about Asia knowing what was going on, he really didn't want to intrude on their evening. "It can wait until tomorrow."

"Now you've got my curiosity up. How about I take a break?"

"That would be great," he answered and walked outside. He felt relieved, not wanting any more time to pass before Jesse or Lisa knew what was happening.

In two minutes, Jesse came out the door. "So, what's up?"

He didn't want it to look like he was digging into their family business, but there wasn't any other way to say it. "Are you aware that there are plans in the works to take Fire Mountain away from your family and make it public land?"

"There was a group of locals that tried to make that happen a few years ago. We beat them though. Is that what's bothering you?" Jesse's face relaxed somewhat.

"I was in a restaurant and heard Angela Basso say she had a state politician who had secured enough support to make it happen—and he wasn't going to put it on the agenda until the last moment." He watched Jesse's face.

"Did she say when?"

"September twenty-sixth." He noticed a serious side to Jesse that hadn't been there during their interactions with Asia or when they were hiking.

Pursing his lips, Jesse said, "I'll tell Mom. This is probably the last thing she wants to handle while she's at this juncture of the Tangle Grove project. I would manage it myself, but she's the only one authorized to deal with it."

"There's one more thing. Angela was talking to Verina Fields, who seemed to be thrilled to take down your mother."

Jesse's expression darkened. "That witch. Mom's saved her tail more than once, calming clients who would've backed out of their contracts because of Verina's attitude. Wait until Mom finds out how she's been rewarded." The frown on Jesse's brow changed to a look of gratitude as he glanced at Taylor. "Thanks for covering our backsides. I've got to get back to work, but I'll give Mom a call right away."

His tension eased. "Is there anything I can help with," he volunteered, wanting to have some action to take.

Jesse clapped him on the back. "I know how you feel. I was still a kid the first time they tried to pull this stunt on us. I remember feeling so helpless, but Grandma Rose handled it great—she was a real tiger and gave them a sound beating. You should have seen Angela and her mother's faces when their side lost. Mom has a different temperament, but I'm sure she'll do a good job. In the meantime, I'd appreciate it if you just keep your ears open."

"I'll do that, and hey, you guys have a great time tonight." Taylor added in mock self-pity, "Just forget about me. I'll find something to occupy my time."

"Don't worry," Jesse said back over his shoulder, "I've already forgotten."

Walking back to his car, the laughter faded from Taylor's face. Jesse was sure about Lisa, but he had his doubts. She may think she was playing a smart game, but he was certain she was inept when it came to dealing with the real world of sharks. Before he could proceed any farther, his phone rang. He answered it and was surprised at the voice on the other end.

"Hello Taylor, this is Thomas Richards." There was a pause before he continued. "Things were a little crazy the other night. I probably had one too many beers. Anyway, I was hoping we could have lunch in town tomorrow and clear up any misunderstandings."

Taylor was about to decline, but decided to find out what he could about this guy and maybe get more insight into Lisa. Sounding friendlier than he felt, he responded, "Sure, what time?"

The relief in Thomas' voice was audible. "Let's make it at a quarter to twelve and avoid the crowds. Could you come to my office, and we'll walk over together?" Taylor agreed and Thomas gave him directions to his office.

Having done enough sleuthing, Taylor decided to get a quick salad at Varano's and go to bed. Again, he marveled at the beauty of the drive back up the mountain.

Anna Varano greeted him at the restaurant with a motherly hug. "You are almost family. Come, sit down." She brought him a glass of wine and his salad. Where's your pretty woman? You're too good looking to be alone."

He laughed and asked, "Do you know anything about the Montebelli family?"

She brightened. "Oh, yes. It has been a long time since I thought of them. They were one of the early families here—very nice people, I was told. Costantino Montebelli was on the climb when we lost Fabio. After the tragedy, he stayed here with my grandfather, Doriano, and sent for his fiancé." She sighed. "They both loved to climb and led groups up the mountain every year. Unfortunately, they were killed in an avalanche. Their daughters, Adriana and Ladonna, were orphaned at an early age."

"Adriana Montebelli!" He pronounced the name as though he had just struck gold.

Anna Varano's eyes popped open in surprise. "Is that something important?"

"It is to me." *And to a lot of other people.* "Anna, do many other people know about this?"

"Could be. Few of the records are around and I am the last of the older people who knew the stories."

"I'd like to ask you for a big favor."

"What are you wanting?" She gave him a sly smile.

"If people happen to come around asking about the Montebellis, could you...forget the information for a while?"

Her grin widened, "You want to play a game of secrets, then?"

He could see she would cooperate. "Yes, I do," he smiled back. "Thank you."

Back in his room, he pulled out his notebook. Next to the entry, *Montebelli Corporation*, he wrote, "Adriana Montebelli married Joren Van Buren, and they had Klara, who had Rose, who had Lisa." He grinned at the progress he'd made. So, Lisa was connected *by blood* to the Montebellis. He wondered who else she was working with and just how she fit in.

Chapter 10

Entering the lion's den. Taylor smirked, wondering what he would discover about Thomas Richards today. He stayed in Mont Castello as long as he could, drinking in the peace of the place and then began the drive down, gauging his time to make certain he was right on time to Thomas Richards' office. He parked his car on the street and walked a half block to the address.

Impressive. Black, gray, and buff-colored marble created a powerful statement. Thin vertical lines of shining steel separated the colors as they wound their way around the building. Brushed steel and glass doors appeared as solid as a bank's, and more marble greeted him underfoot as he entered the lobby. A young and attractive receptionist sat at a sleek mahogany desk in the center.

"May I help you," she asked, leaning toward him with undivided attention.

"Thomas Richards' office," he said politely.

Not achieving the effect she hoped to, the woman sat back and gave a bored response. "Take the elevator to the second floor and go through the double doors straight ahead."

"Thank you," he said and made his way to the elevator. When he pushed the button and looked up, she darted her eyes away and quickly picked up a paper, pretending indifference. He shook his head at the act.

The chrome and mahogany elevator rose to the second floor, and he stepped out. Ahead was a massive door with a brushed steel sign that read, *Thomas Richards, M.D.* Opening the door, he encountered a busy secretary on the phone behind a black marble counter.

Large windows at the far end of the reception room looked down on Bella Vista and up at the mountains that towered above the town. Two large caramel-colored leather chairs flanked the view. Four more chairs convened around metal occasional tables. A light gold color on the walls softened the effect of the black marble counter and the metal furniture, while three oversized abstract paintings pulled all the colors together. He smirked at Thomas' obvious motive for inviting him here.

"Are you Mr. Taylor?" the receptionist asked. She was also attractive but maintained a refreshing professional manner.

"Yes, I am."

"Dr. Richards is still with patients, but I'll tell him you've arrived. You are welcome to take a seat."

"Thank you." He sat near her desk and picked up a magazine. She called Thomas' office to speak to him, which supported what Taylor had guessed—he was *not* with patients.

After a long, premeditated delay, Thomas' enthusiastic greeting bellowed across the empty room. "Hello, Taylor. Please, come into my office and have a seat." Inside, he motioned to one of the butter-soft leather chairs that faced his desk, then sat in a taller one on the other side. "I hope I didn't keep you waiting," he said with mock concern.

"It gave me time to look around your office. It's well appointed." Knowing the answer already, he asked, "Did you use a local decorator?"

"No, no. My architect was definite about bringing in a talented woman from New York. It wouldn't have been appropriate to have anything less in this caliber of a building."

Taylor knew he had him. "Well done. You seem to be at the top of your game."

"Thank you. Of course, it took years and a lot of hard work to get to this place, but it has been worth it."

Taylor stifled a smirk. Apparently, Thomas felt he could play his modesty card now that his accomplishments had been acknowledged.

Drawn into a false sense of camaraderie, Thomas opened up. "I want to thank you for coming today. It was so uncomfortable for me the other night. I hated to have you leave with any misunderstandings, but with everyone there, it was impossible to explain."

"We've all been there," Taylor said with a knowing expression. He listened, feeding out the line.

Encouraged further, Thomas began his pitch in earnest. "You haven't known my family very long, and unfortunately you got embroiled in the middle of a stage we seem to be going through. Lisa is a wonderful woman, she really is, but she has become...unstable. I guess that is the best way to put it. It is this menopausal thing—at least that's what I hope. She seems to live in a fantasy world." He paused, waiting for a sign that Taylor was still with him.

"She did seem over reactive," Taylor put in for good measure.

Thomas embraced his words with increased enthusiasm. "That's just what I mean. For years, she has been lying around in bed, complaining of headaches I'm sure she doesn't have, or she is gone for hours with no explanation of where she has been. We are hardly sleeping together, but that is beside the point. She is so full of resentment that it's hard to be around her. It's usually different with company around, except for occasions like last night."

"So, from your professional opinion, what do you think the answer is?"

"I am at a loss. I have referred her to my colleague across the hall, but she refuses to get help. She is really starting to worry me. I'm afraid she might be suffering from schizophrenia."

At those words, Taylor recoiled. Thomas must have felt the need to add evidence to his conclusion.

"Did you know that a few years ago she almost ran our family into the ground financially?" Watching Taylor's increased interest, he figured he was on the right track. "She went behind my back and took my savings—seventy thousand dollars—and put a down payment on an old, rundown house in town. She thought she could rent it out and make the payments, but there were so many things wrong with it that all the rent money went to repairs. Then she had the nerve to tell me what she had done and ask me to bail her out by making the mortgage payments."

"You didn't, I hope." Taylor tried to appear caught up in the spirit of the thing.

"You bet I didn't! I sold that house right out from under her. How dare she go behind my back—without my permission—and spend that kind of money." His breathing accelerated and light reflected off his moist forehead.

"Did you lose a lot of money?" Taylor tried to sound sympathetic.

"That's the best part," he said with great relish. "I sold that house for over twice what she paid for it—but I never let her know. That's how I was able to pick up the property this building stands on—how's that for karma?" He glowed with the remembrance of his triumph.

Taylor was sick to his stomach but determined to keep up the charade. "That was quite a coup you pulled off."

"It really shook me up. I had her sign a prenuptial agreement before we were married but didn't realize how vulnerable my money was."

"Does that mean you signed a prenup for *her*?"

"No, no. She doesn't own anything of value, pretty one-sided."

Taylor estimated the value of Sweet Elke Park and Fire Mountain alone and fantasized about smacking the smug smile off Thomas' face.

"After that episode, I took complete control of our money. She can't take a penny that I don't give her." He stood and straightened a frame on the wall. "For several years, she seemed subdued, but now I'm starting to hear rumors of her getting involved in the affairs of the town down the road, Tangle Grove." His voice rose again. "You would have thought she'd learned her lesson."

Clenching his teeth, he slammed his fists onto his desk. "How can she think I'm that stupid? I have people coming to me, complaining she has her nose in everybody's business. She's on this committee and that committee and works in some capacity with a corporation in Nevada. It's probably mob-run."

Taylor was aghast at his rant. Thomas noticed and instantly changed his tone to concern. "I tell you, Taylor, she's so naive, I'm afraid she's really going to get hurt, or drag someone else down with her, maybe even our son." He ended with an emotional crescendo.

Thoughts spun through Taylor's mind. Some of the details seemed accurate but were mixed with fabrications. He needed time to sort it out and didn't want to do it with Thomas around. "Well, I'm sorry for the hardship you're going through. Is there anything I can do to help?"

"Thanks for listening," Thomas replied with a sad smile. "The one thing you could do is to keep an eye on Lisa during your stay here. I talked to the kids last night and they agreed to help, letting me know how she is involved and such, you know. It would be awful if everything came crashing down around her."

At those familiar words, Taylor had to mask his surprise. "Yes, it would." He now understood the breadth of Lisa's motives. He wanted to smash this guy. How dare he undermine her with her own son.

"Well, shall we go to lunch?" Thomas had accomplished his mission and was ready to go have an enjoyable meal.

Taylor couldn't believe his eyes at the sudden transformation. Checking his watch, he created a way out. "You know, it's much later than I expected, and I made an appointment at 1:15 that can't be rescheduled. How about we catch lunch next time?"

Thomas seemed let down. Now that he imagined he had another accomplice in his pocket, he wasn't eager to let go. "Well, I am sorry I took up all our time on my problems but thank you for being such a good listener."

"Anytime," Taylor said as he clapped his shoulder. He wanted to lay him out.

As they came out of the office, the secretary reported that she had some papers for him to sign and that a message from the attorney was on the counter. He looked at Taylor and shrugged. "Always work to do," he said and walked backed to his desk.

Taylor passed the counter. A bolt went through him. The note, written on a Spartan Investigations notepad, contained a phone number, a time to call, and a name. *Gary Bristol.* These two men were in contact!

Taylor had to find Jesse. Of all the people Thomas could use to hurt Lisa, her son would be top on the list. Checking his watch again, he knew Jesse would still be at work. He walked at a brisk pace down the street to Zach's. Opening the door, he saw the young man cleaning glasses behind the bar.

Jesse saw him arrive. "Hey."

"Hi, Jesse." He sat down on a stool in a quiet spot. His jaw set hard.

Jesse noticed and asked what was wrong.

"I've just been to see your dad." He paused, feeling the weight of his knowledge. "I'm going to tell you some things straight out and hope you'll act wisely with the information."

"Is it about spying on Mom?" Jesse asked with a grim expression.

His head jerked up. "Yes, it is. Where are you with it?"

"He's full of it. I know he's my father and at some level I love him, but he's always made that very difficult to do."

He sighed audibly and his jaw slackened. "You don't know how glad it makes me to hear you say that. Do you know how much damage he can do—the things he has done, to your mother?"

"What kind of things?" His full attention focused on Taylor's words.

"For starters, it sounds like he's gathering a case against her sanity. As a respected professional, there's no telling what sort of influence he could have in casting doubt on her emotional stability. She could lose all credibility with her business connections." Jesse's tense face reddened. Taylor continued. "Do you know what happened when your mother invested in a rental house some years ago?"

Jesse nodded. "That was a travesty. Mom began to study the real estate market in Bella Vista and could see where it was heading. This was fifteen years ago, remember, and prices hadn't skyrocketed yet. There was this old house for sale by owner, right in the growth pattern for the city. Mom knew that because she'd attended many of the planning meetings and was aware of what was about to happen.

"She kept trying to get Dad to buy it, but he didn't think she knew what she was doing. Finally, she just took some of their savings and put a large down payment on the place. It could have worked, but Dad was furious and refused to help fix the plumbing when the basement flooded. All he would have had to do was keep it afloat for a few months while prices went up—which they did—and it would have been a real score for the family. Mom would have been a hero."

Taylor looked at Jesse full in the face. "He did score."

"What do you mean?"

"When I was in your dad's office, he told me he sold that house for more than twice the amount and purchased the property on which he built his office—and he never told your mom. He made her think she'd lost the family money for all these years."

Jesse's fists clenched, his knuckles white. "That jerk!" he hissed.

Taylor clasped Jesse's fist. "It's important not to let your dad know that you know. Your mom is in a very precarious place. We have to find out what his plans are, so we know how to protect her. Thomas said he asked you and Asia to keep an eye on her and tell him what she's doing. He also told me he has other people reporting to him about the committees she's on in Tangle Grove. And he seems to be checking out her relationship to the Montebelli Corporation."

"How did that come up?"

Taylor shrugged his shoulders. "His secretary gave him a note with the corporate attorney's name on it. I don't know what he's found out or will find out, but I have a bad feeling that Thomas and this attorney are already working on something together. They both used a similar phrase about everything falling in on her, regarding your mother's dealings in Tangle Grove. I met her attorney and he seemed underhanded. I don't trust him."

While Taylor talked, Jesse listened with increasing anger. "Why is he doing this to her? Mom deserves to succeed in something she's worked so hard at." He ran his hands through his hair. "How can we keep him from undermining her again?"

He thought a minute. "My first stop was to see where you were with this. I guess the next step is to warn Asia."

"Don't worry, we already discussed it," Jesse assured him.

"Then I need to get the truth from Lisa. I'm not certain she'll talk to me, or if she's ready to trust anyone." His mind was running in several directions at once.

"Why do you need information from her?"

He held Jesse's eyes while he voiced his suspicions. "I think she owns the Montebelli Corporation."

Chapter 11

"What do you mean she *owns* the Montebelli Corporation?" Jesse's voice rose.

Taylor motioned for him to be quiet. "Maybe I overstated that. It could just be that she owns stock or is an officer, but I believe she's definitely connected as more than an employee."

"That doesn't make sense. How could she keep that a secret?"

"I think it's set up as a Nevada corporation to hide the identity of its investors. With your father's mindset, Lisa couldn't let it be known she had any part in it, but that seems to have placed her at a disadvantage. If the corporate attorney is any indication of the caliber of people she's working with, she could be in a real mess. And he seems to be in league with your father."

Jesse's brows knit together in thought. "That corporation has to be worth a few million dollars. A chunk of that would be a sweet deal."

"And if your father finds out, he will fight to take it all away, just like he did with the rental house—and with no prenup."

Jesse's tone sounded hopeless. "How can she keep that big of a deal hidden?"

"She's managed this far and probably would have continued except for her lawyer. I used to live in Nevada and know a sharp, confidential attorney there, Sydney Wakeham. When I leave, I'll call and get her advice. Then we'll see what Lisa wants to do. Will you call Asia and bring her up to date on this, so she doesn't let any information slip?"

Jesse agreed. Taylor arose and they shook hands. "It's going to be okay." The younger man nodded, but concern tugged on his face. Taylor turned away, hiding the residual rage that belied the calm he'd exuded. Though not prone to violence, he wanted to break something. He needed to get out of here and place the call.

Everyone looked suspicious as Taylor's eyes swept up and down the busy street. People glanced his way, or ignored him, maybe too completely. Thomas gave him the creeps. Who else was in league with him anyway?

He wanted to get out of the downtown area before he called Sydney. A college friend and a trusted advisor on more than one occasion, she was just the person to give him some answers. His stomach grumbled for an afternoon snack and Tangle Grove came to mind.

He drove the quick fifteen minutes along the gentle curves of the Strada del Vino. As beautiful as it was, his mind couldn't take in the scenery today. An avid chess player, he was following moves in his head, trying to locate the best outcome, but there were still too many unknowns.

Siebert's barn appeared on the left. He slowed and made the turn, taking a moment to imagine what Lisa envisioned for this town. It was a great vision. She possessed talent in the area of development, and he longed to see her win this time.

Sweet Elke Café was on the left. He pulled into a parking spot on the right and walked across the uneven street. As expected, the café was empty after lunch. Vacant chairs sat outside in the shade of the overhanging apartments above. "Hello, Lilly," he said when he walked in.

The young woman glanced up from wiping off a table. Her face brightened. "Good afternoon. What can I get you?"

It was nice to be around a genuine person, and he felt his shoulders relax. "I would like a cup of very hot espresso and one of your bear claws there." He pointed to the pastry, noticing the intensity of his appetite. "I'll be outside."

The wrought iron chairs were more comfortable than they appeared. He sat close to the building, eyes shielded from the afternoon sun and punched Sydney's number into his phone. Lilly brought out his food just as Sydney's secretary answered.

"Wakeham, Wakeham, and Billings, this is Karen. How may I direct your call?"

Recognizing her voice, he smiled. She'd been a great support while Sydney handled his divorce. "Hello, Karen, this is Steven Taylor."

"Taylor, so good to hear from you."

He could hear her smile through the phone. "How are you?

"Things are good. There is always more work to be done than time to do it, but I'm finally convinced that is just the way life is."

"So it is. Is Sydney in a place where I could speak with her? I have a pressing problem I need some help with."

"I think I can get her on the line. Can you wait just a moment?"

"Absolutely." Within two minutes, Sydney was on the line, and within fifteen minutes, he had explained the details to her.

"I'll look up Gary Bristol and see what kind of character he is," Sydney promised. "Then I'll examine his expertise in setting up corporations."

"So, are there ways of finding out who actually sets up and owns a Nevada corporation?"

"Yes and no. It depends on how they were set up, and where. Let me see what I can come up with."

"Sydney, I know how your schedule runs, but Lisa—I mean this woman, may not have much time before this guy goes after her."

"For you alone, this goes to the top of my priority list. I'll call you back no later than tomorrow."

Setting his cell phone down, he looked up the street to where the new courthouse would sit and spotted Lisa walking his way.

"Hello," he greeted when she passed.

She averted her eyes. "Hello, Taylor. Nice afternoon."

"Beautiful," he answered without enthusiasm. "Would you care to join me?"

"Thank you, but I really need to get coffee and run home." She went inside, bought her drink, and started to rush by him, but he reached out and gently caught her wrist. Her sweater shifted.

He noticed the black and blue finger marks on her arm. "I really need to talk with you," he said with urgency.

A wary expression altered her face. "About what?"

"About this, for one thing." He pointed to her shoulder and voiced the anger he'd been feeling all day.

She looked down and adjusted her sweater over the bruise. "It's not what you think. I'm not a battered woman. Thomas was angry and grabbed my arm in the kitchen. When the pitcher started to fall, I lunged for it."

He was certain she wasn't telling the whole truth but decided not to pursue it. "I had another matter on my mind." She exhaled her frustration, sat down, and crossed her arms.

Now that she was here, he contemplated where to start. "First off, I want you to know I appreciate the amazing job you're doing here. I don't know all the reasons why you have...set things up the way you have, and it's really none of my business. All I know is that Asia is excited to be working with you. You've given her a huge opportunity and I'm grateful."

"She's a brilliant designer." Lisa folded her hands around her paper cup. "I couldn't have asked for a better person to work with."

He smiled. "She talks about you constantly, that is, when she's not talking about Jesse." They both chuckled, relieving a little of the stress, yet her eyes were still cautious. He gentled his voice, "I have a reason for the personal question I'm about to ask you."

She stiffened and held her breath.

"How long are you going to keep Thomas in the dark about your…interest...in Tangle Grove?"

She gasped. "Well," she hesitated, taking time to compose her words. "Thomas isn't interested in... this sort of thing. He has his practice and needs his peace of mind to focus on his patients."

"Would he be opposed to your being so involved on the level at which you are *engaged*?"

Her breathing quickened, but she spoke evenly. "He doesn't like anything about Tangle Grove. It's my connection. By birth. He likes to be in control. When my mother passed away and I became the...I was put in charge of the family business, he felt threatened. I handle my business privately because I don't want to rub it in his face, but I need to do what I'm doing. For me. Maybe that's selfish, but this is the best solution I could come up with."

Gauging his timing, he asked the key question. "And what solution is that?"

She straightened, very alert. "That's *my* business."

He sighed, had been naive to hope she would simply trust and open up to him. There was nothing to do but come out with it. "What would you say if I told you that Thomas is privy to what's going on here in Tangle Grove?" He watched for her expression.

A flash of fear passed over her face. Eyes cast down, she responded, "Thomas knows that I'm on the town committees and that I'm helping out with the...ideas. He has no objection to any community work I do." Her eyes chanced a quick glance from under the cover of her eyelashes, revealing the hope that her explanation would suffice.

He was sympathetic as he took her to the next step. "He knows about the Montebelli Corporation. He's been talking to their attorney, Gary Bristol."

Her hand went to her throat. "Thomas knows I work for the Montebelli Corporation. It's been on our tax records every year. There's nothing Gary can tell him that can possibly matter to me." Her voice had gone up in pitch with the effort to control her emotions.

Not wanting to add more weight to her anguish but needing her to know the whole story for her safety, he decided to tell her everything right then. "Thomas called me to his office to butter me up and ask me to spy on you."

Fear flash through her and she started to get up.

"Lisa, look at me. I'm not on Thomas' side. You can believe that. I don't lie." She studied his eyes and sat back down. He continued, "This will be the hard part for you. He also asked Jesse and Asia to report your activities to him. He's setting it up as though your state of mind is unstable, and you are acting irrationally. He even used the story of your *ill-advised* investment in the Bella Vista property as an example of the damage you are capable of, and thus, his need to monitor you."

Tears sprang to her stunned eyes. Vulnerable and deflated, she slumped in her seat, her voice barely audible. "That would have been a good investment, but there were things I didn't take into consideration. If he'd only helped, just a little, we would have made a lot of money."

Taylor's chest ached as he watched this powerful woman reduced to defending her decisions needlessly. He reached out and covered her clenched hand with his, feeling the tremors caused from the cruel memory. Holding his temper in check, he revealed the truth. "You *did* make a lot of money, only Thomas never told you. He let you sit in your guilt for all these years while he sold the property for a large profit and bought the lot for his trophy office with the proceeds."

She jolted upright. Anger heated her face to crimson. Her hands shook with fury and her mouth opened, but words refused to form. She searched Taylor's face for truth, and he knew the moment she believed him.

Angry sobs altered her voice. "Do you know the years of humiliation he put me through because of that investment? No, it was further back than that. It started soon after our marriage, all the demeaning comments in front of friends and family, meant to make me feel less about myself. The way he always turned things around, so I assumed they were my fault—and I apologized. I tried to live up to his standards, but I never could have. He has none." Tears streaked her cheeks.

"Lisa, you need to believe me when I say I'm your friend in this." He watched as the anguish diminished.

Her hands stopped shaking and she withdrew from his hold. She was quiet for a few moments, and he let her have her space. Finally, she spoke. "That's it then. How much does he think he knows?"

Taylor let out the breath he'd been holding. "He seemed vague about your arrangement with the Montebelli Corporation, but his secretary gave him Gary Bristol's number while I was there. It seems he has people around who are keeping him informed of your activities, but he didn't mention who."

She nodded and waited for a couple to enter the café. "I've been very careful in my actions and legal dealings. Perhaps I was too naive about my attorney. He seems to be the weak link." She looked into his eyes. "The conversation you saw the other day was regarding his *salary*."

Taylor's brows knit in confusion. "His salary?"

Heaving a sigh of resignation, she leaned closer and whispered, "I created the Montebelli Corporation. Gary is my attorney and he suddenly felt he deserved a larger *percentage*. I refused."

Jaw dropping, Taylor sat back as though struck. She owned the *whole* corporation.

"I mortgaged most of the buildings to get the money for this project, but the rents aren't covering the costs, and I need to refinance at a lower percentage rate. This was *not* a good time for Gary to get greedy and he knew it."

Understanding dawned, explaining her elusive behavior. He pursed his lips. The stakes were higher than he'd imagined. She *was* swimming with the sharks—two of them. "Then it's possible that he was the one who contacted Thomas, rather than the other way around."

"Either way, it's a breach of client confidentiality."

"I hope it doesn't offend you," Taylor began, "but I have a close friend who is a well-connected attorney in Nevada. I took the liberty of explaining the situation—without using your name——and asked her to check into Gary Bristol's background." He waited.

Looking him square in the eyes, she said, "I understand why you would do what you've done, and believe me it's good to know I have someone on my side, but would you do me a favor from now on?"

He cringed. "Of course."

"Don't discuss my business with anyone else until we have an agreed upon plan." There was no criticism in her voice, which surprised him. But what amazed him even more was the sudden change in her demeanor. She exuded confident authority.

He nodded. "You have my word on that."

"And I don't want Jesse and Asia to know yet." Taylor swallowed, wishing he hadn't said something to Jesse. He was about to explain, when she looked at her watch and said, "I need get home to get dinner made."

He did a double take. "Are you certain you can pull that off?"

She sighed. "I've been *pulling it off* for a long time. I can do it a little longer. The main thing is not to alert him. My situation is still tenuous." She paused. "You know what's really sad? When I made that investment, I wasn't doing it to have my own money or hide from Thomas. I planned to surprise him after it was finished. I thought he would begin to value my opinion, but it wouldn't have made any difference. He's a cheat."

"And he kept you off-balance to cover his guilt."

Looking skyward, she mused, "I suffered through the abuse for Jesse's sake, then to give myself time to set my finances in order in case the relationship collapsed entirely. I kept holding out hope that if he saw me in a better light, there would be more respect between us." She swiped at her tears with finality. "With all of Thomas' connections and his influence as a psychiatrist, he could ruin me. All I want now is to be out of this."

Taylor shook his head, not understanding how Thomas could live with himself. "I'll call you tomorrow as soon as Sydney gets back to me. They stood and she wobbled. His large hands caught her shoulders and steadied her. "Are you certain you're all right?"

She looked up and gave a tight smile. "Thank you. I will be." He saw the determination in her eyes and dropped his hands. Pulling a pen from her purse, she asked, "May I have the name and phone number of your attorney? There are some obstacles I need advice about."

He gave her the information and waited for an explanation, but she just gave him a look that said, *Don't ask*, and snapped her purse shut.

"See you later then," he said and watched her charge back to the courthouse, get in her car, and slam the door. Thomas had better hope she didn't have arsenic around the house.

***

Taylor drove back to Mont Castello for dinner at Varano's again. It was becoming a good habit. Anna Varano was the sole hostess. Her face lit up when she saw him walk through the door.

"Hello, Mr. Taylor, you came back to see me," she teased.

He enjoyed Anna's charm and sincerity and gave her a hug. "Just to see you—and to get some good food."

"Then you are in the right place. I have a great seat for you by the fireplace."

"Actually, I want to get some work done while I eat and need to use my computer. Would you happen to have a wireless connection here?"

She smiled broadly. "Of course. We are very modern. Only our dishes are from the old country." With that, she waved him to follow her to the back of the restaurant to a large, comfortable booth. "You sit here where you can have your privacy." Handing him a menu, she said, "I'll send Candice over to get your order." She patted his shoulder as she would a son.

When Candice came to take his order, he recognized her as the waitress Thomas had been flirting with. She smiled and said, "Welcome back. What can I get for you?"

"I'd like the top sirloin steak, medium rare, with a baked potato, and a full Caesar salad. And please bring a glass of Cabernet Sauvignon with my bread."

"My, you must be hungry," she said with her southern drawl.

Taylor laughed. "I haven't eaten much today," he confessed. She left and when she returned with his wine and bread, he acted on a hunch. "When I was in here on Thursday, there was an attractive couple seated by me. He was a cyclist—Dr. Richards. Do you remember them?"

She thought for a second and said with a look of disgust, "Oh, you mean the *doctor*. He came in here the first two nights of the ride."

That piqued Taylor's interest. "Do you know him?"

"Not the way he would have liked, if you get my meaning. He was in here with his wife and tried hittin' on me. When she went to the restroom, he gave me his business card and said to call him if I ever needed *anything*. Like I'd be interested in a married guy." She left to serve another table.

Taylor added this information to the many reasons he disdained Thomas Richards. When Candice set his plate in front of him, he picked up his knife and directed his anger at the steak. The food was excellent, however, and he began to relax for the first time that day.

Opening his computer, he searched out information on Nevada corporations. After a time, he sat back. *Lisa had a brilliant idea.* He smiled at the glimpse into her mind the day's events had given him.

An hour later, he closed his computer and opened his notebook. The list of her enemies was on top. He added Thomas' name. Each of their faces glared out of the page. Setting his jaw, he felt more determined than ever to keep them from bulldozing Lisa's achievements.

Chapter 12

The cold black night swallowed him up as blaring sirens assaulted his ears. On the dark earth, he saw Lisa's white face, blank except for the anguish etched on it. "NO!" Taylor heard himself shout.

Struggling to untangle himself from damp sheets, he opened his eyes and threw them on the floor. He sat up and downed a glass of cold mountain water to rid his mind of the remnants of the nightmare. Still, his hand shook while he reached for his ringing cell phone. The clock read 8:27. Bright sunlight attested to the late hour. "Steven Taylor," he said in a husky voice.

"I trust I am not waking you." He recognized Sydney's crisp, formal tone.

"Good morning. It's been a long time since I've slept this late."

"I have some news for you." She always got right to the point. "Gary Bristol has been investigated twice for fraud and extortion but never convicted. However, he is on probation with the State Bar of Nevada. Apparently, he has a gambling problem. I have seen a couple examples of the corporations he's set up and it looks as though he does a tight job—the husband shouldn't be able to track the ownership unless Bristol hands it to him on a platter."

Taylor was wide-awake by now. "He failed at the extortion angle, looks like he's approaching the husband now. What would I need to prove it?"

"You need written evidence or eyewitnesses of Bristol giving out privileged information."

He stood and paced. "What happens if we can prove that he sold out his client?"

"Then he will be disbarred and possibly prosecuted."

"Thanks for getting back to me, Syd." He stifled a yawn. "I'd like to ask your advice on one more thing."

Twenty minutes later, he closed his phone and punched in Lisa's number, leaving a message for her to call. He showered and headed downstairs for breakfast.

The innkeeper brought coffee and a basket of hot pastries to keep him busy until his omelet was ready. In the meantime, an advertisement in the local newspaper caught his eye. Bella Vista Jewels was offering a rare black opal for sale—at an unimaginable price. A photograph showed the stone, set in a unique design with diamonds accenting the opal's brilliance. It looked a cut above what Angela had been selling. *How would she get her hands on that?*

He ate his breakfast, and the coffee helped his mind get going. Today he needed to make flight arrangements for his next assignment. In a week, he would be traveling to Spain for a major race, but for the first time since he took this job, his heart wasn't in it. The new editor had returned Taylor's preliminary ideas with underhanded comments hinting at incompetence. Taylor grinned at the choice replies he'd drafted, then discarded. He could make this work as long as *he* got to travel, and the guy stuck to his desk.

He finished eating and rose slowly. *Come on Taylor, get the lead out.* Chuckling, he realized that was just what it felt like. His feet felt like lead, as if planted deep into the soil here. "Roots," Stan Harding called it. This was a new sensation for him.

The following two hours sped by while he downloaded information about the riders entered in the Vuelta a Espana. He would arrive in Spain early and change hotels three times over the twenty-three-day race. The magazine had hired a driver and secured a motorcycle for his cameraman. Soon, he felt more enthusiastic about the trip.

At eleven o'clock, it was time for a drive back down the mountain. *Let's go see what Angela is up to.* He tucked his small notebook into his shirt pocket. As he descended into the valley, he turned on the air conditioning, almost wishing he'd stayed in the mountains. He parked his car near the jewelry store and walked in with the ad he'd ripped from the newspaper.

"Good morning," a pleasant young woman greeted.

"Good morning to you," he returned. "Is Angela available?"

"I'm sorry, she's not in today. May I help you?"

He was disappointed that Angela wasn't working, but then decided he might gain more information from this young woman. "Perhaps you can. What's your name?"

"I'm Sandra." She reached out to shake his hand.

He returned the gesture then handed her the ad and asked if she still had that stone.

A huge smile brightened her face, and she led him to the main showcase located at the back of the store. "We keep it back here for security reasons." She unlocked the case with great flourish to add to the sense of value and took out the crystal box holding the stone. "Here it is: one of the *original* Dutchman Mine pieces. Of course, reset in our custom setting."

"Exquisite," Taylor commented, with true appreciation in his voice. His large fingers took the stone and tilted it to catch more of the light. It was as if flames were alive in it. "I was speaking to Angela a few days ago and she assured me that this quality of a stone was unavailable. Is it a new purchase?"

Sandra's eyes sparkled. "Yes, it is, but we were only able to obtain a few of these extraordinary opals. This is the first we've offered. Each piece is literally a work of art."

"You really know your business," he said to score points. Turning it to the light again, he asked, "So, did this come from the estate of one of the original descendants?"

"Normally we don't give out that information, but since you've already spoken to Angela, I'll tell you. One of the Van Burens was having financial problems and, after selling everything else of value, was forced to part with her family jewels. Even then, these were very difficult to obtain. There were many competing buyers, but Angela was determined to have them. She amazed everyone with her triumph," Sandra finished, elated.

His mind was busy trying to think if he'd heard anything of Lisa's relatives selling off their jewels. As the family Guardian, he wondered if she would see it as a breach of loyalty. He was certain she would be furious that Angela now owned substantial family assets. He winked, "Well, good for Angela. That had to be a proud moment for her."

"It was a proud moment for me." Angela came in with a wide smile. She looked gratified to see him back again and singing her praises. "I see you have been viewing my prize. How does that compare to the one you saw the other day?"

Amused, he said, "This one has much more fire and it's larger, isn't it?"

She leaned back against the counter directly across from him. The cream-colored knit dress accentuated her figure, which she made certain he noticed. "Definitely. Thirty-eight carats and the color is superior. This is one of the highest quality stones that ever came out of the Dutchman's mine. Are you interested in making a purchase for someone *special*?"

He realized he needed a reason for being here twice if he wasn't in the market for jewelry, so decided to appeal to her vanity. Feigning embarrassment, he replied, "I don't have someone special. I'm enjoying a short stay in your fascinating town but haven't found anything interesting to do." He knew she'd translate his meaning. Sandra must have been acquainted with how her employer operated and sensed it was time for her to leave.

A languid smile spread across Angela's mouth. Her fingers moved up to the necklace she wore and curled the chain around her long, manicured nails. "Well, we can't have a handsome visitor left unescorted in our friendly town. What sights have you seen?"

"I spent some time in your museum and I've taken a few hikes."

She took the bait. "Deplorable. We need to remedy that."

Giving her the look he knew she wanted, he asked, "Are you available to show me the sights?"

"I might be," she teased. "Would you like to start with lunch in one of our four-star restaurants?"

"I'm starved. Shall we go?"

Keeping her gaze on Taylor, she spoke over her shoulder, "I'll see you tomorrow, Sandra."

They exited the store, and Angela slipped her hand around his arm. "This way," she directed him to the right. He played the game and allowed her to walk close to him, pointing out some of the interesting aspects of her town. He smiled at the things she said, loathing her inside.

They turned into a smart restaurant two blocks away. The young host appeared, and Angela kissed his cheek with a flirtatious smile. "Hello, Brad," she purred. "Do you have a table open by the window?"

"Of course, right this way." He led them to a brocade-covered booth. She slid in to make room next to her, but Taylor moved to the other side, pretending not to notice her frown of disappointment.

Brad handed them menus and laid their napkins on their laps. Taylor looked up at Angela. She raised her eyebrows as if to say, *I told you I knew where to come for the best.* He acknowledged her unspoken message with a nod and then asked, "What do you recommend?"

"The filet of sole will melt in your mouth," she said, dropping her eyes to his lips.

Oh, brother. He said, "I'll trust your good taste."

Her brazen eyes filled with admiration as his wit matched hers. Brad returned and she ordered for them. "We'll both have the sole and my *special* wine," she said with a wink.

Taylor noticed a smirk on the young man's face as he turned away. *I'm with you buddy.* Watching this woman's misguided sense of her own prowess proved amusing. Nevertheless, he needed to make headway. "How long have you lived in Bella Vista?"

Her chin lifted. "I was born here. I am really one of the very few natives. Most of the others are just transplants. My great-grandmother was married to Jochem Van Buren's son. No one goes back further than that."

"That's impressive," he replied, certain it was expected. "You must be acquainted with everyone in town."

"Not everyone," she corrected. "There really aren't that many quality people here, if you know what I mean. It's getting harder to avoid the riffraff. Take this restaurant—you would think that the expense would limit who could get in, but here they are, spoiling the view with their jeans and raunchy tennis shoes." She nodded her head toward a couple of tourists across the restaurant.

"Hmm," he responded, not trusting himself to keep from laughing at her remark. "You must have an exclusive group of friends. What do you do for entertainment?"

She looked out from under her eyelashes. When he acted oblivious to the nuance, she gave a delicate shrug and answered, "People throw amazing parties here. There is a lot of money around, you know. Of course, the theaters provide a constantly changing array of interesting plays and musicals. In fact, Taylor, we should plan to see one while you are here."

"I'd enjoy taking you," he lied.

"I would enjoy taking her," a voice entered their conversation. Thomas Richards stood at their table wearing a lecherous smile. "Angie dear, how are you? Taylor, it looks like we share the same taste in women—isn't she luscious?" He reached for her hand and lifted it to his lips. "Umm," he breathed in her perfume.

Angela laughed. "Tommy, you never change, always the flirt."

"Honey, you know I don't flirt with just anybody—only the most beautiful woman in Bella Vista."

The exchange disgusted Taylor. *What was Thomas up to?*

He turned to Taylor. "This was the restaurant I planned to show you. It looks as though we arrived early enough to avoid the crowds—I hate waiting."

Of course, you do. Taylor had to work to hide his cynicism when he answered. "Angela was gracious enough to show me around town. We might even see a play, right Angela?"

A gleam appeared in Thomas' eye. "I have a grand idea. Angie, why don't you bring Taylor to the country club on Saturday night?"

Taylor was at a loss, but she filled him in. "Thomas is talking about the Bella Vista Ball. It celebrates the end of the tourist season and is the highlight of our social scene—tuxedos and all. Would you like to come?"

"With you? Of course, he would," Thomas said, reaching into his pocket. He retrieved a ticket and handed it to Taylor. "Lucky man."

"Thank you, that's very generous," Taylor said. He would find an excuse to extract himself later.

"Thomas is not all that generous," she cut in. "He didn't tell you it is a fundraiser for his favorite charity."

"What charity am I supporting?" Taylor tried to sound good-natured.

"We are expanding the golf course and adding another nine holes," Thomas laughed. "We need variety here or we may lose some of our membership to other clubs around the county."

The revelation didn't surprise Taylor. He pretended to go along with them. "Sounds like a worthy cause, I'll do my best to do my part."

"That's the spirit," Thomas said, clapping him on the shoulder. He leaned over and kissed Angela on the neck. "See you, Angie," he whispered, and then went back to his table.

Angela blushed when she caught Taylor's probing eyes. "I must apologize for his behavior. He has absolutely no manners and takes liberties he really is not entitled to."

"Should I have hit him and saved your honor?"

She laughed, "No, I've just always hated him calling me *Angie*."

Interesting sense of propriety. "Have you known him a long time then?"

"He moved to town quite a few years ago and was a complete bore. Then he got interesting for a while." She smiled. "Now he's a bore again."

"I see," Taylor said, and he did. He wanted to slap her for Lisa's sake. "Well, he's quite handsome. I get what a woman might see in him." His fishing came up empty.

"Let's talk about the present," she said, setting her gaze on him. "What should *we* do tonight?"

The waiter brought their food and made a production of placing it before them, adding pepper and Parmesan cheese. It saved Taylor having to answer. He busied himself with his meal, complimenting Angela on her choice. "One of the things I was able to do was visit the little community next door, Tangle Grove," he said, watching for her response. He wasn't disappointed.

Her face curled up into what he could best describe as a snarl. "What a waste of your precious time. How on earth did you end up there?"

"The sun was shining, and I decided to take a drive to see what was out and around the valley." He dangled the worm. "It looks like they are starting to update it."

"It will never happen." Her eyes narrowed.

I think I've hit a gusher. "Why is that?"

"Because there is a big scandal just about to break," she whispered in hushed tones and leaned closer. "Thomas' wife, Lisa, spends a lot of time working for the huge corporation that is developing that town. He is suspicious she has wormed her way into owning stock or something. If that's true, half of her assets belong to him and he's going to pull out his share. Her pitiful project will come crashing down around her."

Taylor started, imperceptibly he hoped. *The same words.* There was a lot of communication going around regarding Lisa's plans. "Is that a good thing to have happen? Won't a lot of people be hurt financially?"

"No one that matters. If you knew his wife, you would know it was a *very* good thing. She is the most conceited, too good for anybody person you'd want to meet. Her family goes back almost as far as mine and she makes sure everyone knows it. Thomas has suffered years of humiliation because of her. She even lost his money on a ridiculous investment that almost ruined him!"

"That doesn't sound right," he responded. "It sounds like you're a friend he can confide in."

"Well, yes, I try to be. Poor guy needs some encouragement with a wife like that."

He had a good hunch what kind of encouragement that had been—or maybe still was. He said, "I wouldn't worry. People generally lose when they take what's not theirs."

Oblivious to his meaning, she said, "I certainly hope you are right. It's time *she* loses for once." She raised an eyebrow that emphasized a wicked smile. "Or maybe twice."

"What do you mean?"

"She owns a mountain—can you imagine the audacity to own a *mountain*? We are going to take it away from her and make it public and there is nothing she can do about it. How is that for turning the tables?" Her eyes gleamed with jubilation.

"Has she offended a lot of people then?"

Angela seemed more than willing to gossip about one of her favorite subjects. "Lisa is a secretary for a friend of mine who is a *professional* real estate agent. Lisa shops properties for the corporation I mentioned, but instead of accepting Verina's advice, Lisa chose the seediest places imaginable, cutting Verina's commissions significantly from what they could have been. Can you believe the haughtiness that my friend has to endure from her *secretary*?"

"Must be unbearable," he said, awed at how people could turn things around to fit any way they want to see them. Taking a new tack, he asked, "How does Thomas know that Lisa is connected with this corporation?"

"He said she gets a 1099 from them every year that shows she makes $400 a month. She says she's just an employee, but how stupid does she think he is?" Angela charged ahead with her tirade. "Get this—I heard Thomas is meeting with the corporate attorney on Saturday to get all of the details—even that guy can't stand her insolence."

Tucking that bit of information away, Taylor tried to respond with enthusiasm. "That should finish her off. I'll bet the attorney knows everything Thomas needs to put the nails in her coffin. Who do you suppose will come to the funeral?"

Licking her lips in delight, Angela went over an invisible list and began to count on her fingers. "Well, Thomas and I'll lead the parade. And of course, Verina and her staff, who have had to work with Lisa, will be delighted to see her put in her place. Oh, and then there are the people she has irritated in Tangle Grove. Foolhardy Jim, the mayor, will be happy to have her out of his hair. He should never have gotten involved in that town in the first place."

Her breathing became fast and shallow. It reminded Taylor of a cat about to pounce. "Lisa led the corporation's decisions to scoop up properties in the *old town* section of Tangle Grove and then, by bribing the members of the committees she's on, pressured everyone to make *that* area the renovated town center. Many people invested in land in the sprawling growth path to the south, thinking it would host any new commercial development. They stand to lose money, Verina and Jim included."

She leaned even closer. "Jim owns several buildings in the south part of town. He thinks he has a buyer for his *old town* corner office so he can be out of the firing line when Lisa's little project collapses." She sat back and laughed. "When Thomas gets finished with her, Lisa's reputation will be worthless. And Fire Mountain will be gone." Her eyes danced. "She will have to sell her opals to dig herself out from under the financial mess she has made." Angela ended with triumph in her voice.

"That's some comprehensive plan," Taylor said and gave her a convincing look of admiration. "You seem to have orchestrated quite a coup." It was nearly two o'clock and he was not sure how much more play acting he could sustain. Glancing at his watch, he pretended surprise. "Angela, I was enjoying your company so much, the time got away from me. I'm sorry to rush off like this, but I need to be back in Mont Castello by two-thirty to meet a cyclist for an interview. Thank you for sharing your town and its intricate secrets." Standing, he tossed a few bills on the check the waiter had left and strode out the door. Without a backward glance, he knew she would have a stunned expression on her face that would soon change to livid anger.

He stepped outside and breathed deeply, trying to exhale the venomous conversation he just concluded. *That woman is evil, pure evil.* His body gave a shudder as he walked back to his car and drove away, eager to distance himself from the contamination he felt. Driving toward Tangle Grove, he opened his cell phone and called Asia. It would be good to hear a cheerful voice.

"Hello, Daddy," her voice sounded stressed and tired.

"What's wrong?"

"I'm still here in a conference, but can you meet me at Sweet Elke's?"

"I'm on my way," he said and increased his speed. "Be there in ten minutes."

"Thank you, Dad. Gotta go."

His mind searched for things that would explain Asia's upset. He pressed even harder on the gas pedal and was soon pulling into a parking space across from Sweet Elke Café. He could see that Asia was already inside.

When he walked into the café, she was almost in tears. He pulled her into a protective hug and held her. She was shaky but soon began to calm. Letting her go, he stood back and studied her.

Her big brown eyes looked worried as she explained the situation. "Lisa had to take off today for some pressing business. I went ahead with our meeting, but it's all wrong. Jim Cook, the mayor, is trying to change everything. He's pressing to move the whole downtown to a site south of town. And Verina says most people are in agreement with him."

She sighed. "It puts me in a very difficult spot. My company was hired primarily with Montebelli Corporation money, and I know they want the plans to remain as they are. The committees have already voted and agreed to this location. I don't understand why he's doing this." She shook her head slowly. "He said Lisa has dealt underhandedly with the town and is guilty of a conflict of interest. Is that true?"

Taylor rubbed the back of his neck. Lisa was desperate, but bribing and coercing didn't fit the person he was getting to know. Even though the café was empty, he led Asia to a table in a far corner. "I'll tell you some of what's going on." He tried to sound calm, but inside he was fuming. Not only were these people attempting to undermine a woman who seemed to be doing them an enormous service, they were undermining his daughter. He explained all that Angela told him, leaving out the *small* part about Lisa's company.

Asia's eyes widened with fear and bewilderment. "I've never heard of anything so sickening. We have to stop this."

"I think that's where Lisa might be today. However, to my knowledge, she doesn't know about this segment of the attack on her. Once we inform her of their plans, she'll need to decide how to handle this. Until then, are you strong enough to go back in there and scoop up as much information as you can? It will be very helpful to Lisa to know who's going to stand with her."

Determination replaced her fear. "You bet I can."

His head jerked back to get a better look at his daughter. He hadn't seen fire like that since he lived with her mother. It startled him at first, but then he smiled. "I'm glad to see some tiger in you when it's called for." Asia laughed, relaxing her shoulders. "Okay, I'm going back into the fray." She leaned down and kissed him goodbye.

"That's my girl." He continued to sit at the table, rehashing the details of the day, then took out his notebook and recounted the information. The list of Lisa's enemies increased by the minute.

The afternoon was difficult. He tried to reach Lisa a couple of times and had to settle to leave messages. Then he worked to get his mind to focus on some sort of plan but couldn't settle down.

Knowing that Asia was in an adverse situation didn't help. Although there was no doubt that she would do well, it would be taxing.

Restless, he decided to walk out the frustration. Outside, an old pickup tore past him, then slammed on the brakes and backed up. The truck came to a sudden stop even with where he stood, and an old woman leaned out her window. He recognized Gale Wallace from the Design Team meetings. She looked like she could spit bullets.

"Mr. Taylor, I'm so mad I could shoot somebody, and I just might do it! Do ya know what that no-good mayor of ours has done?" She didn't bother waiting for an answer. "He just stabbed Lisa and yer daughter in the back. The coward waited 'til Lisa wasn't here an' then started turnin' the others over to his side. He came back from lunch with a whole crowd of his cronies and starts gettin' them all riled up about the huge cost of this project. I know what he's doin', he's tryin' to get this project moved to where more of his property is! I'm tellin' ya, he won't get away with it—I've got lots of friends here—we'll stop him!"

Taylor was shocked that Mayor Cook would be that conspicuous. He must be confident that Lisa was going down. Gale's behavior was true to her name—she proved a force to be reckoned with. She huffed, red in the face, and her hands pounded on the wheel to accentuate her words. The exchange would have been comical except for the gravity of the situation.

He leaned on the door of her rusty truck. "Remind me never to cross you," he said, in an attempt to diffuse her emotions. Then he patted her arm, "You don't know how good it is to find someone on Lisa's team. Asia just told me what was happening, and I've placed calls to Lisa but can't reach her. Do you know what started all of this?"

Gale thought for a minute. "It makes no sense," she said, still fuming. "Jim was on board all last week and then comes in today with second thoughts."

Taylor's mind began to spin. Thomas' inquiries to Lisa's attorney might have coincided with Jim Cook's change of heart. His focus fell back on Gale, who was staring at him with impatience. "Sorry. I was just searching for some clue to why this happened."

"What happened is Jim Cook's abandoning the ship and lookin' out fer his own interests—not the town's. She was just as flushed as when she began her tirade. "I'll have a recall, I tell ya!"

Taylor was not certain how to help but letting Gale loose on Jim Cook and his associates seemed like a great idea. "That's the best news I've heard today. I'd like to suggest, however, that you calm down for your health's sake and get organized. Is there anyone you trust who can help you get the word out?"

"You bet there is, lots of folks."

He watched her mind whizzing through her friends. "Good." He opened his wallet and handed her a business card with his cell number on it. "If you need anything, please call me."

Gale gave him a toothy grin for the first time in their conversation. "We'll get this turned around, so don't worry about yer daughter. She's doin' real good this afternoon—cool as a cucumber."

He smiled and Gale drove off, but his stomach knotted when he thought about Asia dealing with a whole group of outsiders pushing a different agenda. He wanted to help, but his presence there might undermine her confidence. Rubbing the back of his neck, he took off on a brisk walk.

Thirty minutes later, he slowed to a stroll as he passed Siebert's barn and imagined Lisa rummaging around this old place with Jesse six years ago. A fierce longing to protect her swelled within him. *Stop this. Now.* He pulled his emotions back from those thoughts, surprised that he'd arrived at the place where he was willing to let himself care again. Wrong woman, wrong time. *But she needs protecting,* he argued.

Memories of his mother's faith surfaced, and a sudden prayer slipped from his lips, "You know all the things coming against Lisa. Please, shield her from her enemies." Reluctantly, he walked back into Tangle Grove. The sound of his cell phone pulled him out of his musings.

"Hi, Dad," Asia sounded excited. "Wait 'til you hear what I've found out."

Relief spread throughout his being. He smiled at the exuberance he heard in her voice. "Tell me."

"Let's wait until dinner, I want to go back to Bella Vista and have a long, soaking bath."

That gave him time to shower and change in Mont Castello. "Great, I'll pick you up at six."

***

Jesse worked that evening, so Taylor and Asia planned dinner by themselves. They arrived at a small, vine-covered restaurant with leaded glass windows. Candlelight, burning softly on each of the tables, illuminated the room as they came through the door.

An elegant man greeted them at the reservation desk. "How may I help you?"

"We don't have a reservation," Taylor said. "Is that a problem?"

"Not tonight." He glanced at Asia and his face lit up, belying his formality. "We have a wonderful table with a view. Please come this way."

He sat them at a table in an intimate brick alcove that looked out over a private garden. An eight-foot-high stone wall enclosed the landscape, which was designed with Tuscany in mind. The same vine on the front of the building reached around to the garden. Italian cypress trees anchored two of the corners, otherwise the garden was asymmetric, giving it a sense of artful randomness.

A lemon tree stood as a centerpiece for a lavish flowerbed, which boasted the late summer colors of reds, oranges, and yellows. Flagstones created a path that wound through the evergreen shrubs and under the lacy overhanging branches of red Japanese maple trees. They hinted at hidden views around each bend.

"Look," Asia directed, when the outdoor lighting turned on for the evening. Inconspicuous spotlights directed their beams onto profuse yellow rose bushes that climbed up and over the wall. Other spotlights aimed upward to accentuate the intricate patterns of shadows cast from the various trees and flowering vines. Taylor had been looking. The scene drained the tension of the day from his neck and shoulders.

Their waiter took their order and brought them each a glass of red wine and basket of bread. Taylor smiled at his lovely daughter and raised his glass to toast her. "You fill up my heart with happiness." He blinked the moisture from his eyes and chuckled. "Pretty sentimental."

She smiled softly and gazed at him. "I love you, Dad."

"Okay, tell me about your day," he said, wanting to move onto something concrete.

Radiant, she began a blow-by-blow story of the afternoon with Mayor Cook, Gale Wallace, the original Design Team, and the new recruits that Jim Cook brought to the meeting. "They stated that their reason was the insurmountable costs that accompanied the larger plan," Asia explained, with a look of disgust. "The Montebelli Corporation has put up most of the money for the town. It's costing them far less this way than if they move the whole thing to the southern location—plus there's no way for the town to grow and be cohesive there. It would destroy any possibility for it to become an attraction."

He listened, making mental notes.

"Dad, is there any truth to the rumor that the Montebelli Corporation may have to withdraw its support of Tangle Grove?" Her eyes pleaded for reassurance.

Without breaking his promise, he said, "Lisa indicated they have formidable foes, but from what I gather, they've been diligent in their business dealings." He wished he could offer more certainty. He smiled at his daughter and watched her breathe a gentle sigh of relief.

They finished a fabulous dinner and had to forego dessert. Relaxed and warm, they exited the restaurant and strolled arm in arm down the sidewalk. Asia's face was aglow. "Can you imagine how wonderful it's going to be walking down the new streets of Tangle Grove? We can know we played a big part in making it happen."

"I like the sound of that," he responded, looking in the attractive shop windows as they walked. "As charming as Bella Vista is, the openness of the valley in Tangle Grove has more appeal to me. Imagine sitting on your front deck every night watching that amazing sunset." He could see the picture in his mind's eye.

"That's the second time you've talked like that, Dad. Are you seriously thinking of moving here?"

He thought for a moment. "I might be...it's tempting." He glanced at her. "I'd certainly be closer to you."

Her smile engaged her whole face. She almost squealed with delight. "We'd only be a few hours apart. That beats Arizona any day."

He laughed aloud at her enthusiasm. "That assumes you don't end up somewhere else," he teased.

"Who knows," she tossed back, "maybe I'll be your next-door neighbor."

He laughed again. They reached his SUV and he opened the door for her. She gave him a big hug and got in. He walked toward the driver's side and watched a white Cadillac drive past. A woman was craning her neck to see who was in his car. She was past them before he recognized Angela Basso. Realizing what she must be thinking, he laughed. This was the perfect ending to a troubled day.

Chapter 13

Time was running out. It was Friday and nothing was resolved for Lisa and Asia. In fact, it was getting more complicated by the hour. Taylor had put off his own work as long as he dared and now forced himself to spend the hours it would take to write out questions pertinent to each of the cyclists he would interview in Spain.

After a few hours, his stomach growled. "Enough of that," he declared. He stood and picked up his phone to confirm his plane reservations. Moments later a quick call from Asia relieved some of his angst. Gale was getting the natives riled up to *mount an attack*, as she put it.

Lisa's call was more disconcerting. "Yesterday, Thomas came home early with roses for me. At first, I thought it was a ruse, but he took me to a movie and dinner. Then he wanted to hang out and talk about my work and…everyday things. He was actually pleasant—like he is with other people. He held my hand all evening."

"What do you make of it," Taylor asked, hoping she wasn't going to fall for it.

"I don't know. He was his old charming self—like he was when we were first dating. He says I've changed, become more self-assured and interesting. Maybe he wants to bury the hatchet. Or, maybe I want to believe him. No matter what he's done, there's still a place in me that hates the idea of failing in my marriage."

Knowing what he did about Thomas and Angela, Taylor doubted anything good could come from Thomas, but it was not his place to discourage her. Thomas had done plenty of that already.

***

Lisa went downstairs on Saturday morning, but Thomas wasn't around. A note lay on the counter, "*Went to see a client in a crisis.*" Her stomach rolled over. Occasionally Thomas needed to see clients on the weekend, but she hoped against hope that he would not follow through with his plan to meet Gary Bristol. He had been so attentive and romantic last night—it wouldn't make sense.

The apprehension pushed her to get some exercise. She changed into a swimsuit and dove into the water, swimming back and forth until she exhausted herself. Breathing hard, she hung on the side of the pool and let the calming effect of the physical exertion overcome her. She was so close to building her financial freedom, but what if Thomas had changed? After years of abuse, could she make herself love him again?

He came home and poked his head out the door. "Hi, Babe." She waited to discern more of his mood. There was no sign of guilt or friction between them. Instead, he remained cheerful. "I'm taking you to the ball tonight, did you remember?"

She flashed him a smile, "Yes, I bought a new dress for it."

"Great." He came out and gave her a fabulous kiss. His handsome eyes appraised her, boosting her ego. "I have some work to do, then I'll see you after my bike ride." He went back inside, his charm leaving her equilibrium off-balance.

***

Lisa dressed and went downtown to pick up the dress that the store had altered to fit her slender figure. She hummed with the radio while she drove, parking just as her phone rang. Recognizing Sydney's voice, she sobered. "Yes."

"The private investigator I hired just got back to me. He followed Thomas this morning and emailed me photos of him meeting with Gary Bristol."

Lisa's heart stopped. "Maybe he just met to call it off," she suggested in a weak voice.

"It doesn't look that way," Sydney said, trying to be gentle. "The photos show them looking over papers. One was clear enough to see the letterhead of the Montebelli Corporation. It is pretty conclusive."

Closing her eyes, Lisa shook her head in disbelief. Tears fell onto her lap.

Sydney waited.

"What do we do now?"

"The PI saw them go into your husband's office. When Thomas came out, he had no papers with him. I need you to retrieve those documents. Carefully. We need to get Gary and Thomas' fingerprints. Also, he probably paid Gary today. It would be lucky for us if you could find any evidence that would prove it—check book entry, receipt, you know."

Lisa sat stunned as she thought back over the last twenty-four hours. Why would Thomas purposely deceive her like that? He could have just continued along in his old rude way. There was only one answer. "He's won, hasn't he? He's playing me." The world started to cave in. Thomas' belittling remarks echoed in her mind. Maybe she had been fooling herself that she could succeed in this endeavor. How he would laugh with his friends again about her failures.

"Lisa," Sydney's voice was steady.

"I'm here," she whispered.

"Are you going to be able to do this?"

"What's the use?"

"Remember what it felt like when Thomas took over your investment? Taking the gain and degrading you? That is exactly what he plans to do again, only worse. He wants to tear down everything you have worked for."

Thinking about the way he had abused her, anger seeped in and emotional heat traveled up her spine and into her neck. Strength replaced the weakness she'd felt.

Sydney added one more thing. "You started this project in Tangle Grove and worked hard at it for six years. You convinced your friends to get onboard. If you are not strong, many good people are going to be hurt."

Her clammy hands shook. The picture of the loss and disappointment on the faces of her friends and those who'd trusted her, moved her back to sensibility. She drew a breath. "Okay, Sydney, I'll get it done."

"You are doing the right thing but be careful not to give anything away. We're not out of the woods yet and it is imperative to keep him in the dark as long as possible. I need more time to secure your interests."

***

Thomas was ecstatic. He waited until after Lisa left for town, then called his attorney and filled him in on the information that Gary Bristol had given him. "I have the proof and every detail of her corporation," he bragged. The attorney gave him the good news that he had been able to schedule a court date for October 5.

Hanging up the phone, he planned his strategy. If this ploy didn't work out, he would just divorce her and take half of everything she had accumulated. It appeared she owned considerably more than he did, and he was certain to score—big time.

Maybe she'll need to support me with alimony." He laughed at the thought as he headed out on his bike but couldn't escape the memory of Lisa's face when he gave her the flowers. She still believed him. He wobbled as he steered onto the road, increasing his speed until he was back in his groove.

***

Still in shock, Lisa retrieved her dress from the shop. Driving to Thomas' office, fear gripped her. He often rode by his office building. What if he caught her in his desk? What would she say? His angry face loomed large in her imagination, producing an agonizing feeling of dread as she rode the elevator to the second floor. She glanced up and down the hall and then listened at his door. Nothing. Unlocking the door, she quickly stepped in, closing it behind her. No lights were on in the reception area or in his office. The sun illuminated the golden room but brought no cheer.

She stopped a moment to consider the office. Thomas always bragged about this building, but he never could have built it without her efforts. It was small consolation. With trembling hands, she unlocked the safe and pulled out the documents, tossed without a care on top of the other valuables. She glanced back toward the door. Careful to limit her touch to one corner of her incorporation papers, her eyes caressed the words, *The Montebelli Corporation*. They had held such hope for her. They *hold* hope for me, she corrected, then slid them into a folder and laid them on Thomas' desk.

Next, she opened his business checkbook—and froze. A door closed. Holding her breath, she waited. Footsteps. She ducked down and strained to listen. They paced down the hallway and bypassed Thomas' office. All was quiet again. With renewed determination, she continued her task.

Sydney said she would be surprised if Thomas made it easy, but apparently, he didn't regard Lisa as a threat. The check stub was handwritten for $25,000 to GB Enterprises with a notation for *business consultation.* Lisa removed the stub and put the checkbook back. Closing the safe, she left with the papers.

In the lobby, she glanced out the glass door. Feeling exposed, her heart pounded, but she saw her chance. A large group of tourists passing the front door would provide cover. She opened the door and stepped outside but dropped the keys. The group continued down the sidewalk, leaving her in full view of the busy street. She glanced toward Angela's store, fumbling while she locked the door. It took all her effort not to run to her car.

The bright sun that slanted through her windshield diminished in the dark and dread she felt. Where did she think she was going? She couldn't face Thomas at home. How could she get through an evening surrounded by the very people secretly bent on destroying her? Her phone rang three times before she could answer.

"Hi, this is Taylor." His voice sounded concerned.

Choking back her tears, she blurted, "He did it. He paid off Gary and plans to destroy me. I don't think I can handle this."

He fell silent for a moment. "Can you meet me at Sweet Elke Park?"

She took uneven breaths through her sobs. "Yes, that's a good idea." After turning her car around, she journeyed blindly down the Strada del Vino, heading for her place of refuge.

***

Taylor was already there when Lisa arrived. He swung out of his car and sprang her door open. Reaching for her shaking hand, he pulled her out and held the trembling woman. "I'm so sorry." Great welling sobs escaped, and her shoulders shook violently. He led her to a bench in the park. Sitting down, he let her cry until the sobs began to subside.

She tried to wipe her eyes, but the tears wouldn't stop. She gave up and let them fall. Taking even breaths to calm herself, she whispered, "Thank you."

"You *will* get through this." He pulled her chin up and smiled into her red, watery eyes. "You're a mess," he said and got the humorless chuckle he hoped for.

The warm sun and the gentle sound of the creek soothed their raw nerves. Peace encompassed them, bringing a sense of hope out of nowhere. He broke the silence. "Amazing. I've never been in a place like this." He gazed at her face, softened with a serene glow. The tremors had vanished.

Her voice quiet, she filled him in. "I recovered the papers, but I don't want to touch them again. Would you mail them to Sydney?"

"Of course. Syd's the best, you know. You can count on her advice. At first, I found her strategy uncomfortable, but in the end, she saved me money and my sanity."

"I know. We spent Thursday going over my legal documents and accounting books. She asked some hard questions that forced me to come up with contingency plans in case Thomas..." her voice faltered, "...in case he took this course of action."

Taylor wanted to snatch her away from this turmoil but couldn't think of any place that would ease the situation. He spoke the obvious, "The only way out is through."

She nodded. "I know. I just don't know how I'll make it." A light breeze passed over them like a soothing balm. They sat in the silence for a while until she spoke, "I need to go and get ready for the ball tonight."

"You're not still going?"

"If I don't, it will tip my hand and he will know something's up." Her voice sounded drained, but her eyes looked determined. "I can't have him speeding things up until some loose ends are in place." She chuckled without smiling. "It helps viewing the situation like a game of chess."

"That came from Sydney," he smiled.

"Yes. It's good advice."

They stood and he said, "Thomas invited me to go tonight. I was planning to come up with an excuse to get out of it, but I think I'll hang around in case you need anything."

She smiled her gratitude.

He rubbed the back of his neck. "I was having lunch with Angela to get information out of her when he invited me. He set it up as though I was taking her. I just want you to know that I loathe that woman."

A mixture of emotions passed over her face. Taylor knew that outside of Thomas, Angela was her worst enemy. A deep sigh escaped, and her shoulders drooped. "Then we'll both be actors tonight," she said with resignation.

He hated the thought of what they would be going through this evening. "We can take comfort that we know what's going on and they're in the dark, okay?" He gave her a confident smile, hoping to lift the mood.

She nodded. "If I start to get overwhelmed, I'll look at you and remember that." She drove away first, leaving him alone in the park with his thoughts.

He looked up. "We need help tonight," he whispered. Reluctantly, he left this place of solitude and drove back to town to rent a last-minute tux for their theatrical ordeal.

Chapter 14

Thomas was still out on his ride when Lisa arrived home. Relieved to see his bicycle missing from its storage hook, she took a long, hot bath and let the bubbles repair her emotions.

Later, she dressed for the ball and checked out her image in the mirror. The red dress she bought fit tight to the waist then flared out when she twirled, showing off her slender legs—as did the red stilettos. The vibrant color was a vivid contrast to her black hair.

Lifting the famous black fire opal, known as *The Dutchman,* out of her locked jewelry safe, she gazed at the two-inch long, 58-carat stone that her great-great-grandfather had cut out of his mine. Electric blue ignited the brilliant red and orange flames, and a simple band of 18-carat gold surrounded the stone. Fastening it behind her neck, it hung at her throat. The combination with her dress was dazzling. Surveying herself once more in the mirror, she was satisfied with the effect. She needed as much feminine power on her side tonight as she could muster.

The sky was darkening, and she began to wonder if Thomas was going to make it back in time to change and get to the celebration. She grasped at the hope she'd be spared the humiliation of her enemies watching her, but he burst through the door.

"Had a great ride," he said, avoiding eye contact. "I'll be ready in a second." When he came down again, he grinned, "You look fantastic."

Her heart tore at the corners, but anger took over. "Not so bad yourself." While they drove to the country club, she set the stereo louder than usual so they wouldn't have to talk. They smiled, but she was the only one who knew they were *both* playing a part.

The attendant took their car and Thomas led her through the impressive glass door of the country club. Other members greeted them, and Thomas stopped to talk with two of his golfing friends. "Let's get to the bar," he said, and directed her toward the laughter coming from the room ahead. He ordered a whiskey sour, which he downed quickly, then ordered a second one. "That's better."

"Everything all right?" she asked, indicating his second drink.

"Just need to calm down from all the excitement of the day," he said and gave her a quick smile that didn't light his eyes. He spotted another friend and hailed him. While they talked, Lisa pretended to listen. However, more pressing matters occupied her mind.

Looking past Thomas, she spotted Taylor and her pulse quickened. He followed Angela to the bar. She wore a dress with a low-cut halter-top and returned provocative smiles to the men who were ogling her as she passed. Centered prominently in her cleavage was one of the larger opals Lisa had arranged for an agent to sell to her—for an exorbitant price.

Thomas' eyes strayed from his conversation and his attention focused on the arriving couple. "Hello Taylor, glad you could come. Hi, Angie. You look spectacular." He reached for her and gave her a kiss.

***

Jaw tense, Taylor watched with apprehension for Lisa's reaction to Thomas' hand caressing Angela's waist in a familiar way. Angela was quick to catch the startled look on Lisa's face.

"Tommy," she oozed, "you always know how to make a girl feel beautiful. Her eyes darted to Lisa's opal, and she smiled, touching her own necklace to draw attention to her new acquisition. "Oh, hello, Lisa."

"Hello, Angela," Lisa replied, her voice calm. She showed no reaction to the necklace.

Angela seemed disappointed. Turning back to Thomas, she asked, "How do you like my new trinket, Tommy?"

"Beautiful," he said, not even glancing at the gemstone.

Lisa must have had enough. "Oh, I see you bought one of the seconds I released from our stock." She looked more closely at the stone. "Nice job covering up the flaw with a diamond. It's almost unnoticeable."

"How dare you!" Angela sputtered. "This opal is flawless!"

Lisa lifted one eyebrow. "I certainly hope that's not what you're telling your customers."

Angela was speechless. Taylor covered a grin, but Thomas scowled at his wife, his shaking hand clenching into a fist. Taylor stiffened, ready to intervene, when a woman he had never met interrupted the intensity of the moment.

***

Lisa dodged Thomas' scathing expression and smiled at Deanne Archer when she joined them. A descendant of a local well-to-do merchant, Deanne was enamored with her historical significance. Her manner was usually overbearing to the point of rudeness, but for once, Lisa was happy to see her.

"Lisa, dear," Deanne gushed. "May I introduce Cynthia Bennett. She is new to town from Boston and from a *very* old family. Cynthia, this is Lisa *Van Buren* Richards."

Her heart still racing, Lisa acted more gracious than she felt as she extended her hand. "I'm pleased to meet you, Cynthia," she smiled. "Welcome to Bella Vista."

"It is a lovely town," Cynthia said. "I think we will enjoy the climate more than Boston, although I'll miss the shopping." The three women nodded in agreement.

Sensing Thomas' pressure, Lisa said, "Cynthia, this is my husband, Thomas Richards. She glanced at Angela and couldn't see any way around introducing her. "And this is…" but Deanne cut her off, clearly disapproving of Angela, and her dress.

Turning her back on Angela and Thomas, Deanne spoke to Cynthia. "Lisa's family is one of the oldest in Bella Vista and certainly the most famous." She glanced at Lisa, her face glowing. "The Van Buren's discovered a mine that produced fabulous opals." Her eye caught the famous black fire opal. "Is that *The Dutchman*?"

Cynthia's eyes widened at the spectacular stone before her. "I have never seen anything like it," she said, and moved closer. Even in the dim light of the bar, the lights reflected off the gem, making it look like fire on Lisa's throat. "You are a fortunate woman. The fact that it is a family heirloom makes it even more valuable. I have a few cherished pieces myself, dating back to the Civil War."

Lisa could tell she would enjoy Cynthia as a friend. She was unpretentious but confident. "Thank you, that's just how I feel about it." She caught Angela's fuming eyes, and a small smile tilted the corners of her mouth. Deanne took Cynthia off to introduce her, and her heritage, around.

Thomas was irate and had ordered another drink. Lisa hid a nervous swallow. He hated it when someone raised the subject of her family. Lifting his glass to Angela he said, "The only thing important about *old* family is that they're all dead." Angela caught on and clinked her glass on his. Lisa couldn't disguise the stab she felt. Thomas' expression was dark and jubilant.

"Oh," he said, "another good thing about old family, at least Lisa's, is how protected they are. Angela, do you know her family has their own personal guardian angel at Sweet Elke Park? Isn't that right Lisa?" His voice slurred.

"You're out of line, Thomas," Lisa said, fighting to keep a cool head.

The authority in her exhortation seemed to surprise him. He flung back, "You have no right to tell me I'm out of line. From where I sit, you've been out of line for six years. Lying, cheating, and pretending you're some kind of executive. Ha, you'll see where all your scheming gets you." He threw back the rest of his drink. "After I'm finished with you, you'll have *nothing*," he hissed. Bringing Angela's hand to his lips, his eyes darkened. "Did you know, Angie's been my *lady* for some time?"

Lisa's mouth dropped open in disbelief. He laughed and threw the final dagger. "Oh, and we have a hearing on October fifth. That's when everything you own gets put into my name, just like your little investment project fifteen years ago—and wait till you hear..."

Angela's eyes widened, apparently not knowing how much of their plan Thomas was about to give away. "Tommy," she said, "come with me, there's someone you *have* to meet." He didn't seem to comprehend what Angela was doing but allowed her to put her arm through his and lead him away.

The scene was so surreal that Lisa just stood there and watched them leave together. People stared in her direction, curious about the argument. For the most part, Thomas kept his voice low enough, so the poisonous words were nearly inaudible. She felt embarrassed but was too numb to move. A sound attempted to cut through the fog.

Someone took her elbow and said, "Lisa," with more insistence.

Still bewildered, she turned to see Taylor and said, "He admitted it. All of it."

"I know. I heard him." His eyes darted around them. "Let's get out of here."

His warm, sure hand on her back seemed to pulse life into her. She glanced up and saw him mask his concern with a broad smile at the groups of people who watched them move through the party. She was also smiling—at first to cover up, but then laughter began to bubble up inside, like a mild hysteria. Instead of grief, surprising relief hit her.

Concern clouded Taylor's face and he let his hand drop to take hold of hers. "Are you all right?"

She gazed up with a delirious smile. "Better than I've been for years. And you know what I want to do?"

He smiled tentatively. "What?"

"Dance. Do you like to dance?"

"Yes," he said, his eyes wary. They reached the ballroom, and he led her onto the floor. The orchestra was playing a waltz. He moved through the basic steps until she got her bearing. After following his flawless lead, he began to move her around the floor, twirling her and pulling her back into step. She gloried as her beautiful red dress and the large, handsome man in a black tuxedo, caught everyone's attention.

Linking eyes with him, she drank in the admiration she found there. The dance seemed to emulate the emotions swirling inside her. Thomas' admission of his infidelity had been a gift that broke the last thread that tied her to him. She was free. Her fingers enmeshed with Taylor's and the whole world vanished. She wanted the dance to last forever.

When the music ended, they exited the floor and people standing near them nodded and smiled. Lisa looked around, abashed at the attention. She continued to hold his hand as they wove their way through the crowd to the open doors that led to the formal gardens outside. Once there, she let out a long breath she hadn't realized she'd been holding. "That was wonderful, like a dream."

***

Taylor looked down at her glowing face, not trusting himself to speak. This afternoon, it became obvious to him how deep his feelings had grown. He ached to tell her, but it would only make a messy situation worse. Instead, he said, "*You* were wonderful."

The cool evening air felt refreshing after the exertion of the dance. They leaned against the marble banister that edged the patio and looked down at the lighted swimming pool. Her small frame seemed so fragile. He knew if they stayed much longer, he wouldn't be able to stop himself from pulling her into his protective arms. "Should we go back inside, or would you like me to take you home."

Sobering, she thought for a moment. "I think it would be good to get home before Thomas. I want to take a few things and leave the house tonight." Her voice held firm resolve, but there was also a trace of fear.

He studied her, thinking of the scene that might ensue if Thomas walked in while she was packing. "I'll stay with you while you gather your things and drive you wherever you want to go."

"That wouldn't look too good—as much as I would like that." She stumbled over her words and blushed. "I think it would be better if Jesse took me to a hotel."

"Good." Changing the subject, he said, "I liked the way you handled yourself tonight. The look on Angela's face was priceless."

"Thanks. It helped having you there. I might have bludgeoned her with one more *Tommy*." She started to laugh again. "They were so pitiful."

It was good to hear her laugh. He hoped the hardest part of the night was over. They walked to the large lobby, and she called Jesse, but only got his voicemail. Taylor called Asia's number and got the same. He looked at her and raised an eyebrow. "Looks like the kids are out on the town. What do you want to do?"

She glanced around. The lobby was empty with everyone engaged elsewhere in the clubhouse. "I guess I need a ride to my house."

The parking attendant brought Taylor's SUV and opened the door for her. Taylor got in the other side, tipped the young man, and drove off.

***

Lisa held her stomach, trying to suppress the anxiety that gripped her. Things were happening too fast, and her emotions were starting to catch up. The closer they got to her home, the more grief came to the surface. "Taylor, I'm not doing too well," she wailed as a wave of uncontrollable emotions threatened to overwhelm her.

"I thought you were getting out of this a little too easily." He looked sideways at her and took her hand. "Look at me. You're a strong woman and you *will* get through this pain. Don't be afraid you won't. Believe me, I know what it's like."

She nodded and focused on controlling her breathing. They pulled up to her house and he came around and opened the door.

When her legs peeked out from under her red dress, he grinned and said, "If it's any consolation, you were the *Bella* of the ball."

She was tired but stood and swished her skirt playfully. Her arms felt heavy as she walked to the front door. "What a roller coaster weekend." She missed the lock when she tried to open the door, so he took her key and unlocked it for her.

Looking around her home, a fresh wave of sadness hit. "Twenty-one years in this house and tonight I'm leaving." She began to sob. He opened his arms, and she buried her head on his chest, letting his strength infuse her. After some moments, it took all her effort to back away from him. She glanced around. "I don't know if I can trust him with anything he knows I value."

"It wouldn't hurt to have Jesse stay here tonight," he suggested.

She tried calling him again, but with no luck. Climbing the stairs, she started packing clothes, jewelry, and toiletries. She was just dragging her suitcases out to the landing, when Jesse returned her call.

"What's going on, Mom? You sounded frantic."

"I'm moving out of the house," she stated with as much calm as she could. "Dad made it plain tonight that he plans to ruin me." She began to sob again. "I'm sorry Jesse."

"Don't worry about me, where are you?"

"I'm at home," she sniffed. "Taylor drove me because we couldn't get hold of you. I've packed my things and I'm staying at a hotel tonight until I can think of what else to do." Then she had an idea. "Do you know if there are any rooms at the Raffinato, where Asia's staying?"

"I'll check and call you back." Jesse hesitated and asked, "Taylor isn't staying with you, is he?"

She felt a shock wave go through her. "No—he's leaving here as soon as he helps me put my bags in my car."

"Good. Are you okay to drive?"

"I'll be fine, but I need a favor. Could you stay at the house tonight? There's no telling what Dad will be like, but he'll act civilized if you're here."

"I'll be right there." He hung up.

Taylor climbed the stairs, carried her suitcases out to the garage, and put them in her car.

Jesse called back to say that all the rooms had been rented for the ball and that he was on his way over. Lisa sank onto the sofa to think. She had no choice. Turning to Taylor, she said, "I'm going to have to explain this to my dad and ask if I can stay with him."

"Once you tell him the situation, there won't be any question in his mind that you're doing the right thing."

It was still early in the evening when she called her father and briefed him on what had happened. She felt so weary, but his voice was reassuring.

"Honey, what on earth would make you feel like you couldn't call me? I should be the first one you run to—always."

She started to relax a little and stood up, pacing. Being alone all night in a strange room had been frightening in the state of mind she was in. "I'll be right there, Dad."

When the conversation ended, Taylor put his arm around her shoulder. "See, you're already being taken care of," he smiled.

At that moment, Jesse walked in the front door and saw Taylor standing with his mother. His confused look spoke volumes. Taylor's arm dropped from her shoulder as he spoke. "Your mother's been through quite an ordeal. She's going to need a lot of support."

"I can give her all the support she needs, so you can go."

"Jesse," she scolded. "What's gotten into you? Taylor's done nothing but help us in this mess. He's been one of our only friends."

Jesse's angry look faltered. "I'm sorry. It's just that you're here with my mother and my dad isn't. I didn't know what to think."

"You have a right to be confused," Taylor said. "However, you do know what Thomas did to her fifteen years ago, and tonight I heard him promise to do the same thing again. There's nothing confusing about that."

Jesse nodded with tight lips. He walked to his mother and surrounded her in his arms.

***

Taylor's gut and jaw took turns tensing. He had zero power to protect Lisa from Thomas—just as he was unable to protect Asia from her mother's devastating decisions that broke up their family. At least Lisa would have Jesse and her father to lean on during this impossible time. Watching Jesse doing his best to comfort her, Taylor knew his own presence would only complicate things, and possibly cause more problems. Still, his feet felt nailed to the floor. She looked so vulnerable. "Are you certain you want to drive yourself?" he asked one last time.

She withdrew from Jesse. "I'm a little shaky, but it won't be a problem." Then she said with a gloomy face, "I hate running home to my dad after a failed marriage."

Jesse's head perked up. "Going to Grandpa's is much better than a lonely hotel room, Mom. That was bothering me."

The weight of the evening stooped her shoulders, but she straightened and looked at both of them. "Thank you for your concern, but I promise I'll be fine. This week has just been such a terrible shock. People have directed more venom at me than I ever thought possible. By tomorrow the worst will be over and by next week I'll know what direction my life is going to take."

She handed Jesse another bag to put into her car. When he left the room, she turned to Taylor. "I don't know what I would have done without you this week." The look she gave him pleaded for a sign that he might be part of that new direction.

He studied her, sensing this journey was something she needed to finish on her own. His heart argued, but when she searched his eyes, he knew he couldn't give her what she wanted.

Not now.

Ever? There was no answer. Reluctantly, he followed his head. "You have a strong family with a lot of love—that's what will get you through this. It's not my place to be in the middle of it." He rubbed his neck and frowned, "Besides, I'm scheduled to fly to Spain tomorrow."

Her eyes filled with disappointment, but she attempted a brave smile. "I know."

Things felt like they were crashing inside, tearing at his resolve. She stepped to him and kissed his cheek lightly. "Thank you for everything," she said, holding his eyes one last time.

"Goodbye, Lisa." He pulled her to him and kissed the top of her head, longing to shield her. *God bless and keep you*, he prayed silently and forced his arms to release her. As she moved away, his heart followed. It was a good thing he had to be in Spain for a month, otherwise he wouldn't have been able to leave her like this.

They drove away at the same time but veered off in different directions. He watched the lights of her car move out of sight, wondering if she was doing the same. A lump filled his throat as he made his way back up the mountain, knowing he would continue down the other side the next day to meet his flight.

He called Asia to say goodbye and wish her well on the completion of the project. They were both sad that they were not able to say their farewells in person. "I'll be back to Portland in the spring," he promised. A wave of guilt and helplessness swept over him that he couldn't offer more to anyone right now.

***

After Lisa left, Jesse waited for his dad to come home, but he never did. His sleep was light and fitful, worrying about what would happen in the next two weeks.

He called Asia in the morning and made plans to meet at her hotel for breakfast. Just before pulling out of the drive, he saw Angela drop off his father. That was the last straw. Jesse threw a disgusted look at his father and sped away.

Chapter 15

Lisa's father, Jess Sorensen, had hot tea waiting for her. He helped bring her luggage into the guest room. After setting her things down, she fell into his comforting arms. She looked into his concerned face, still handsome with his white hair, and was again thankful for the source of her family's startling Danish blue eyes.

They sat in the cozy living room, reminding her how much she enjoyed her parents' home—at least when her mother wasn't being critical. She never understood how her father was able to stay so cheerful and positive while living with such a demanding woman. Leaving for a distant college had been Lisa's escape. She shook her head. Those quarrels seemed ages ago.

The large front windows afforded an expansive view of the valley below and the host of stars that hung in thin air above them. Tonight, only white pinpoints of light blinked up from Bella Vista.

In the safety of her dad's home, she explained all that had taken place. The light of dawn was just starting to touch the tops of the mountains when they stood to head for bed. Hours of tears and sorting had depleted her of all emotion, and she slept without dreaming until nearly four o'clock in the afternoon.

Waking up was a slow process. She washed her face with cold water to help her mind get started, then found Jess in the kitchen, reading the paper. He looked somewhat rested although the redness in his eyes testified to the lack of sleep the night before. She looked more closely. *Or was it from the tears he'd shed after she went to bed?* "Dad, I'm sorry to have brought this on the family," she told him for the tenth time.

Jess surveyed her face, his jaw set, and his mouth stretched to a thin line. "That's the last time I want to hear that. You've taken responsibility for your part in this, now Thomas has to take his. This self-abusive habit of taking the blame for everything is what got you into this. Stop it or it will end up destroying you, Lisa. Am I clear on this?"

She took the exhortation without protest. He was right. Sitting down, she said, "I keep getting the same advice. I guess it's time I take it." Her thoughts turned to Taylor and her heart wrenched. He should be halfway to Spain by now. *Stop,* she reprimanded herself. She was still entangled in this shredded marriage and had no idea how long it would take to sort her life out again, if ever.

Rising to get her a cup of coffee, Jess said, "I've made a list of things you'll need to take care of. It's Sunday, so Thomas will be at home, but if you need to get anything out of the house, I'll go with you."

Thinking about her home, she realized there were few possessions she wanted, but those were very important to her. "Thomas is angry about anything associated with our family," she said. "I'd like to get the dishes and heirlooms that came from Mom and Grandma Klara. I took the photographs last night."

"Okay, then," he said. "Let's get some boxes and drive over. I doubt Thomas will make a scene if I'm there." He paused, "Where do you plan to live while this gets sorted out?"

Her mind was clearing with the coffee. "One of my apartments over Sweet Elke Café will be vacated at the end of the month. "I'd like to stay here until then."

He grinned, "That sounds like a good plan. I like those apartments and you'll be happy watching over your building project." Looking at the notes he'd written down, he asked, "Have you thought of an attorney you want to use to defend your corporation?"

"I'd like to continue using Sydney Wakeham. She's been in contact with the Van Buren Estate attorney. I trust them both." She paused. "Thomas said he had a hearing set for October fifth. That doesn't give us much time, but Sydney already had an audit scheduled for the early part of next week. "Your investment has grown a bit," she grinned. After selling some of her personal opals, she was still short at the beginning of her business plan. He'd leant her money to buy the coffee shop building, then decided to leave it invested, claiming it was rewarding to see her happy. She'd kept him in the dark, knowing it would have worried him to see the extent to which she had expanded their first purchase. When she gave him an approximation of his earnings, his eyes widened with a look of new appreciation.

"This is big stuff. Are you sure Thomas can't take over these like he did your rental house? The thought of him tormenting you over that property still infuriates me. I don't want to see that happen again."

"I'm pretty sure I'm protected," she said, her brow furrowing. "Sydney said I may have to give up something, but she hasn't finished going through all the paperwork. We only met last Thursday. Thomas' date is rushing things."

She thought back over the events of last night. "For once, it's a good thing that Thomas got drunk. He spilled the beans, which gives me a heads up on his plans. At least they don't know I have any idea about Fire Mountain." At this, her brow furrowed more deeply. "Angela seems to have a lot of support. I have the Van Buren Trust attorney, James Morley, researching what our options are."

Jess smiled encouragement, "Don't worry, Honey, you're in good hands and you've got a good head on your shoulders."

She appreciated her father's confidence. Still, a deep sigh escaped. After gathering some boxes, Jess, Jesse and Asia drove to her house to move her possessions. Thomas wasn't home, and she jerked to alert with every new sound that creaked in the house, every car door that slammed shut outside. Thankfully, he never showed. They unloaded the boxes into a vacant corner of Jess' garage. The remnants of her life.

***

The next week was a whirlwind for her. Jesse and Asia met with her for a private gathering afterhours with Lilly and Joe at Sweet Elke Café. Gale Wallace and several of her friends attended, along with the property owners who were still on board with the original plan for Tangle Grove. Jess came as moral support.

In a surprising move, Frank Harding, the realtor in Verina's office, called Lisa to inform her that Jim Cook and Verina Fields had sold their downtown Tangle Grove properties to another corporation on Friday. He also reported that Jim had purchased another property adjacent to one of Verina's in the competing southern area. Frank felt he needed to remain anonymous for now because of his job, so Lisa was pleased to report the information at the meeting without revealing his name.

"That snake," Gale railed. "Jim's in it all fer himself!" This fueled the fire hotter than ever.

Denny Chapman, the attorney who planned to build his office in the current downtown area, spoke up. "Last week, Jim came to see if I was interested in moving to the new area." He scoured Lisa's face for truth. "Jim indicated that the Montebelli Corporation was somehow in jeopardy, and they needed a second option that was less costly. Is that true?"

Lisa swallowed and took a deep breath. She addressed the meeting with a straightforward and, finally, honest approach. "What Jim was alluding to is a plan that my husband devised to take over the assets of the Montebelli Corporation." She steeled herself for the next question.

"How does he have any connection to the corporation?" Denny asked with a wary expression.

Meeting Jesse and her friends' eyes, knowing that she had worked among them deceptively for six years, she prepared herself for the worst. "The Montebelli Corporation was formed by me. I worked through it to create the vision for Tangle Grove.

"What!" Jessie and Asia exclaimed in unison.

She winced. "There are personal reasons for remaining anonymous—the same reasons that now threaten to jeopardize this plan." Instantly, murmurs and sideways glances encompassed the meeting. "I'm sorry I deceived you, but this is very important to me, and my husband has no... interest in Tangle Grove. I want to assure you that he can't overturn anything I have committed to do here." She let her breath out and watched their expressions.

The whole room was quiet as the information sank in. Finally, Gale Wallace spoke up and addressed the group. "I've had an idea all along that Lisa was the one runnin' the Montebelli Corporation and

I've had no problem with that. She's put her heart and soul into our town—at great expense to her personal life, it seems. I've known her to be an honest and trustworthy member of our team," she paused, "except fer this one, rather big, deception." She chuckled and soon many of the other members joined her. "I imagine that some of ya might be peeved with her fer keeping us in the dark, but I'm willin' to trust that she had her reasons and that her motives were fer us, not agin' us."

Denny was one member who had not laughed at Gale's comment. "How do you know the corporation's assets are out of his reach?" Lisa knew he, along with many others, had invested in this area based on the sizeable financial commitment made by the corporation. They stood to lose a lot if this was blocked.

"I've had good counsel all along and even now, my attorneys are looking into every aspect of my business," she answered. "They've been set up legally and thoughtfully." She paused and then gave them the rest of the information they needed. "I can't go into the specifics, Denny. You understand the need for confidentiality in these matters." He nodded and she continued, "My husband has set a hearing date for October fifth to try to get control of my properties." Again, a buzz broke out in the room.

"What happens if he wins?" questioned Mari Harris.

Lisa hesitated, "I'll still own a portion of my properties, although I may have to sell them to keep my commitment to the downtown area. But I will keep my commitment." She noticed her hands were trembling.

"Is there a real possibility that the downtown area could be moved to Jim Cook's place?" Lilly asked.

Asia, who had been listening intently, asked if she could answer that question. "The signatures on the contract that hired my company are binding on the city. They include Mayor Cook, Lisa Richards, Gale Wallace, and two other city council members who are not here tonight. These people signed that they would endorse the plan presented by the Design Team. We have minutes of the meeting that show the current downtown area won the majority of the votes. That is not to say that the Mayor couldn't call the matter back for further consideration and through a new vote, move the site, but it's unlikely for him to get that kind of support."

"Thank you, Asia," Gale said. She had been the mayor in Tangle Grove years ago. Lisa noted that out of habit, she guided the meeting.

Asia spoke up again. "There's one other thing I'd like to bring up. At Thursday's meeting, Mayor Cook produced another set of plans that he and his group had been working on. Another engineering firm had used many of the designs created by Baker and Thymes. It's illegal for them to use those designs."

"Did they leave you copies?" Denny asked, instantly alerted.

"No," Asia answered, "but I was able to get clear photographs of the designs with the name of the other company." She produced copies made from the digital pictures she had taken with her cell phone.

For the first time during the meeting, Denny smiled. "Well done," he said, examining them. "May I keep these?"

Asia nodded, "They've been emailed to my company, and I can make more copies if you need them."

"The last thing we need to cover," Gale said, "is the recall of Mayor Cook. We have scheduled a town meeting fer all parties to speak their piece. Denny, I was hopin' that you might be the spokesman fer us."

Denny looked up from his tablet with determination. "It would be a privilege to take this on." At his announcement, relief spread through the small group. The rest of the meeting consisted of Denny gathering any other information that anyone had to contribute.

By the end, many of Lisa's anxieties had eased. Her associates had stuck by her and had not pressed too hard for the details of her corporation. Gale was a true friend to take her side. She felt forever indebted. Once outside, Jesse and Lisa waited for Asia to exit. Denny needed to ask her a few more questions, but at last, she joined them.

"Okay, I'm free. It looks like we're still on track." The relief in her voice was tangible.

Lisa hugged her and they began walking to their cars. "You did a great job, Asia, clear and concise. Everyone was able to understand, and it put them at ease."

Jesse shook his head. "Look who's talking. That took real courage, Mom. I think I would have run the other way and let my attorneys make the announcement."

"I'm through hiding," she said. By the time they reached Jesse's car, the adrenaline was wearing off and she felt exhausted. In the darkness of the evening, sadness again encompassed her. Since Sunday, she had been pushing hard to help prepare for this meeting. Now the loss of her twenty-nine-year marriage, with all the good and bad, crushed her. "Good night, Jesse. I'll see you tomorrow, Asia."

"Actually, my company called just before the meeting, and they want me back in the office tomorrow by noon. They scheduled a flight in the morning."

Lisa's shoulders slumped further. "I wish you didn't have to leave right away." She took Asia's hand in hers. "Come back soon," she said and hugged her. "I'll miss you terribly."

Asia's eyes misted. "I'll miss you too," she whispered.

***

Last week's pace proved leisurely compared to the nearly overwhelming number of things flying at Lisa this week. Meetings with attorneys and her accountant filled her schedule. She printed documents from her computer and brought boxes of files to their offices to check dates and amounts paid for supplies and services on all her properties. Six years' worth. Though a grueling and tedious job, they finished the worst of it by late afternoon on Friday.

Sydney had flown back to Bella Vista on Thursday morning to supervise the handling of Lisa's case. "Thank you, Sydney," Lisa said, looking up at the imposing woman with short, precision-cut platinum hair.

Tired from the long day, she nodded in a matter-of-fact way. "Under normal circumstances, I would not have taken on this responsibility personally, but Taylor is a close friend. And *you* are important to him."

She swallowed the threatening emotion. "I owe him so much."

Sydney's voice softened. "I know you've been told this a lot lately, but you *will* get through this. You have more pressing on you than I would wish for my worst enemy, but you are holding up because you *are* a strong woman. And there is a lot of power behind you—from your family and friends, and your legal team. We're all on your side, so don't feel alone."

She nodded. "You've all been great."

Sydney cocked her head and asked, "Have you heard from him?"

Lisa's tepid smile vanished altogether, and she tried not to let her disappointment show. "No, we haven't talked since he left on Saturday night. He's in Spain covering the race there and I..." she paused and lifted sad eyes. "Things were sort of...strained between he and Jesse."

Sydney raised an eyebrow for more information.

Lisa sighed and laid it all out. "Jesse had just found out I was leaving his father and I think he wondered if Taylor had something to do with my decision. None of us talked about it, but I imagine Taylor knew..." Her voice got small, "...and then he left." Unbidden tears came to her eyes as she thought about the rock he'd been during her crisis. She missed his strength, but she couldn't ask him to clean up her mess.

Sydney smiled. "I don't imagine he'll be gone long."

Lisa thought of the emotional tempest that lay ahead of her. "That's the problem. I don't have anything to offer him, even if he does come back."

***

Labor Day weekend proved to be just that. Lisa's renters moved out on Saturday, and she spent the rest of the day cleaning. By Sunday afternoon, her back was stiff from scrubbing. She stood back and looked at the apartment from the entryway. The afternoon sun shone through the large front windows of the living and dining rooms.

Ten-foot ceilings made the space feel even larger—all a blank canvas for her to paint. Her excitement grew as she realized she could decorate this apartment in whatever way she wanted. A genuine smile came to her face for the first time in weeks, maybe years.

She stepped to the front window and gazed onto Maple Street, soon to be renamed *Main Street*, and envisioned the new courthouse building. It was going to happen, and she would have a front seat view of all the progress. Unexpected exhilaration bubbled up inside. She hugged herself and gave a small squeal of delight.

Turning around and studying the empty rooms, she made a decision to paint. Filled with new creative energy, she bounded downstairs, which landed by the side of Sweet Elke Café, and gazed up at the lovely Tuscan style building that was her new home. She smiled again and drove off to get the paint.

***

"Are you going to sleep *all* day?" Jess' voice reached through the fog in Lisa's head.

She looked up from her pillow with half open eyes. "Hi, Dad. What time is it?"

"Almost noon," he teased with a chuckle. "You haven't slept this late since you were in college."

"Well, it wasn't a party this time, unless you want to call it a painting party." Sitting up, she stretched and felt the aches in her arms and neck from rolling on paint and cutting in the corners with a brush. The last room was finished at five-thirty this morning. It was a push, but she wanted it done before her dad and Jesse helped her move the few things she owned.

They got a later start than planned, but Jess and Jesse were able to get her things moved in by 4:00. The extensive wooden cupboards in her kitchen were barren, except for the few decorative antiques that sat on the granite countertop. The apartment was one big, empty canvas. She bit her lower lip in exhilaration, imagining what it would look like after a few shopping trips.

Jesse leaned against the counter, frowning as he scrutinized her face. She had seen the dark circles that lay under her eyes and knew she had lost too much weight, yet she felt stronger and more at ease than she could remember being in a long while. He put his arm around her shoulder. "Mom, I think that's enough for one day. Let's go to Jake's for dinner—okay with you, Grandpa?" He looked from one of them to the other.

"Perfect," Jess said. They gathered up the empty boxes and headed to Bella Vista for Jake's special: Harvest Stuffed Pork Chops and Orchard Salad. Lisa ate as much as she could, but only made a small dent in her plate, taking the rest home. That night, laying her head on the pillow in her father's guest room, she determined to sleep in her own place by tomorrow—even if she could only find a bed and blanket.

Her strength had returned fully by Tuesday morning. Discarding the jeans and T-shirts she'd lived in while moving and painting, she felt like looking good and dressed for her shopping trip. The first store she entered carried a large selection of mattresses. After trying several, she settled on a king size set they had in stock that could be delivered at four-thirty that afternoon. The bed frame would have to be ordered, but she didn't care.

Browsing through their sheets, she was surprised to find a luxurious 600-thread count set. White would go with whatever pattern she settled on for her comforter and curtains. After adding a couple of blankets to her order, she left the store feeling she'd accomplished a major task.

It was close to lunch, but wanting to keep on a roll, she headed for her favorite furniture store. Nadine, the owner and a friend, took her hands when she walked in. Concern in her eyes reminded Lisa that Bella Vista was a small town. "I heard about Thomas' scene at the ball. Are you okay?"

There was no use pretending all was well. "I moved out last week."

"Well, it's about time. No one expects you to stay with a man who flaunts his lover all over town."

Her mouth opened as a new stab of pain hit.

Nadine colored. "Don't tell me you didn't know—I'm so sorry I blurted it out that way."

What had Jesse heard? Swallowing the hard lump in her throat, Lisa let her anger override the hurt. "It's not your doing, Nadine. This has been very difficult, but I do better if I don't dwell on it."

Nadine got the message. "Well then, what can I do for you?"

She refused to let Thomas rob her of any more joy. "I need some furnishings for my new apartment." A smile relaxed her lips, replacing the familiar tightness.

"I can help with that," Nadine said. They spent the afternoon choosing living and dining room furniture, plus nightstands for Lisa's bedroom and guest room. She also picked out a glorious inlaid wooden desk and filing cabinet for her office. By two-thirty, workmen had stored the lamps, area rugs, and accessories in the back warehouse to deliver the next day.

She felt drained but satisfied as she paid her bill with her credit card. "This was just what I needed," she said, hugging her friend. "Thank you so much, Nadine."

The woman returned her hug. "I'll come over tomorrow and help you pull everything together. How's that?"

That was not the normal protocol for the store and Lisa appreciated the kindness. "You're on," she said with grateful surprise and left.

A wave of hunger hit, causing her to feel lightheaded. She ducked into the coffee shop across the street and ordered an espresso drink and a warm brie and chicken croissant. What a constructive and exhausting day. Oblivious to the other customers' chatter, she sipped hot coffee and nibbled the sandwich, willing her mind away from scenes of Thomas and Angela. Instead, she imagined how everything she purchased would look in its own place. In her own place.

She checked her watch. The deliverymen would bring her bed in one hour. Though her appetite had disappeared, she needed to get groceries in the house. Frustrated that she'd cut the time so close, she headed for the market and then made the short drive home to Tangle Grove.

***

The furniture van sat parked next to the café when Lisa drove up. "Have you been waiting long?" She was sure the time had been set for four-thirty.

"No, ma'am, we just got here," the younger man answered. "Where do you want this bed?" He was affable and burly, the teddy bear type. Lisa learned his name was Ben and directed them up the stairs.

By the time the movers climbed the stairs the third time with all the pieces and parts, they were red-faced and sweating. The day was still sweltering. She asked, "Can I get you a drink of water?"

"Thank you, ma'am, we could use it," Ben responded for both of them. The young men drank the ice water in the living room and looked out over the dusty town of Tangle Grove. Finally, Ben said, "This is a real pretty apartment building, but it looks kind of out of place in this town, if you don't mind me saying so." He blushed, probably worried he'd offended a customer.

Well aware of the discrepancy, she said, "You're right, but we have wonderful plans for this town. She pointed below them. "This will become Main Street. Over there, we are building a beautiful courthouse and all of these buildings will be rebuilt." She said it with the pride of ownership, causing a swell of joy to bubble up.

Ben's interest was aroused. "When's all this going to happen?"

"We've already got the plans, but just have a few loose ends to deal with and then we can start construction. We'll start with downtown and work out as people are attracted to the area. It will provide a place where families can afford to own a nice home at a decent price."

"My wife and I have been renting a *hole* in Bella Vista and paying through the nose," Ben said. "There's never been any hope of owning our own place."

"You should check into getting something here before the prices take a jump. The commercial properties are already getting high, but the outlying houses and building lots are still a bargain."

Gulping the last of his water, Ben handed her the glass and thanked her for the tip. They left and she watched them drive the van up and down some of the nearby streets, then head out to the countryside for a better look at the area. She grinned. It was starting to catch on.

After a light dinner, she opened the packages of sheets and blankets and made her bed. Mentally and emotionally exhausted, she fell onto them and snuggled into the softness. The evening light cast a glow across the ceiling with the pinks and oranges of sunset. *What an inspiring place*, she thought, grateful to have a part in it.

A pounding knock at the door startled her. Who would visit this late? Who even knew she was here? She arose quickly and peeked out the front picture window. The streets below were deserted, and the closest streetlight was too far to cast a glow in front of her building. "Jesse?" she called through the oak door. No answer. Her heart thumped against her chest. Was someone waiting on the other side of her door, just inches from her? She listened for movement, not daring to breathe.

Catching a glimpse of her panicked face in the entry hall mirror, instant anger overrode her fear. She would *not* be intimidated any longer. She reached out a shaky hand and pulled open the door as wide as the chain would allow, then flipped on her porch light. It flooded the stairwell leading to the street. No one. A letter lay on the threshold. She undid the chain, picked up the letter, and relocked the door.

There was no writing on the envelope, but when she read the short note, she gasped.

You won't come out of this well.

***

After listening to every noise throughout the night, Lisa pushed out of bed early and trudged down to the cafe for a quick coffee and a bagel. *Who would threaten her?* She didn't think Thomas would stoop that low. Angela would, but coming to Tangle Grove at night seemed too odd, even for her.

At nine the next morning, relief washed over her raw nerves when Nadine showed up with her crew of movers. "Good morning," she said, stifling a yawn.

Nadine did a double take at Lisa's face, but thankfully decided not to comment. Instead, she took a good look at the apartment from the front entry. "This is charming." She stood on the elegant tiles and gazed across the space. Turning to Lisa, her eyes held real excitement. "You're very gifted. I can't wait to see what you do with the rest of this town."

Her mood lifted. It felt amazing to share her plans in the open. "It wouldn't be a bad place for a furniture store," she teased.

Nadine surveyed the old street from the front window. "You know, you're right. With all the building going on, it would be good to have a presence here. Hmm…even if it's only a small shop, it would attract customers to us rather than to some other store that's likely to move in." She grinned. "You're contagious."

As the movers brought items up the stairs, the women directed them where to set the furnishings. By eleven o'clock, everything was in its place. Nadine sent the men back to the store and sat down on the new sofa with Lisa and a cup of coffee. "You couldn't have made better choices for this room. The colors and scale of these pieces make it look like they were commissioned for the space."

She grinned. "With your taste and experience, I'm flattered."

Nadine sipped her coffee. "What's your sense of this place, now that you're living here?"

"Honestly? I've believed in Tangle Grove and worked hard on it for six years, but when it came right down to moving here, after years of living in Bella Vista, I felt apprehensive. I know it *will be* a great place to live, but the harsh reality is that it isn't—yet."

Nadine contemplated her admission. "Without planning it, you've done the most brilliant thing you could have for your project. By moving here, you're setting an example to others that this is a quality place to live. And you're showing how far your commitment goes."

"That's a good point," she replied, letting the thought sink in. She smiled and looked around. This building had been her lynchpin, the first of many attractive commercial structures downtown, and now she had furnished the first of many upscale homes that would occupy the second stories of those buildings. A sense of order was coming out of the chaos that had blown through her life like a *Wizard of Oz* tale.

They finished their coffee and Nadine rose to leave. "Thank you for bringing me in on this undertaking." Once outside, she studied the old, but squarely built buildings that lined the street. Lisa could tell she was seeing the vision. She turned and said, "I'd be very interested in being part of the revamping if you need any help."

"I'll take you up on that," she said. She couldn't imagine anyone else who would be as enjoyable and inspiring to work with. The two women hugged, and Nadine left for Bella Vista.

***

Lisa spent some time organizing her office that occupied an alcove off the guest room. The new wooden file cabinet matched the desk she'd chosen for this space. She moved her files out of the boxes and arranged them neatly in alphabetical order. Plans had been set for a phone conference with Sydney in the early afternoon, so she made certain everything she might need was in reach. Promptly at one o'clock, her cell phone rang.

"Hello, this is Sydney."

She savored the strength in her attorney's voice. "Hello," she replied, and they began to discuss the problems she might encounter at the town hall meeting on Tuesday night.

Sydney filled her in. "Jim Cook's main attack will center on your inability to cover your commitments because of Thomas' claim against the Montebelli Corporation."

"What assurances can I give them without tipping my hand before my hearing with Thomas?"

Sydney briefed her on how to present things, so they appeared in the most optimistic light. "I spoke with Denny Chapman and he's more than qualified to handle this. That will give me a chance to prepare the rest of your case."

Lisa chewed on her lip, hoping she was right. After Taylor's high praise for Sydney, and then working with her, Lisa had put her full trust in her new attorney's capabilities. It was hard to count on anyone else, even James Morley, whom she'd known for years. Sydney had discovered some breaches in the wall of protection Lisa had felt secure behind. The question remained if they could be repaired in time. Her mind whirled at the multitude of legal facets that were in play at the moment. "Sydney, thank you for handling all of this. Honestly, I don't know what I would've done without you."

"I have confidence that you would have managed but thank you and you are welcome."

They ended their call, and she sat back in her new leather office chair. Her eyes drifted out the window, over the part of town to the rear of her building. Farther to the southeast lay Bella Vista. She wondered what Thomas was doing today.

When they were first married, she used to call him at work to say hello. He was always too busy to talk, but it had been nice to touch base during the day on occasion. Was he as stressed as she was? Feeling just as betrayed? A wave of loneliness flattened her mood. Dropping her head, she realized she'd been lonely for years, covering it with busyness. Could he have been feeling the same way? She felt sadness for them both.

Chapter 16

The battle was on. Tuesday evening came all too soon for Lisa. A great deal was riding on the outcome of the meeting in Tangle Grove. No one really knew how prepared to be, so there was the sense of not having studied enough for a final exam. In two hours, she would have a better idea of what the future held.

At the meeting in the crowded old courthouse, she watched Gale Wallace head up the contingency for the recall of Mayor Jim Cook. Red-faced, she slapped the podium while stating the reasons that led to their decision. "Mayor Cook has purposefully undermined the plan that the Design Team and City Council adopted. It's a sorry fact that he acted purely out of self-interest, trying to persuade everybody to move the new downtown to the south, where he *now* holds premium lots!" A high volume of derision filled the hall after her announcement. Happy that her words carried a good amount of emotional weight, she gave a stiff nod with a, *so there,* message at the mayor.

Denny Chapman stepped in to recount the mayor's conversation, wherein the mayor tried to sway him and others to abandon the adopted plans and join a new group working at odds with the first team. "This man was entrusted with leading this process forward—in the direction your elected officials decided."

On his own behalf, the mayor came to the platform. He laughed off the importance of the charges brought against him. "If that's the case, then it can be argued that Lisa Richards acted out of self-interest when she, using the Montebelli Corporation, pushed to have the improvements where *her* properties were situated." He adopted a stern expression and gazed across the audience, landing on her. She held her breath. With a flair for drama, he dropped the whole problem into her lap.

"Mrs. Richards has deceived the residents of this city for six years by working with the teams under false pretenses. She set up an illegal corporation to hide money from her husband and work undetected to push the downtown development to the location of *nine* properties that she owns." A loud buzz of surprise filled the crowded chamber.

"Because of Mrs. Richards' deceit, Mr. Richards has been forced to take her to court to retrieve half of the ownership of the corporation, which is legally his. I have a notarized letter here from Mr. Richards, stating that when he comes into possession of the Montebelli Corporation properties, he will *not*, under any circumstances, financially support the growth of Tangle Grove."

Jim's smug face revealed his assurance he'd hit his mark with superb timing. He took a deep breath for another jab. "Lisa Richards, under the guise of the Montebelli Corporation, led us to believe that she would be contributing a substantial amount of money to this project, which is the *only* reason we felt it was fiscally responsible to move forward with these plans in the first place."

Lisa knew it would be a difficult meeting, but she had no idea how personal the attack would be. She was shocked at the extent that Thomas was fighting her.

By this time, Jim had worked the crowd into a crescendo. He peered down at her stricken face and gave them his final defense. "When Verina Fields and I learned of the difficulty between the Richards, we felt it was our responsibility to look for a less expensive alternative. We hired another firm for appreciably less cost and did our best to convince the rest of the team to be reasonable. I've been dismayed by the irresponsibility of the others in their refusal to listen." He sat down, head held high, and gave Gale Wallace a menacing smirk. He looked around and smiled at the people nodding their heads in agreement with him.

It was not boding well for Gale and Lisa. The comments around them showed that the people were convinced of Jim's good intentions, and that Lisa was clearly at fault for the trouble brewing in town. She overheard two people congratulate Verina and Jim for their quick response in heading off a near crisis. It took several minutes for the moderator to restore order so he could present the next speaker, Denny Chapman.

"That is a nice *story*," Denny began. "But I think you are out of touch with reality, Jim." He addressed the crowd. "Before I say anything else, I want to assure you that as an attorney, I have reviewed Lisa Richards' corporation and it is perfectly legal. It is within her right to set up a private corporation, married or not, for whatever reason she chooses.

"Furthermore, even if Mr. Richards were to control half of her assets, I have an affidavit from Mrs. Richards committing to the same financial support she had originally offered. Having seen the audit of her corporate books, I can tell you that she is quite capable of keeping this commitment. I am sure many of you are aware of the enormous contribution that Lisa's Montebelli Corporation has made to our town."

She dropped her eyes as Denny went on to give an account of the funds she had already donated and the major improvements she was committed to during the first phase of growth. The sum sounded staggering, even in her ears.

For the first time in the meeting, silence settled over the listeners. It was obvious that agreement in the crowd had turned back toward her. There were thumbs up gestures from those who were amazed at the amount of money she was offering their town. "Way to go, Lisa," came from team members and residents. She nodded her thanks and tried to keep her focus on Denny, who allowed the crowd time to immerse itself in the magnitude of what he had just revealed.

"The second thing I would like to address is the mayor's insinuation that Lisa secretly schemed to get her way. You all know how tirelessly she has worked on the committees for this project. Yet just like everyone else, she had only one vote on the city council and had only one vote on the Design Team. She didn't strong-arm anyone into voting for the area around her properties. It was decided by a majority vote, and until recently, the mayor was for it, or at least he pretended to be.

"Why was it only when he could get a premium price for his properties on Maple Street that he sold them for properties at the second site that had previously lost their value? The only answer is he was certain he could manipulate the council to back him." Lisa stifled a smile. Denny also had a great deal of flare.

"That said," and here he paused for greatest affect, "I have a letter of intent to sue the City of Tangle Grove, brought against us by Baker and Thymes Architectural Firm. It states that they entered a contract in good faith and at considerable expense to furnish a design proposal for our city. They have evidence that at a meeting last week, led by Mayor Jim Cook, he and Verina Fields produced an alternate plan created by an alternate firm. During this meeting, they exhibited plagiarized designs that were the property of Baker and Thymes.

"What this says," Denny summarized for the crowd, "is that they will sue us if we follow Mayor Cook's half-baked plan. If we recall him and condemn this act of betrayal, then he can deal with their suit personally and the town will not be at risk. I urge the citizens of Tangle Grove to recall Jim Cook and vote in a mayor with a stronger moral compass."

Denny's powerful words were persuasive. The meeting soon ended. Those who had been congratulating Jim and Verina, now avoided them and rushed over to thank Lisa for her efforts on behalf of the town. People swamped her with questions as they worked to rectify their perceptions of her—now that they knew she owned the Montebelli Corporation.

A local reporter worked his way to Lisa and asked, "Where did you get the name for your corporation?"

"From one of my ancestors," she replied. "My name is Lisa Adriana after my great-grandmother, Adriana Montebelli. She married my great-grandfather, Joren Van Buren."

The reporter followed that lead. "Did Adriana grow up around here?"

Joyous at the opportunity to share her secret with the world, Lisa answered with enthusiasm. "Yes. She was the daughter of Costantino Montebelli, one of the original climbers of Mt. Thurman. When I got the vision for Tangle Grove, I knew it would be an uphill challenge, like my great-great-grandfather had faced. It seemed fitting to name my corporation after him."

People were excited to hear the *rest of the story* and be in on the unveiling of the mystery that had surrounded the Montebelli Corporation for the last six years. She could hear the residents' relief that one of their own was helping develop their town, rather than an outside corporation.

"One last question, if I may. Why did you set up and keep your business a secret from your husband?" The reporter held a microphone to Lisa's mouth.

As she looked at all the curious eyes, her face blazed hot. She knew there were differing opinions out there regarding her motives and she wanted to set them straight. On the other hand, Thomas had to live in this town and do business here. It would not be wise to smear her son's father in public.

"I was afraid...and headstrong. My son was grown, and I desired to do something of value with my life. This is what I wanted to do and, as Jim Cook read to you, my husband would have opposed me so strongly that I couldn't have accomplished my goals. It was the way I chose to..." At this point, her voice broke and diminished to a whisper, "…appease two very stubborn people." She turned her watery eyes away from the reporter to gain composure.

"I think we've put Lisa through enough tonight," Gale Wallace said and ushered her out the door and into her truck. "Honey, let's just go fer a little ride until they all clear out, okay?"

Lisa nodded, her mind numb. "I feel so foolish breaking down like that—just like an emotional schoolgirl."

Gale glowered at her and said, "You stop that right now. You got every reason to cry like a baby if ya want, and I won't let ya stomp on yerself, along with yer husband and everyone else on that side of the fence. You need to stick up for yerself. Give yerself some grace."

She had never been on this side of Gale's admonishment and was glad of it. Yet, the word *grace* sang to her. That was indeed what she needed. Lots of it. Tears flowed freely. Tears for everything—the trauma of tonight, the weight of the deception she'd carried, Thomas' wrath and unfaithfulness—all flooded out. Gale continued to drive around the darkened streets of Tangle Grove, serving as a silent witness for Lisa's release of her shadowy deeds.

***

Lisa could hardly keep track of the events that filled the following week. Voters made their opinions known and recalled Jim Cook. A new election was underway to replace him, and Gale Wallace was running for the office. Baker and Thymes withdrew the threat to sue the city but sent a strong demand letter to the other architectural firm, who argued they had been under the impression from Jim Cook that the plans were his. Eventually they dropped the matter, in spite of a string of complaints from Gale at the city council meeting.

Because of the mystery that had surrounded the Montebelli Corporation, the reporter had gone to Thomas for his side of the story. The newscast was set to appear on the local TV station. Lisa sat alone in her apartment, dreading what would come.

The reporter asked, "Do you agree with the reasons your wife stated that she hid her corporation from you?"

Thomas gave his practiced look of anguish and said, "I am sorry the good people of Tangle Grove got dragged into this...travesty. I am a psychiatrist, you know. For years Lisa has suffered with delusional tendencies, manic-depressive behaviors, and now, I am afraid she may be a borderline schizophrenic."

Lisa gasped. Thankfully, there was a look of disbelief on the reporter's face, but Thomas quickly backed up his claims. "This is not the first time she has done something like this. The last time, she stole my money and made a risky investment that almost ruined my finances. Now she has promised these people all of this money and it just is not there."

"Then why are you going to court on..." the reporter checked his notes, "...October fifth—to get control of *nothing*?" Skepticism laced his voice.

"That is purely to take control of a situation that has gotten out of hand. Lisa needs protection from herself." Anger infused his voice. "I've stuck by her for twenty-nine years and faithfully supported our family. Now, I've been given the information that she has not only lied to me about this situation, but she has an *associate* on the side and had plans to make her money and leave me." He jerked open the door to his office building, then turned back. "I can promise you, she won't come out of this well."

***

Lisa's hand went to her throat. The note on her doorstep *had* come from Thomas. A chill sprinted up her spine. She'd seen glimpses of the rage he kept under control—a control it now appeared he was losing. His plans for her financial ruin were clear, but this felt like a physical threat to her well-being.

Fear and grief flooded and spilled out. On top of everything else, here on TV the reporter exposed their dirty laundry for all to see. And Thomas added his lies just for spite. He knew she wasn't unstable. She alternated between fury and grief. How could he say those things?

Hours of ruminating brought seeds of doubt that took hold and sprouted in the rich soil of pressure and fatigue. Thomas had been such a pragmatic man. Had her betrayal hurt him to the core? Unstrung his rationality? Plagued with guilt, she fought the belief that her actions had driven him to this harassment.

During the day, several good friends called to tell her Thomas' performance was unbelievable and not to worry, no one would fall for such lies. She thanked them and then turned off her phone.

Jesse showed up in the afternoon and held her while they both cried. "I can't believe Dad said those things. I don't know this man." His phone rang and he put Asia on the speakerphone.

"Is there any way I can help?" she pleaded. I need something concrete to do."

"Not until the hearing." Jesse's lips pulled tight with grim tension. "Thanks again for your firm's help in this initial fight. Now we…well, we'll see."

Lisa watched him battle a myriad of emotions. It destroyed her, seeing her son so miserable. Regret hit hard that she'd ever started this mess.

Jess arrived at her apartment a short time later and pulled his little family together. "You're going to have to face the fact that something's gone haywire with Thomas. This isn't normal behavior, even for an alcoholic. Lisa, you can't take responsibility for him. If you hadn't placated him over the years, I have a sense this would have erupted long ago. I'm not a psychologist, but this seems like much more than just revenge. There's something vicious behind what he's doing." He looked from one to the other. "For your sakes, I suggest that you think of him as a sick man. Feel pity, pray for him, but don't take on what he says as having anything to do with reality."

It was a sobering moment and Lisa sensed that Jess had hit on the truth. As understanding dawned, the calm of acceptance started to take hold. On Jesse too. It gave them a solid base to make sense out of the chaos that was continuing to strike at their lives. After more discussion, she rose from her new sofa, "I feel like I should eat something. Are you guys interested?"

Jesse nodded. "I've been nauseated all day, but now I'm famished. Can I help you with anything?" She had him make grilled cheese sandwiches while she opened a can of tomato soup.

Jess watched them from the dining room table. "We will weather this storm. Whether Thomas does is another question. Lisa, you'd be wise to steer clear of him for now."

Chapter 17

The first swell of the tsunami had struck and now the second was almost on top of them. Lisa trusted that the opposition was still unaware she knew of their plan to take Fire Mountain. She worked feverishly for days with James Morley and Sydney to research every argument they could use to battle the attack.

James was working to discover what kind of support Angela had been able to garner. He called Lisa at her apartment to give an update. "So far, everyone is closed mouth about it. That in itself is worrisome. If the lawmakers were given false information and there was not any debate on the floor to speak of, there would be no way they could vote knowledgeably. It would be easy for someone to slide his agenda through.

"Even worse, the politician I believe Angela is working with has been using a recent change in the law to swallow up private land with little compensation to the owners. So far, the outcry from the landowners hasn't been enough to counter his moves."

Gazing out the dining room window as she listened, she was well aware that sentiment toward the private rights of individuals had been waning, while the move toward grasping land for urban boundary growth and open space was gaining popularity. She hung up.

God, will it never end? Worry over Fire Mountain and her responsibility as the Guardian weighed on her, as did her upcoming court hearing with Thomas. Her beige shirt sagged, and she bunched a handful of extra fabric around her middle. Her family and friends had expressed concern, but she couldn't keep much food down.

The phone rang again, but after checking caller ID, she didn't answer. Well-meaning friends had been calling to report seeing Thomas and Angela together around town, not caring how their affair affected their reputations. Lisa couldn't understand Thomas. People knew he was still married and there had been no mention of divorce, only the hearing to get her property. He was looking seedier all the time. His clientele was sure to decline.

She'd just made an afternoon coffee when Jesse plowed through the front door of her apartment. His face tight and strained, he flopped on her sofa. "Every time I see Dad, it's more obvious how sick he is. I tried to reason with him to back off this stupid attack and to work toward reconciliation."

"And?"

He shook his head and stared at the floor. "He flew into a rage and threw me out of the house."

She sat next to him and prayed. "Lord, please help us to hold it together and get through this." After a short time of blowing off steam, he left for work. She tried to keep her mind on Tangle Grove and the details that still required her attention but gave up.

Flipping through the mail, she smiled at the announcement that the citizens had voted Gale Wallace in as the new mayor. Lisa was glad on one hand, but it would create that much more work for the city council members to bring her up to speed. At the end of each day for the past week, it was all Lisa could do to put herself to bed.

***

Judgment day hovered over them for Fire Mountain. Lisa, Jesse, and Jess joined James Morley at the capitol building and walked up the steps and into the grand building. They met beforehand with their representative, but he couldn't give them any idea one way or the other of how he expected it to go.

"Mom, what if they win?" Jesse paced the hall. "It isn't fair. Our family has benefitted this town for over a hundred years. This is *our* inheritance." The ramifications of losing were hitting home hard.

Her throat constricted and her hand pressed against the ach in her chest. She had nothing to say. The anguish in Jesse's face burned its image on her mind. Was this also her fault? With her mind so focused on her goals, maybe she hadn't paid enough attention to her responsibilities as the Guardian.

The legislature worked arduously through a variety of issues the whole day and were tired and in a hurry to leave by the time the Fire Mountain question came up. Angela's man skillfully brought up the subject as a minor but necessary move and suggested they include Fire Mountain along with the other properties they had already targeted under the new law.

Lisa's representative did his best to counter it, but to no avail. Fire Mountain would be acquired by condemnation to be available for public use in Harding County, effective on November first.

It was over. Lisa's heart sank. In less than twenty minutes, she watched her family heritage grasped from her hands. No one was able to offer any comfort as they drove home silently. She drifted off to sleep under the weight of the decision that had become too much for her mind to deal with.

***

Jess brought her to his house where he could keep an eye on her. She slept for two days, waking just long enough to eat a little and collapse again. When her body had rested and refused to sleep anymore, her waking hours revealed the toll the event had taken. For days, she shook constantly and cried until her strength was gone.

Her doctor prescribed a sedative, which only helped relieve part of the stress. Jess kept up a constant vigil of prayer. *God, be close to her. Strengthen my daughter through this trial.*

A few days later, Jesse visited his grandfather. Agitated and pacing in the kitchen, he shouted, "They had a *party,* Grandpa. Look at what they've done to my mother, and he's out there partying! In a week, he's taking her to court. I'd like to beat him to a pulp."

Jess had caught wind of the *Fire Mountain Party* that Angela and Verina had thrown. Thomas had been whooping it up and throwing insults at Lisa and the Van Buren family right along with them. Jesse was being pushed beyond his limits.

***

Lisa's breath caught in her throat. Standing at the door, she'd witnessed Jesse's outburst. She straightened as her resolve clicked back on. She'd had a week to recover and knew she couldn't keep hiding like this, for Jesse's sake. In a stronger tone than she felt, she stepped into the kitchen and admonished her son. "Jesse, that's not the way to talk, and it's unnecessary. I'll be fine. It's just been a huge disappointment." He walked across the room and wrapped her in his arms.

She kissed his cheek. "It will all work out. We still have Sweet Elke Park," she said with as much lightness as she could garner. She pulled back and looked at him. "Let's not sink to their level, okay?"

His body shook with adrenaline. "Okay," he answered and flopped into a chair.

"I could use a good, solid meal," she teased her dad. "Don't you have anything besides soup around here?"

"You bet," Jess smiled.

They were just finishing dinner when James Morley called on her cell phone. "I've been trying to get hold of you," he said with some frustration.

"I've had my phone off."

"Well, I've got some news. Your representative is incensed at what they did to you and is doing everything he can to make it right. He found an obscure clause in the new law that prohibits, among other things, the taking of productive mines. So, if you could prove..."

Lisa was ahead of him. "…that the mine is producing again," she finished with growing excitement.

"Is that possible?" James asked. "I thought the mine was depleted."

"We'll see what we can do." Her optimism resounded through the kitchen. "Thank you *so* much. You don't know what you've done for us." They hung up and she shared the good news with two men who looked awestruck by the change in her energy.

"How does that make any difference, Mom? We've been digging for years. You took us up there all the time, remember? We couldn't find anything."

She gave them a mischievous smile. "That was *before* I was made the Guardian and had access to the family *secrets*," she teased, laughing with relief.

Jess dropped his fork. "You mean there really is a family treasure and your mother never told me?"

"You never heard it from me either, Dad. But I think tomorrow would be a great day for a picnic." Her eyes sparkled as she imagined the shocked expressions on the faces of Angela and Verina, but more importantly, she thought of having her mountain back in the family, safe and sound.

***

October first was a glorious day. The air was crisp in the morning when Lisa and Jess made their way to Sweet Elke Park. Jesse had to work but promised to go with them the following day.

"Why are we going here instead of to the mine?" Jess asked.

She just grinned and trudged on to Elke Van Buren's grave. Leaning down at the foot of the tombstone, she traced the lines radiating out from the compass up to where the cross was on the headstone. She looked beyond it, trying to get a bearing, then frowned and squatted down to get a better angle.

Reciting a poem in her head that her mother made her memorize as the new Guardian, she went through the lines one by one, but with no revelation. "Dad, this is going to be harder than I thought."

"What are you looking for?"

"Some sort of light on the mountain." She knew she couldn't tell him everything, but this was only a small piece of the puzzle. She and the mountain needed his help.

Kneeling down next to her, he looked up at the mountain past the top of the headstone. His head moved right and left. "I don't see anything either," he said and looked to her for direction.

She sighed. "Well, let's get a bearing from here and make our way up the hill. The line-of-sight points to that tall tree to the right of the peak." She looked at her dad who was well into his seventies and revised her plan. "Why don't you stay here, and I'll make the climb. Once I get there, you can motion for me to move right or left. Okay?"

***

Jess was grateful for his daughter's thoughtfulness, but sorry he couldn't be of more help. "Okay," he said and watched her hike up the mountain until she disappeared beneath the underbrush. He wandered around the gravestone looking at the symbols engraved in the marble slab. Maybe these women did have some kind of key to work with.

The sun rose high in the sky as he studied the markings on the marble. Rose never mentioned anything about the signs on the grave, while Lisa had always wanted to know everything, even before Rose passed on the Guardianship to her. It appeared as if it was going to be a challenge to decipher the code, even with the key.

Half an hour later, a faint shout came from the mountain. Jess shielded his eyes from the sun and tried to spot Lisa. He was just able to make out her waving arms. She was in a clearing about a hundred yards to the right of the large tree they were using as a reference point. He motioned for her to keep walking in the direction she was going.

She lowered her arms, and he caught glimpses of her ducking in and out of the shadows. A few minutes later, she was at the base of the tree, and he could see her searching around the area, moving brush aside here and there.

His neck ached and he lowered his head to stretch it. Realizing this was going to take a long while, he rambled back to the car. He returned with a water bottle and slumped down near the creek in the sun. The day's warmth had replaced the morning chill long ago and soaked into his muscles. He smiled at the peace of this place and lay back on the bank.

"Some watch dog you are," Jess heard Lisa's laugh as he opened his eyes to see her.

"I'm sorry, Honey. I didn't mean to fall asleep. Did you find something?"

"No. There must be a different angle that I'm supposed to be looking at, or..." she let her voice trail off and changed the subject. "I'm going to get our sandwiches out of the car."

He sat on the ground and thought about Rose and the times they had come here for picnics. His heart still carried the dull ache of loss. She'd been a handful, but he loved her. Releasing a deep sigh, a rustle in the leaves caught his attention. A sense of foreboding overcame him, raising the hair on his arms.

He searched for the source of his dread and jerked his head toward the thicket. Across the stream, he saw yellow eyes watching him. The tales of wildcats in this area flooded his mind. He rose with caution and started for the car to warn Lisa. He saw her striding toward him with a lunch sack. "Lisa, get back to the car!"

***

Lisa couldn't tell what her dad was saying, but he looked distressed. She ran toward him, then saw the rising of the brush paralleling her father's course. He was still some distance away.

Pacing herself, she shouted, "Dad, stop running. Wave your arms." Her father slowed and did as she said. Her heart thumped against her chest, and she seemed stuck in molasses. When at last she reached him, she grabbed his hand and used loud, bold words while they made their way back. They were still a way from Jess's car when the fear lifted and the peace they were familiar with returned. "It's gone," she whispered.

"I saw it," her dad said. "It was a cougar!"

"I only saw the brush," she said, her voice still quivering from the fright, "but I've glimpsed him before. He's huge."

Jess turned her toward him. "Listen to me. I don't want you out here by yourself ever again. Do you understand? Not ever! And I don't want Jesse up here unless he's got his rifle with him."

She could understand her father's concern. He was right. She'd felt that same protective instinct for him just now, and for Jesse during the times he went hiking around here. Yet, for herself, she'd always felt shielded. She didn't flaunt it and didn't take unreasonable risks, she just knew she was watched over.

"Okay, I'll make sure I bring someone with me—and a rifle." Her father's suggestion was a good one, no matter how safe she felt. It would have been helpful today to protect him. She made a mental note to retrieve her gun from the garage at her house.

That thought brought her back to the reality of her life. Thomas had their house now. It was a sad thought after so many years of caring for their home and raising their child there. The sense of adventure vanished. "Let's come back another time. We've done enough looking for one day."

He didn't need to be asked twice. She thought back over his pleasant nap by the creek and what that could have ended up like. A tremor passed over her as they drove back to her apartment. They ate a late lunch in her dining room and gazed out the window onto Tangle Grove. Neither spoke and he soon left.

What would she have done if the cat had attacked him? The thought of losing him brought a painful lump to her throat and stinging tears to her eyes. She took a hot bath to dispel the last of the jitters. Eventually, the warmth and the bubbles did their job and she floated undisturbed until the water grew cool. "I'm a prune," she chuckled, looking at her crinkled fingers and feet.

Exhausted from the day and still recovering from the Fire Mountain trauma, she dressed in her softest silky pajamas and slid under the sheets for a solid night's rest.

***

Jesse agreed to meet at Lisa's after his lunch shift that ended at two o'clock. She knew Thomas would be at work this morning and took the opportunity to get her rifle out of the garage. Feeling like a thief, she had to remind herself this was still her house. She put the gun in the trunk of her car and took the time to go through the house alone.

Unlocking the door, she crept into the living room. Thomas hadn't changed anything since she left. The house was in more disarray than when she occupied it, but it wasn't in complete chaos. In the kitchen, she went through the cupboards and drawers, laying the items on the counter that she planned to take, then moved them to the car a few at a time.

After an hour, her anxiety grew. With every creak, she held her breath and listened for him. What had she been thinking coming here alone? She moved faster and was just setting the last load on the back seat when Thomas pulled up and squealed to a stop. Her throat constricted, and she dropped the box.

"What do you think you're doing?" he screamed, red-faced and shaking with rage.

She swallowed and forced her chin up. "I'm taking *my* things," she shouted back.

"This is not your house anymore, so stay out of here unless you want to be arrested for trespassing." He stalked toward her.

Remembering her father's words, she tried for a pragmatic tone. "You're delusional. No one's going to arrest me for entering my own home." The calm and strength in her voice stopped him. "I got what I came for," she said, then got into her car and locked the doors. She matched his glare and started the car.

To her relief, he stormed toward the house and threw open the door. It bounced off the siding and hit him. He swore, turned, and raced toward her. Heart pounding, she stepped on the gas and backed out quickly.

He stopped and grimaced. "You'll get yours."

She sped away, hands trembling on the wheel.

***

The day clouded over, matching Lisa's emotions. She wondered how long the weather would hold. Jesse showed up at two-thirty, ready to go digging in the cave. She transferred her gun and ammunition to his truck, not speaking of the encounter with Thomas.

"Grandpa said you guys had a close call yesterday," he said.

"We did. Dad could have been in real trouble. I'd like you to remember to bring your gun whenever you come up here, okay?"

He put his hand on the butt of his rifle. "I'm on it," he assured. "Do you know where we're digging today?"

She could tell he was holding his curiosity in check. "Not exactly. Dad and I were unable to locate anything outside from the clues yesterday, so I thought I might try from inside the cave today."

With a hint of disappointment, he asked, "You mean you only have *clues* to go on? No actual map with an, *X marks the spot,* to follow?"

She shrugged. "There's a lot of information. As far as I can calculate, the clues seem to indicate that the area we are looking for is in the cave toward Elke's grave and high up in the ceiling."

"If you say so." He opened the door for her, and they headed toward the mine. A short time later, he unlocked the vault door with his key, and they turned on their flashlights. Inside, he lit several of the kerosene lamps that hung at intervals throughout the main room.

After putting on hard hats, they grabbed picks from the old iron hooks that the Dutchman had mounted on the front wall of the cave. Off to the right, she followed a small tunnel that the miners abandoned when it proved to be unproductive.

Most of the tunnel was high enough for Jesse to stand up straight, but he ducked when his hat scraped a low outcrop. Shining their lights upward, they looked for any signs of the sparkling gems. They reached the end, and she realized nothing would be given to them.

She chose what she hoped were the most likely spots for finding their prize, and for the next couple of hours they chipped away overhead. They used the frequent breaks to rake fragments away from their work area.

Although the cave was cool, they worked up a sweat and continuously needed to replenish their bodies with bottled water. Jesse took off his long-sleeved shirt and she removed her jacket. They started at it again, looking for any fleck of colored light that might show itself.

Frustrated after hours of toil, she called a halt to their search. "I think that's about all I can do in one day." The look on his face reminded her of summers long ago when she had to persuade him that it was time to go home. "Come on," she laughed, playing their old game, "let's give it fifteen more minutes."

He smiled and forged ahead with extra vigor, racing the clock. She chuckled to herself as she watched him. When the inevitable time came, he lowered his pick, and they started back to the main cavern. They extinguished the lights and stepped outside into the drizzle. Pushing the door closed together, Jesse locked it and they ducked into the truck.

"That wasn't bad for a first attempt," she said with more cheer than she felt. She had no idea how long it would take to find the opals, or if they were even moving in the right direction.

"What makes you think we were in the right tunnel, Mom?"

Without breaking her promise to her adamant mother, she felt there were some things she could share with him. "There's some kind of...line from the gravestone toward this mine. Jochem knew of one more vein. He directed the Guardians to keep the location a secret. Even then, he hid its position with clues. It was to be used in the event that the family needed the funds to preserve the mountain, the mine, or the park."

Jesse tilted his head. "I've looked at the lines on her grave a thousand times and they go in several directions. Are you saying there's something that indicates which line?"

"Something like that," she answered, afraid of giving away more than was permitted.

"Can we come back tomorrow and take a look at the markings again? Maybe I could help you interpret something." He cast a sideways glance as he drove her back to Tangle Grove.

"That's just what we should do, but don't think you're going to pry anymore information out of me." They were laughing as she got out of the truck in front of her new home.

Denny Chapman walked toward them, his expression grim. "Sorry to interrupt you, Lisa," he said in a tense voice, "but this was brought to my office today, regarding the financing of our construction project." He summarized it as she read the text. "It was sent to the City of Tangle Grove from your bank, saying they are withdrawing their funding. They indicate that the Montebelli Corporation appears to be an unstable company and is likely to be a poor risk."

She looked at the bottom of the page. It was signed by the vice-president of the bank. "Thomas' golfing buddy," she said aloud. She looked up at Denny. "This won't stand. They can't run a bank on friendship and hearsay." Determination took over. She thanked Denny for the letter and bid Jesse goodbye. His face exhibited the pain of another blow from his father.

She marched up the stairs to her apartment. "That..." she said under her breath but didn't finish the description of Thomas that crossed her mind. It was too late to do much about this tonight, but she spent the evening making a list of her options and what documents she would need to provide for an alternative lender if it came down to that. It was a short list.

Her arms felt like jelly from the strenuous work, and Thomas' continual assaults produced a throbbing headache. At her desk, she lowered her head onto her folded arms and let the tears come, never dreaming in a million years she'd be in this position.

***

Lisa moaned as she stretched her neck in all directions. She phoned Jesse to call off their treasure hunt, needing to handle the curve ball that Thomas had thrown. Gathering the files, she headed for the bank to talk to the president. He said there was no way he could consider funding her Tangle Grove project with a pending hearing and an *uncertain outcome.*

"I'll tell you what," she said, "this will be resolved in a few days, and you can be sure you'll wish you'd made a different decision." She left the bank furious, but also worried.

Nadine's store was two doors down, and she caught Lisa before she reached her car. Reacting to the look on her face, Nadine asked, "How about lunch and a sympathetic ear?"

Lisa considered the offer. "Okay, if you think you can withstand a tornado."

"I think it would take a lot to blow me over." She put her arm around Lisa's waist.

They ate lunch and Lisa shared the sum of her worries. Nadine sat in silence, meeting her eyes as she talked. When Lisa finished, Nadine shook her head and said, "This is pure nastiness. I don't know how you can take on all of it."

They had just requested the check, when Angela Basso sauntered up to the table. Lisa and Nadine glared at her with disgust, which only seemed to please her more.

"Looks like you're finished, Lisa," she purred as she threw her poisoned darts. "It would have helped if you had friends in high places. Guess you've lost your mountain, your mine, and..." she licked her upper lip, "...your husband." She left before either woman could overcome their shock in time to respond.

When Nadine could speak, her mouth stumbled over the words. Her hands shook with rage. "I can't believe the diabolical insensitivity of that woman. How can you stand this?"

She felt relieved that she'd had a witness to Angela and Thomas' malevolence. "Thank you for being here. It's impossible to explain how they've been." Somehow, her burden seemed lighter now that someone else knew.

Nadine rose to leave and gave her a solid hug. "Hang in there. They haven't won yet."

Her mind went over all the areas in which they had won, but she knew her friend was trying to cheer her. She smiled and thanked Nadine again, then got into her car and drove home. Her energy was depleted, and she knew she couldn't continue the plans she'd devised for the day.

Entering her apartment, she looked around at the welcoming rooms. If Thomas won two days from now, she might not even have this. The thought was too much. She started to tremble. Taking two sedatives, she curled up in bed and let the blackness overtake her mind.

Chapter 18

"Open this door!" a voice roared through the fog in Lisa's head. The vague sound of a phone had been ringing off and on all morning, but she had ignored it and continued to sleep. Eventually, however, she couldn't dismiss the insistent yelling and pounding. Getting up with unsteady steps, she pulled her robe on and headed for the front door. Her gait quickened as she heard Jesse's desperate voice shouting for her.

When she opened the door, he took one look at her and swore. "Mom, I won't have this," he shouted. "I won't let them do this to you." He rushed in and pulled her toward the sofa. His expression was fully distressed as he held her hand and looked intently into what she knew was a fatigued face. "I don't know what to do. I went to Dad again to plead for him to be reasonable and call off the hearing tomorrow, but he won't listen to anything I have to say regarding you. He said you put me up to it and accused me of taking sides. He thinks *he's* the injured party. I can't fathom how he can twist the truth so drastically."

She rubbed his shoulder, trying to relieve some of the strain. "This isn't your battle. I was the one who chose to keep secrets from your father, and he was the one who chose to demean and manipulate me. We're each facing the consequences of our actions, but you don't deserve any of this. The best thing you can do for me is to stay out of it."

"I don't know how you think I could do that. I wouldn't have a heart if I wasn't disturbed by what's going on between you two."

She felt heartsick for what he must be going through. "Then all I can wish is for this to be over quickly." Her gaze fell to the floor, not knowing what else to do, until a spark of hope lit her dark mood. Head lifted, she said, "When this is all over, we'll just start again with our lives and move on. Help me hold onto that thought. That's your task, okay?" She attempted to imbue her words with enthusiasm.

Her entreaty worked. Returning a resigned nod, he said, "Okay." His chin came up and he straightened his shoulders. "I've always loved your optimism, but *truly* appreciate it right now."

"I need a shower and some coffee," she said with more energy. "Do you want to hang around and get some espresso downstairs?"

Looking at his watch he said, "It's one o'clock. Lunch sounds better."

"There are cheese and crackers in the kitchen," she said and left to shower and dress. A short time later, she came out feeling refreshed, having quickly curled her hair and added makeup. She wore a brightly colored dress pulled tight with a belt and had slipped on leather sandals. Swinging a small silk bag over her shoulder, she hoped her emotions would soon catch up with her looks. "Okay, let's go." They made their way down the stairs and followed the scent of coffee into the Sweet Elke Café.

"Hi, Lilly," she called.

Like always, Lilly seemed genuinely happy to see her and asked, "What can I get you?"

Jesse and Lisa placed their order and decided to sit outside in the sun, which had finally chosen to poke its rays through the clouds. Scanning the street and old buildings, she was surprised at the good humor returning to her. They talked about the plans for Tangle Grove and their enthusiasm started to climb.

"I wonder who bought Jim and Verina's properties," Jesse said.

Lisa thought about that for a moment. She hoped the new owners would want to adopt the plans that Asia had drawn up for those buildings. They were kingpins in the scheme of the street. She made a mental note to look into it.

A thought had been tugging at the corners of her mind and she decided to give voice to it. "If I had to, I wouldn't have any problem selling all my opals to help complete this project—except the *Dutchman*, of course. I can take them out and wear them for an evening, or I could make something wonderful here that people can see and use every day."

"That's a surprising turn," he said. "We've all grown up with the family's sense of value for the Dutchman's opals, are you sure you could do that?"

"After I'm gone, they will belong to you and your children. My only concern is what would be more important to you." She waited for his response.

Jesse studied the old buildings. "I think I'd like to see this town flourish. In fact, it seems to me that the important part of our inheritance is here, in the people and town of Tangle Grove, and not just in the treasure we took out of the mountain."

She smiled at her son. It was good to share this vision with someone—with family. She watched his eyes sweep up the street and knew he was seeing it in its completed state. Her heart felt lighter than it had in a while. "You're right, you know. Even the Dutchman said the treasure was in the real property you could buy with the gems. That's why he insisted on setting up the Van Buren Trust the way he did, so the stones would always be available to protect the land." A cloud darted across her face as she thought of the impending appeal for Fire Mountain.

Jesse noticed it. "Don't worry about the mountain, Mom. I have a strong feeling we'll be successful in finding those opals. Even if I have to plant some to be found," he laughed.

"That's an idea," she replied with dry humor. They talked and laughed together. A rare magic surrounded them. No matter what trials she faced tomorrow, she was glad for this time today with her son.

Her cell phone rang, and she retrieved it from her purse, not recognizing the number on her display. "Hello."

"Hello, this is Cynthia Bennett. We met at the Bella Vista Ball. I hope I am not interrupting you."

Lisa remembered her immediately. "Not at all. It was such a pleasure meeting you. I was planning to invite you to lunch, but my life got rather...busy," she finished. A stab of embarrassment pierced her chest, certain the scandal had spread throughout their small community.

"I hope you will not consider me rude for the late invitation, but there is something I would like to discuss with you. Could you join me for dinner this evening? It is very important."

"I would enjoy that." Something about Cynthia had attracted Lisa during their brief encounter. The timing to begin a new friendship couldn't be worse, but she relished the distraction. "Where shall we meet?"

"Would you mind if we stay in and eat at my home? I would like a quiet dinner where we can talk privately."

"That would suit me just fine," Lisa said, thankful she wouldn't be running into any more surprises from Angela. Or Thomas.

"Wonderful." She gave Lisa the time and directions to her home.

She hung up and explained the call to Jesse. "That was an interesting woman I met a few weeks ago. She's invited me to dinner tonight."

Jesse grinned and shook his head. "You have no idea how interesting *you* are." He paid their tab and kissed her on the cheek. "Have a good time tonight." He kissed her cheek and left.

Feeling the need for a boost, she called her hairdresser for a fresh color and cut and lucked out on a cancellation. For the rest of the day, she refused to think about tomorrow's hearing. Sydney was coming to town in the morning, James Morley was set, and they had spent weeks getting as ready as was possible. "God, it's in your hands," she whispered as she drove off to the salon.

***

The evening boasted a soft orange and rose sunset while Lisa made her way to Bella Vista. Cynthia's directions took her up into the hills on a comparatively new road. For years, developers had combed this area for every possible lot on which to build the mini-mansions that were in demand. Slowing, she thought she must have missed the turn, but the road dropped into a small valley.

The lights of the immense house greeted her. It was set like a fairytale castle nestled amongst the fir and pine trees. Ornate gates, hinged to massive stone pillars, stood open in expectancy of her arrival.

"Wow," she said in awe. Many wealthy people had moved to this area and built great houses, but Lisa was certain this was the largest and grandest in Bella Vista. She turned off her car and walked to the front door.

A butler greeted her. "Please come in. Mrs. Bennett will join you shortly," he said and led her through an entry hall and up three marble stairs to an ornate sitting room.

This is a first. She gaped at the opulence and felt like she must be in the presence of royalty.

"Hello," Cynthia said and crossed the room to take her hands. "Thank you for accepting my invitation."

"Believe me, it's my pleasure." She felt baffled at what Cynthia's interest in her might be, but grateful for a friendly face. "Your home is exquisite. I had no idea anything like this existed here."

Cynthia laughed, "It really is ostentatious, but I love it. It is something I always dreamed of building and when I found this town, I knew this was where I wanted to build it."

"Did you design it yourself, then?"

"I did the conceptual part, but had an architect pull it together for me. Would you like a tour?"

This was eye candy. She grinned. "Lead the way."

Room after room of beautifully designed and decorated suites greeted her as Cynthia led her through the mansion. In many places, inlaid panels of various woods lined the walls, ceilings, and doors. Hand-carved wooden arches separated rooms and housed leaded glass windows.

"This could hold its own against any castle," Lisa chuckled.

When they came to one door, Cynthia gave a gentle knock and called out, "Robert?"

A man's voice bid them to come in, and Cynthia introduced her husband to Lisa.

"I am very pleased to meet you," he said in a formal but friendly manner. "Cynthia has not stopped talking about you since the ball. Thank you for joining us for dinner."

Cynthia looked at Lisa and smiled. "He isn't exaggerating. I have been hoping we could be friends."

"I'm flattered, and honestly, I had the same thought," she said.

They made their way to the living room, which overlooked a large pond behind the house. Weeping willows overhung its banks, accented by hidden floodlights that bathed the branches in a soft glow. A huge bronze fish served as a water fountain and sprayed a beautiful pattern onto the surface from the middle of the pond. Lisa gasped at the sheer beauty. "Cynthia, this is too much," she said with appreciation.

"Yes, but what good is it, unless I can share it with friends?"

She understood. She'd done so much but hadn't been able to share any of it—none of the joys, the triumphs, or the disappointments. She sighed. That was all behind her now.

"What was that sigh about?" Cynthia tilted her head.

She glanced at her kind face. "I'm sure you're aware of the recent...events that have occurred in my life," she paused, inviting a response.

"I'm aware that you expended a huge effort, pulled together a struggling town and have turned it into a place of pride and community—and that you have a bully of a husband who is bent on destroying your vision." Her voice rose with agitation as she finished her sentence.

The intensity of Cynthia's response left Lisa speechless for a moment.

"Please excuse me," Cynthia said, "but I have little regard for suppressive and small-minded people—which is one of the reasons I wanted to speak with you so soon. Let's sit down over here until dinner."

They sat on high-backed chairs, upholstered in richly woven tapestry of a soft French blue. It would have been a peaceful setting, except the problems she had planned to escape for the evening were about to be thrust on her again.

"Do you mind if I speak freely?" Cynthia asked.

Knowing she would anyway, and curious of what she had to say, she nodded.

"When Robert and I visited here three years ago, we searched the area for a home site. We drove up and down the hills and had to hike back here to find this spot. As soon as I saw it, I knew this was the place I had dreamed about.

"While exploring, we heard about the plans for Tangle Grove and about the mysterious Montebelli Corporation that was so involved in the development. That caught my imagination, and I began to think how challenging it would be to create a whole town and not just a house.

"Then I read about you in the newspaper, and I cannot tell you how happy I was that you were behind the Montebelli Corporation. I have been cheering you on and was delighted with the recall of that mayor." She had been exhilarated up to this point, but now she paused, apparently not sure how to continue.

"Lisa, I hope you are not offended by this," she cast a furtive glance, "but Nadine and I have become good friends, and not to gossip, but just because she was so incensed, she told me about that Basso woman and the loss of your funding."

Sympathetic with her concerned expression, Lisa sighed. "Don't worry, I'm past being surprised about the publicity around my personal affairs. It's created irreparable damage," she said with resignation.

Cynthia's eyebrows rose and a smile lit up her face. "That is just what I wanted to talk with you about. It is not beyond repair."

"I don't understand."

"Let me back up a little. Remember when we were introduced and were talking of family lineage?" Lisa nodded. "Well, my family name is *Vanderbilt*." She waited a moment for that to sink in.

Her eyes opened wide in amazement, "*The* Vanderbilts?"

Cynthia nodded, smiling at her reaction. "When I heard that your husband's friend at the bank had pulled his support of your project, I was determined to salvage the financial end of your plans." She leveled her eyes at Lisa and with full sincerity said, "I would like to finance Tangle Grove."

She stared, dumbfounded and stammered, "You know I have a hearing tomorrow in which there's a chance my husband may take control of a large portion of my assets?"

The expression on Cynthia's face turned more serious. "I took the liberty of checking out the public records before making you this offer. My accountant is not excited about my decision, but knowing I would not be dissuaded, he said he felt my investment would at least break even."

The magnitude of Cynthia's proposition began to sink into Lisa's mind. Wonder and relief hit. "I don't know what to say. How do you want to...?"

Cynthia held up her hand. "We will talk about the details later. I just wanted you to have an appetite, which, from the looks of you, has disappeared over the last few weeks."

"Thank you, Cynthia." She marveled at the kindness this complete stranger offered and suddenly realized her desire for food had returned.

Dinner was excellent. The butler served it, no less. She felt giddy inside for the temporary reprieve of her problems and chatted throughout the meal with Cynthia and Robert. They were an interesting couple and traveled most of their married life until deciding to build *her kingdom,* as he called it. It was obvious he adored her.

The candlelight and conversation cushioned Lisa's spirit. She left with a promise to get back to Cynthia the day after the hearing to go over the particulars. Before she drove home, she called Jesse with the tidings. He was delirious with joy, not just at her news, but Asia was flying in tonight to be with them at the hearing. They hung up with a mutual feeling of hope.

Arriving at her door, she reached her key to the lock and froze. Another envelope lay at her feet. This time, she refused to read it and ripped it to shreds. *Thomas is insane.* Inside, she stuffed the pieces down the garbage disposal and ran hot water down the sink. Angry tears followed his cruel tactic down the drain.

After splashing cold water on her face, she dried her eyes and stared into the empty sink. She desperately wanted out of this tempest, but the results of tomorrow's hearing might sink her into a whirlpool too strong to overcome.

***

The weather had deteriorated, and rain poured all night. With all the fear and anxiety that took turns seizing her stomach, Lisa had found it impossible to sleep. She'd realized too late that she needed a sedative, then feared if she took one at such a late hour, she would oversleep and miss her appointment with Sydney and James. As a result, her head was groggy this morning and she couldn't shake the jitters that made her insides shudder.

Jess called to find out when to meet her at the courthouse and ask what he could do to help. "Just pray, Daddy," she said, and hung up, knowing he took her request seriously.

The meeting with her attorneys lasted from ten until noon. They broke for lunch. The hearing was at one. Lisa couldn't eat and excused herself. She met with Jesse and Asia and huddled in a quiet corner of a coffee shop with a cup of soothing tea. Her cup shook as she tried to bring it up to her mouth, forcing her to use both hands to keep from spilling the hot liquid. Asia laid her hand on Lisa's when she gave up and rested them again in her lap.

Red-eyed, probably from lack of sleep, Jesse tried to cheer her. "It's okay, Mom, remember? No matter what happens it will still be okay."

She was thankful he kept his promise to remind her. "Right," she said with a small smile, but she couldn't get it to reach her heart. So much was riding on today. A dark thought continued to plague her. No matter who won, they both lost. Regardless of how bad their relationship was, she couldn't shake the grief of its demise. Tears came to her eyes, but she refused to let them fall. It was time to go. She had to pull from any inner strength she could find to get through this.

Jess waited in front of the courthouse and joined the trio as soon as they arrived. The attorneys were already in the courtroom when they walked in. Thomas sat stone-faced on one side of the room. Angela sat behind him.

"What's she doing here?" Jesse cried out an accusation at his father.

"That's my business, not yours," Thomas flung back.

Lisa took Jesse's hand and whispered for him not to bother. "It really doesn't matter to me anymore," she lied.

The hearing began and Thomas' attorney read a long list of claims, finishing with a demand for damages due his client. Sydney had briefed Lisa on what to expect, except for the last point. Thomas was claiming damages done to him and his reputation, resulting in a loss of income from his practice. He was suing for ownership of *all* her holdings.

Even Sydney's head jerked up from her notes at that. She had obviously seen a lot in her career, but it appeared to Lisa that this was over the top. It only took a moment to recover, however, and Sydney made a couple of notes while the opposing attorney finished.

"That is an interesting perspective," Sydney commented when it was her turn to speak. She stared straight into Thomas' eyes, which darted away. Sydney addressed the judge. "What we have here, Your Honor, is this." She systematically addressed every argument that Thomas' attorney had brought. As she spoke, she handed the judge a memorandum with exhibits that supported her statements.

Lisa sat in awe as she watched Thomas' hopes pulled apart one by one. His face grew angrier, and he glared at his attorney, whispering to him several times to *do* something.

Angela grew uncomfortable in her seat. Frown lines deepened in her face, exaggerating her age. Lisa was transfixed at how the previous haughty expression had now taken on the look of pure misery.

After listening to both sides and reviewing the information, the judge summarized his perception of the case. "What I see before me," he referred to the stack of verified documents that had been presented to him, "indicates that Mrs. Richards created a Nevada corporation and funded it with her money, yet it was held in common with her husband, Mr. Richards. With those funds, she purchased the property located at..." and he gave the legal description. "As I see it, Mr. Richards is entitled to half of the ownership of that property..."

Thomas threw a triumphant look to Angela.

The judge continued. "However, Mrs. Richards does not own that property anymore..."

"Her corporation does." Thomas shouted out of turn.

The judge shot him a quieting look. "No, Mr. Richards, neither she, nor the Montebelli Corporation own that property. It was sold..." he looked at the record of sale, "over four years ago to the Van Buren Trust."

Thomas was incensed. "She owns that too," he cried.

"No one *owns* a trust, Mr. Richards," the judge said, keeping his voice even. "Mrs. Richards is the trustee of the trust and handles the affairs for the beneficiary, who in this case, is your son and his two cousins."

The information was coming at Thomas too fast. He acted desperate to find a new argument, but before he could say anything, more bad news flew at him.

"As far as damages go, my judgment is that they lay just about even." The judge had lived in Bella Vista for years. After a few more instructions, he stood up and left the courtroom. Sydney and James were smiling.

Thomas' face showed disbelief, "What does this mean?" he screamed at his attorney.

"It means," his counsel said, "that you are entitled to half of Mrs. Richards' profits when she sold the building to the Van Buren Trust."

"How much is that?" he demanded.

Sydney handed him a cashier's check for $1,500. "That's half of what Mrs. Richards made on the sale of the property," she said.

Thomas started to protest, but Sydney cut him off. "The books have been audited by an independent accounting firm from which we have a signed affidavit that the court is in possession of." Handing him a second document, she said, "This is a summons for you to appear in court. Mrs. Richards is suing Gary Bristol for breach of client confidentiality. You are required to take the witness stand to explain your possession of Mrs. Richards' corporate documents and a check stub she found in your office for payment of a large sum to Mr. Bristol."

Lisa had sat in shock, surprised that Thomas wanted *everything*, and that the possibility had existed. It made her wobbly as she stood.

Sydney left him and walked over to her. "Congratulations, Lisa." She gave her a gentle hug. "You have nothing to worry about from him anymore," Sydney looked over at the scowl on Thomas' face as he argued with his counsel. "I heard you were able to find a new financier," she said, loud enough to be heard throughout the room.

Thomas' head swung around to their direction. Daggers pierced Lisa and he cursed her. "I'll make sure you never finish your plans!" He started toward her.

Jesse and Asia stood and moved closer to Lisa in a protective gesture.

Guards immediately escorted Thomas out of the courtroom. Angela had already left, disgusted by the judge's decision.

Lisa cowered against the back of her chair. She shook from the emotional impact of the hearing, and from seeing Thomas in such a state. It was not the first time she'd been physically afraid of him, but this was far worse. "What's happened to him?" she whispered.

"The guy hates to lose," Sydney said. "I think we should get a restraining order—just for a couple of days, until he settles down and accepts his losses."

"His losses?"

"Yes. He paid Gary Bristol $25,000, his attorney fees are well above $10,000, and he will have to defend himself with Gary Bristol," Sydney calculated. "Looks like he should have left well enough alone."

Lisa sat stunned. "I don't think a restraining order is necessary," she said in a quiet voice. She didn't want to antagonize or humiliate him further.

Sydney's expression showed she disagreed, but she let it drop. "Do you realize you won *everything*? Your corporation, your properties, everything is right back to the way it was before Thomas launched this attack. You can move ahead with your plans."

Lisa knew Sydney was endeavoring to encourage her, and that she had done an amazing job. She gave her attorney as much of a smile as she could muster. "You were brilliant. I wouldn't have been able to make it through this without you." She clasped Sydney's hand. "Thank you."

Sydney gave her a solid hug, infusing some of her calm and strength. "What will you do now?"

"I think I'll go for a drive." They said their goodbyes and Lisa left the courtroom, got into her car, and drove off toward Tangle Grove.

***

The cold intensified. Rain continued to drizzle, yet Lisa knew there was only one place that could bring her comfort. Passing up Maple Street, she headed to Dutchman Mine Road and drove to Sweet Elke Park. She inched across the bridge and noticed the creek had risen, churning wildly as it gathered runoff from the many rivulets pouring out of the surrounding mountains. Though experiencing some misgivings about this plan, she continued over the bridge and parked her car in the old gravel parking area.

Too cold to make it to the peaceful creek, she moved her seat back and pulled her chilled knees against her chest. Conversations from the hearing drifted through her mind—all the accusations Thomas had made through his attorney. He said she was mentally unstable and needed supervision. That she was a danger to the community, willful and manic. That he had had to watch her the whole twenty-nine years they had been married. That she was untrustworthy. Each pronouncement ate at her certainty.

Her mind started to argue Thomas' side. She *had* acted in many of those ways. Blame gripped her for the travesty that had overtaken their lives. She *was* willful and untrustworthy—look at the massive deception she had orchestrated. He *had* always tried to corral her. Was that because she needed supervision? Had she *really* put her friends at financial risk? Black thoughts pulled her confidence into a pool of self-doubt. She slumped further in her seat. What if his declining mental state was all her doing?"

Two hours passed. The darkening sky mirrored her musings. She sank into a haze of depression with random thoughts tormenting her conscience. Icy crystals formed on her windshield, building on the ones below them.

Out of nowhere, car lights bolted up the road and interrupted her thoughts. They crossed the bridge at top speed. She wrenched around and stared out the back window. "Oh God, no!"

Thomas' Mercedes whipped in behind her and rammed the back of her car, slamming her forward. She screamed at the impact. Realizing she couldn't drive away and would be at the mercy of his anger, she threw open her door and fled into the park. His furious screams howled after her.

As she groped through the freezing rain, his wild, incoherent shouts pursued her. Frantic, her eyes pleaded for a place of refuge. Seeing a possibility, she threw herself under a dense covering of brush. Scurrying back up against the mountain as far as she could, she crouched under the wet thicket. The leaves funneled their pools of fresh raindrops onto her head and under her open shirt collar, sending further chills down her spine.

Thomas' shouts were close. Ominous footsteps pounded the ground as he approached her hiding place. Her breath labored to expand in her tightened chest. He stopped. She could see his muddy shoes and the patterns of moisture the long grass made on his pants. She froze, not daring to move a hair. An opening through the brush revealed his clenched fist and menacing white knuckles. She could feel those fingers closing around her throat.

After a lifetime of seconds, he darted off again, yelling more curses. Her tears mixed with the rain on her face. She couldn't comprehend the nightmare she was in—that Thomas was in. Fear and grief racked her body as she gripped her shivering knees to her chest. *God, please help us.*

At first, it sounded like the roar of the water had intensified. She perceived a change in Thomas' screams. There was fear in his voice—and pain. Growls were unmistakable now. She launched out of the brush and stopped, gasping at the scene of Thomas trying to fight off a large cougar.

Propelled by a shot of adrenaline, she ran screaming and waving her arms. Anger replaced the fear, which moments before had paralyzed her.

The cat was on top of him, dragging him into the water. Thomas stopped fighting, his body went limp.

"NO!" she screamed repeatedly and closed the distance between herself and the struggling cat. The animal turned toward her, its teeth sunk deep into Thomas' body. It stood, protecting its prey, releasing an angry growl that pierced her ears.

She made one last hysterical lunge at the cougar. It backed onto its haunches and dropped Thomas' body in the water. Leaping to the far side of the swollen creek, it disappeared into the woods.

She clamored into the rushing water, tears mixed with rain. The current tugged at her legs and harsh rocks tripped her. Struggling to keep her footing, she managed to grab Thomas and prevent the water from dragging him down the frigid creek. Using all her strength, she pulled and heaved, hauling him to the muddy bank.

Her clothes soaked through, she fell backwards against the slope, pulling his limp body on top of her. A sharp rock pierced her arm when he fell. The bone snapped and she screamed. Nausea threatened, but her attention focused on him.

"Thomas, Thomas" she cried. "Can you hear me?" She felt his chest rise. Blood flowed from the claw and bite wounds on his neck, turning his shirt a dark crimson. His arm made a small movement and indiscernible sounds gurgled out of his lips. Bending her ear toward his mouth, she could tell he was struggling to breathe. Hissing noises escaped from the gash in his chest.

"Lie quietly." She tried to calm her own hysteria and think of what to do. "Don't talk. I'm going to lay you down and get help." She tried to move him off her, but with her broken arm, he was too heavy.

He groaned out in agony, "No."

Great sobs escaped her. "Please, I have to get help for you. You're hurt——do you understand?"

"No," he groaned again.

Rain joined with her hysterical tears as she surveyed the jagged gashes. "I'm so sorry. I didn't mean for any of this to happen."

His lips moved again, and she heard, "Lisa."

"I'm right here," she whimpered and gave his arm a firm squeeze with her free hand. "I'm here."

His head angled toward her, and she peered into glazed eyes. Fear gripped his face as he attempted to talk. "I'm sorry, Lis'," he rasped. "Forgive me. Please."

The heartache that had been imprisoned in her chest broke through as a tormented moan. "I do, Thomas. I do forgive you."

He inched his left hand across his body to touch her free arm that rested on his chest. His words came out in spurts. "Why…didn't your God…save me?"

She gazed at him with anguish. "You never believed."

Fighting for breath, his eyes held intense sorrow. "I do believe," he whispered. "You couldn't forgive me if your God wasn't real." He gasped in pain. His hand slid off her arm.

Frantic, she scoured his face for signs that he was okay. While she watched in disbelief, the light in his eyes diminished until there was nothing. His body went limp in her arms. She clutched his still warm shoulders to her. "No," she wailed in agony. "Don't die," she pleaded as her heart cried into the night. Deep sobs continued to shake her until the last of her strength left.

She remained on the muddy bank, bleeding and holding him. Unable to move, her sodden body shivered violently. A cold breeze numbed her lips, penetrating its effects deep into her core. She grew quiet in her grief, ignoring the pain in her arm and the dull ache that moved from her feet up through her legs.

The last bit of daylight faded. She welcomed the darkness that matched the emptiness inside. A thick fog cloaked her mind and the recent events in grey. Then in blackness. Her head slumped sideways, her arm still wrapped protectively around her husband.

***

After the hearing, Jesse had helped Asia retrieve some documents her firm needed from Lisa's attorney. Though there were no emotional winners, they felt the judge had settled the uncertainty that had plagued them for weeks. When they finished, Jesse dropped her at the hotel and returned home to call his mom. That proved unsuccessful, as did calling their family and friends to locate her. He rubbed his temples. The rage on his father's face outside the courthouse had unnerved him. He'd never seen anyone so vengeful.

She won't get away with this, his dad had hissed. *Don't ever come to my home again. You chose your side.* He stormed away, yanked open the door of one of the downtown bars, and disappeared out of the rain.

Jesse remembered his mother exiting the courtroom, murmuring she had to find some peace. He understood she needed time to let it all sink in, but that was hours ago. Ringing his father's phone gave him no answers either.

He ran his fingers through his hair in frustration. "God, where can they be?" A sudden premonition swept over him, causing a wave of dizziness that threw him sideways against the wall of his apartment. His face broke out in a sweat and his hands shook with such violence that it was almost impossible to open his cell phone. With great difficulty, he called Asia's number.

"How are you guys doing?" she asked.

Unable to speak, he uttered a couple of slurred syllables.

"Are you all right?"

"It's Mom," he finally managed.

"What's wrong?"

"She's hurt," he screamed. "I had a dream—a vision. I need to get to Sweet Elke Park right now. Call an ambulance!" He dropped his phone while picking up his keys and lunged out the door on shaky legs that threatened to buckle.

After struggling to untangle the truck key from the others on his key chain, he started his truck and headed toward Sweet Elke Park. Dread left his mouth dry. Remnants of the devastating vision he'd seen replayed in his mind and he fought to keep them at bay. Instead, he focused on the road that grew dimmer by the minute. His headlights were on, but the darkness seemed to envelop the light, obstructing their illumination.

He raced along the Strada del Vino at a blinding speed. Siebert's barn flew past him. Dutchman Mine Road would appear any second. He slowed, but not fast enough and overshot the turn. Jamming on his brakes, his truck screeched and fishtailed right and left several times before it came to a stop on the wet pavement. He waited for a second to quiet his pounding chest before maneuvering the truck around, then made the right-hand turn toward the park and sped through the darkness.

Before he even reached the bridge, panic gripped. Two cars belonging to his parents sat smashed together inside the park entrance. "Oh God," he cried out, "No!" He floored his truck over the bridge and raced toward the cars, skidding to a stop in the gravel.

He was already crying at the top of his voice as he exited the truck with his flashlight, "MOM! DAD!" No answer. He ran along the bank, searching and calling out. Then, rounding a bend in the creek, he saw them in the beam of light.

The scene was unearthly. A mist crept up from the water. His mother lay on the ground with her head slumped sideways. His father was lying against her, eyes open. Staring. Blood covered his shredded white shirt. Jesse turned aside and heaved.

He scooped a handful of water from the creek and washed his mouth while he stumbled to where his parents lay. Moaning, he took his father's hand. Ice cold. Fearing the worst, he cradled his mother's face in his hands. She moved. "Oh God, oh God, PLEASE." he shouted, "PLEASE."

He heard the sirens and saw a flicker of red pulsing lights as he tried to revive his mother. She was ice cold, her lips white-blue, but he could detect shallow breathing. Footsteps fell heavy on the ground behind him. Men's shouts became louder, but he couldn't decipher any words. His mother appeared ghostly, ethereal. Fear like he'd never known grabbed his chest like a bear hug. He sucked in a strangled breath.

A hand gently tapped his shoulder. "Jesse." He looked up to see an EMT who'd been a classmate in high school. "We'll take care of them. Move over now so we can help."

A dreamlike state hung over Jesse's mind. Things moved in slow motion while he sat on the ground. His friend moved his father's body to one side and rubbed his mother's hands, then took off his uniform jacket and wrapped her in it. Soon a stretcher arrived, carried by two more men.

Another siren sounded in the distance and soon a group of police officers reached the park and ran to the scene. Their lights flashed over his father as they bent to examine him. "He's gone," one said after a quick examination. "Look at this—lacerations everywhere."

"Man, oh man," his partner said. "Claw marks. A cat from the looks of it."

Jesse was sick again.

The men turned and someone whispered he was the son. They quieted their voices and came over to him. His legs couldn't support him, so two officers held his arms and helped him back to the ambulance.

***

Asia had called 911 the moment Jesse hung up, then sped to the park. She was just getting out of her car amidst a multitude of flashing lights when she saw him being half-dragged to the ambulance. "Jesse," she cried and ran toward him.

One of the officers shouted, "He's all right, Miss, but he's had quite a shock."

She reached him, her eyes wide with fear. "What happened?"

"Dad's dead. And Mom is, well, I don't know," his voice broke. He embraced her and cried into her drenched hair. They stood, holding each other as grief racked their bodies.

The rest of the night continued to be a blur. Unable to drive, they rode back to Bella Vista in a police car. The officer asked a few questions, but Jesse had no answers. After an hour, an officer drove them to his parents' home, where they slumped onto the couch and cried themselves to sleep.

Chapter 19

"NO," Lisa screamed, seeing the cougar tearing at Thomas. She clawed the air, unable to reach him. Invisible hands grabbed her wrists and held her arms against her chest, preventing her from helping him. She cried out again, sobbing.

***

"Give her another sedative," Dr. Bill Grey instructed the nurse. "I think it would be good to put the restraints back on. These attacks seem to be coming back."

His brow furrowed as he gazed at Lisa. She had been in the hospital for five days with little improvement. Yesterday had offered some hope when his patient was peaceful all day. She had even opened her eyes twice and tried to speak. He felt it safe to remove the protective straps that kept her from pulling out the tubes that delivered nutrients and medication. However, today he saw a regression in her anxiety level.

Her attendant secured her arms and checked her vital signs. "Everything seems normal, so what's keeping her this way?"

"She's suffering from delirium—acute confusion and disorientation," he explained. "There are no symptoms of physical injury to her head, but it seems the emotional trauma she sustained was enough to throw her into this state."

"Will she come out of it?"

"These cases are usually short-lived. Let's hope so. She's been through so much these last couple of months, it's probably a good thing she's able to rest for a while."

Bill frowned as he studied his patient. He had been Lisa's physician since she moved to Bella Vista and had been treating her for the anxiety and sleeplessness that plagued her since Thomas began his onslaught. It was still hard for him to think about Thomas without anger.

With the delay in her recovery, he encouraged Jesse to move ahead with burial plans for his father. He knew it was hard on the family, burying the father with the mother still in the hospital, but it seemed to be the best decision.

***

Asia followed Jesse and entered Lisa's room as soon as visiting hours began. "How's she doing?" he asked again. They had been here every day since she was hospitalized. He gazed with tired grief at his mother. Taking her fingers, he kissed her cheek.

Asia moved behind his chair and laid her hands on his shoulders. They had buried his father this morning, without Lisa. Asia wasn't sure that was such a bad thing. Thomas had been horrid to her. Maybe it was better that she didn't have the choice to attend his funeral.

Jesse's shoulders shook as he sobbed. She couldn't imagine the grief he suffered. They left an hour later, hoping for a better day tomorrow.

***

Summoned by the nurse, Dr. Grey rushed into the hospital room near noon the next day. Lisa was awake, lying solemnly in her raised bed. He studied her face, pale and hollow, and took her hand. "You've been through quite a lot, dear. How are you feeling?"

A look of bewilderment spread over her face as her anxious eyes skimmed across the blanket and settled on the far wall. "I thought I'd died. I was holding Thomas when he…" Patting her hand, Bill Grey's mind raced to determine how much she could take. She flitted her eyes up at him. "I know he's dead, Bill. I should be too." Weak tears trickled down her cheeks.

He gazed with concern at his patient, trying to understand her anguish. "What do you mean?"

She swallowed hard and struggled to speak. "My son's father is dead and it's my fault. I should have died too." Her face contorted into agony.

He reached over and gently touched her cheek. "Nonsense. That is too much responsibility for anyone to take on. You need to be thankful you're alive."

She wagged her head in disagreement, tears now flowing hard. "No. I can't bear this. I don't want to live."

He leaned closer and peered into her eyes, his words stern. "Now you listen to me. Thomas made many bad choices, as I'm sure you did, as we all do. His death was an accident, not your fault. I cannot explain why he is gone, and you are here, but it's done. The only thing you can do now is offer him forgiveness—and receive it."

She held his eyes. "He was so demeaning, even ruthless, but with his last words he expressed regret—and faith." She swallowed. "I have forgiven him." A new tear escaped down her cheek.

He pressed further. "And what about you?"

She said nothing but looked hopeless and miserable.

"Lisa, you didn't die. You've been given an opportunity to start over with a clean slate and the chance to be a stronger person. God has offered that to you. Will you take it?"

Her conflicted expression revealed a tremendous struggle. She looked away and shut her eyes.

Outside the room, he asked the nurse to bring Jesse to his office.

***

Asia rubbed Jesse's forearm softly and hoped for a positive report today. She gazed at his sad blue eyes as they sat down with the doctor.

"So, she's better?" Jesse asked, his expression a mixture of anxiety and hope.

"As I told you," Dr. Grey said, "she'll be fine physically. Emotionally, she's still traumatized, but there's something else. She thought she had died. Emotionally, she went through the process of dying and she's struggling with guilt associated with your father's death. That may take a lot to work through."

Jesse nodded and stared at the floor. "I saw it."

"I know." Dr. Grey answered, "I read the police report. It's a horrible thing for you to have witnessed."

Jesse shook his head. "What I mean is, I was still at home, and I saw her lying there, dying with my dad. That's when I called Asia and drove to the park. How can that happen?"

Asia tilted her head, not quite understanding.

In the quiet room, Dr. Grey studied Jesse. "What were you doing when you saw it?"

Jesse's eyes dropped to the floor as his mind recounted the events of that evening. "I was trying to telephone her and beginning to panic...then..." he paused for a moment, searching. He looked up at the physician. "I prayed," he said in a bewildered voice.

"I guess you have your answer." Dr. Grey sat back, eyebrows raised. "That prayer saved your mother's life."

Asia and Jesse linked eyes, sensing the wonder of this revelation. "It was God," he said with certainty. "Mom talked about Him, but I never…" A tremulous smile appeared, accompanying his misting eyes.

A nurse knocked on the door and reported Lisa was awake and insistent about seeing her son. Dr. Grey smiled at Jesse. "Go on."

Asia followed as Jesse rushed to his mother's bedside. He took her hand in both of his and scoured her face for signs she was aware of him. Asia stood to the side, watching Lisa. She looked pale and old. Dark circles drooped under her dull eyes and limp skin hung from her frame caused by the weight loss over the past weeks. Asia wanted to cry at the change in the vibrant woman she'd worked with. She swallowed, trying to displace the knot in her throat.

They talked for a short time, Lisa completely coherent. Her voice held no animation though, and she soon grew tired. Reluctantly, they each kissed her goodbye.

Asia remembered something just before leaving. She leaned down and whispered into Lisa's ear, "My dad's flying back in a few days." The slightest flicker of light passed through Lisa's eyes, then faded. She drifted off to sleep. They left, encouraged she might be coming out of the haze.

***

Taylor paced his room, stricken at what had transpired with Lisa. He should have come back after the three-week bike race instead of catering to his editor's demands. Asia's words tormented his mind. *She's a skeleton, and not just physically. Her mind is only half there and she's in some sort of vague stupor. It's unbearable, Daddy.*

His hands clenched into fists, angry that he waited to cover another race, cursing himself for agreeing to a mountain climb that put him out of cell phone reach. All he could do now was get home as soon as was humanly possible. He slumped in the chair and rubbed his throbbing forehead. Bad choice to leave Lisa to fight this battle alone.

The plane from Spain landed him in the States the next evening. After that, the flights were full, so he spent two more sleepless nights in a hotel. "How could this have happened?" He'd known this would be hard for her but was convinced he would only complicate things. Instead, it was worse than a nightmare. He paced the floor, trying to expel the anxiety that had gripped his stomach since Asia's frantic call. Hours later, he dropped into bed, only to toss and turn. Images of Lisa, touched with the pallor of death, jerked him in and out of sleep.

The next flight only got him as far as Chicago, where he had to wade his way through another sluggish night. In the morning, he couldn't tell if he felt better or worse from the night's sleep. His body seemed to have more energy, but his mind and emotions were beat.

Finally, he landed within driving distance to Bella Vista. The dread of seeing her in the state that Asia had described was nearly as strong as his desire to be there to comfort her. It was a quick one-hour drive, and he sped straight to the hospital.

"I'm looking for Lisa Richards' room," Taylor told the receptionist.

"It's Room 105. Go down this hallway and it's on your left."

A knot formed in his stomach as he neared her door. The doctor was just coming out. "May I help you?"

"I'm Steven Taylor, a friend of Lisa Richards." He searched the doctor's face. "How's she doing?"

Dr. Grey answered, "You must be Asia's father. She said you'd be in today. I'm Bill Grey." The two men shook hands. "To answer your question, she is fair. She's sleeping better and we've been able to get some solid food into her. Her mind is still foggy, but some of that is the medication. She will recover, it's just a matter of time."

Taylor took a deep breath, exhaled slowly, and walked into the room to find her lying against the raised head of her bed. Dull black hair accentuated ghostly pale skin. She looked small and weak. Her eyes were closed, so he approached her bed silently. When he sat down next to her, however, he bumped the bed with his knee.

Opening her eyes, she started. "Taylor," she gasped with relief.

He touched her shoulder and searched her face. She returned his gaze, tears spilling out. "Did they tell you what happened?"

"Yes." His eyes filled and every muscle in his face tensed. "I never should have left you. I thought you needed to do this on your own and I would only be undermining you, but I underestimated Thomas. How could I have been so wrong?" His voice rose with desperation.

Covering his hand with what little strength had returned, she tried to calm him. "None of us anticipated his reaction. Lying here, I've had time to think about things." She paused, searching for words. "Thomas had been out of our marriage almost from the beginning, justifying his affairs, lying to me. Then it all came to light. Everyone knew the truth. He became increasingly agitated and obsessed over the last few weeks. I know he'd been drinking heavily—especially the night of the...attack. But…" Her face crumpled. "But in the end, somehow…he turned around. Found faith." She swallowed her tears but couldn't hold back all of them. "He asked me to forgive him."

Taylor's mouth dropped open, but he couldn't speak. He knew how much this meant to her. He also understood the grief and horror she was experiencing from the tragic way Thomas died. He leaned over and kissed her forehead. "It's over now." They sat in silence for a few minutes as she dried her eyes and he pulled his emotions together. "How long do they want you to stay here?"

"They haven't given me a time yet. I think I'm supposed to gain some weight back. It seems they're feeding me every twenty minutes." She gave a weak laugh.

That tiny fleck of encouragement was all it took to help him look ahead to brighter days. "Well, how about I bring you the largest box of chocolates I can find, and we'll ditch this place for some fresh air?"

A spark ignited in her eyes, and as he held her hand, a deep longing surged between them. A true smile parted her lips when their eyes connected. Then her gaze fell to the tightness in his jaw and concern clouded her face. "Are *you* okay?

"Now I am, but honestly, I don't think anything in my life has caused me more distress." Anger stabbed his chest again. He took a deep, shuddering breath and tried to shake it off.

"This wasn't your battle."

He gave her a thin smile to avoid arguing. "I'm just glad you're recovering."

Her fingers linked with his. "Thank you for coming back."

"I won't leave you again."

Her mouth opened in surprise.

"That's a promise." He leaned over to kiss her lips, but as he gathered her in his arms, she cried out, her head falling back against the pillow.

He jerked back. "Have I hurt you?"

"Just a bit," she said through a full but tired smile. "I cracked a bone in my arm, and I don't have much strength right now."

Frustration hit him for not paying better attention. He brushed a stray hair off her eyebrow with his thumb. "You are so special to me."

Her expression turned serious. "I never, ever wanted to be in another relationship, but I need your strength and your...*care*," she blushed.

"You have me." His heart beat hard at the impact of the revelation.

An ironic chuckle spilled out of her, dissolving the tenderness of the moment,

He hesitated. "What?"

"I look worse than any time in my entire life, and I have the most attractive man I've ever known telling me he cares for me. It's just hard to fathom," she said. More quiet chuckles emerged from both of them, altering the energy of the hospital room.

Jesse walked in and stopped. Studying the change in his mother, his eyes flitted from her to Taylor and a look of gratitude transformed his face. Nodding to Taylor, he said, "We'll need to call you the miracle worker."

Taylor noticed that apprehension had filled Lisa's eyes until she saw the change in Jesse's expression. She relaxed again when the two men shook hands.

"How was your flight?" Jesse asked.

"Too long," Taylor replied, glancing at Lisa. "I think I'll stick to covering rides in the States, the overseas flights are grueling."

The conversation was comfortable, like it had been before the ball at the country club. Taylor sought information from Jesse while steered him away from painful memories.

Exhaustion again overtook Lisa, and she drifted off to sleep. The men noticed and quietly left the room.

"How about lunch?" Jesse invited. He called Asia, who was in Tangle Grove for the morning, and they decided to eat in Bella Vista.

***

"Hi, Daddy," Asia said as she walked in the door of the restaurant. She seemed happy.

Taylor rose and gave her a long hug. "I've missed you so much." He didn't ever want to let those he loved out of his sight again.

"Don't I get a hug?" Jesse asked her.

"You get more than that," She teased and gave him a mock passionate kiss. All three laughed at the lightness they felt in each other's company again. "Jesse told me on the phone what an effect you had on Lisa," she grinned.

Taylor realized his feelings had been obvious to Asia, maybe even before he'd acknowledged them to himself.

"You should've seen Mom," Jesse recounted. She dropped ten years in ten minutes." Relief continued to bathe him like balm. Their missing appetites returned full on and they ordered dessert on top of everything else.

"From the looks of all of you, we'll have to get used to eating like this until we get some meat back on your bones," Taylor teased.

"That would mean a lot of additional exercise for me," Asia laughed.

Jesse stopped eating and became thoughtful. "Mom will need exercise too, but I'm not sure how she'll feel about going back to the mountain. It's her favorite place to hike."

Taylor thought about that for a moment. "Have they found the mountain lion yet?"

"No, they had quite a few volunteer hunters out there, but most have given up. No one feels safe at the park now that..." Jesse stopped, his breathing speeding up.

Taylor realized too late that he'd taken a wrong turn in the conversation. He laid his hand on the younger man's shoulder. "There's a lot of healing that needs to come. It doesn't all have to happen at once."

Jesse nodded, but Taylor noticed moisture gathering on his upper lip. Asia's eyes pleaded with Taylor for help. Moving away from the subject, he commented that there were a number of walking paths throughout the town that would get Lisa out and exercising. Then looking outside at the rain, he smirked, "There's always the gym."

Asia and Jesse looked to him for the meaning and then followed his eyes to the wet sidewalk. "Oh, she'd love that," Jesse stated with dry humor, knowing Lisa hated being cooped up indoors.

The rest of the meal went without an upset. Asia pushed out of the booth. "Since my firm has been good enough to pay me for hanging out down here, I better to get back to work."

After Asia left, Taylor and Jesse lingered in the comfortable booth. Shielded by the low lighting in the restaurant, Jesse filled him in on the details that had occurred since he left for Spain. Much of the information brought anger and pain to both men.

"One of the hardest things for me to face was how my father left me outside the courtroom. Those angry words can never be undone." his lower lip quivered.

He remembered something Asia had said that made him curious. "It's still unclear how you knew where your mother was."

Jesse's mood lifted as he recounted the miracle of receiving the vision. "God showed me. I've never experienced anything like it."

He remained silent for a few moments, seeing the dreadful and amazing events of that night in his mind. His heart filled with immeasurable gratitude at the outcome.

Jesse asked, "Do you believe in God?"

"Yes, I do," he said. "Your mother had a lot to do with bringing me back around. She's a treasure."

At the word, *treasure*, Jesse brightened. "We could take Mom out as a group to Sweet Elke Park and try to make some sense of the clues. We only have a short time to find more opals. Mom's mind would be so occupied, it would take away the fear of the place and help her get used to it again."

He doubted the wisdom of Jesse's suggestion and wasn't certain he wanted to put Lisa through anything that would cause her more pain.

"We could take our guns and post a lookout," Jesse continued after Taylor's delayed response.

"Let's think about it awhile and approach the subject when she's had more time to recover, okay?"

Jesse's enthusiasm receded, but not by much. They hung out a while longer, making plans for Lisa's recovery.

***

Taylor, Jesse, and Asia made another trip back to see Lisa that evening. As they approached her room, they heard laughter coming through the door. They rounded the corner and saw Jess sitting by Lisa's side, both in stitches, attempting to keep their chuckles low.

Following Lisa's eyes, Jess turned around and grinned at their surprised looks. "We were just recounting some old family stories," he said in answer to their unspoken question. He continued to chuckle.

Taylor's shoulders relaxed. It sounded good to hear laughter like this—hearty, from the belly. Lisa was still holding her stomach, whispering, "Shush."

"Here, sit down, Asia," Jess said, rising. She hesitated, but he insisted. They all moved in closer to the bed.

The improvement in Lisa's demeanor from this morning was startling. The nurse must have helped her shower and wash her hair. Lipstick gave her face some appearance of life and brought out the blue of her eyes. Seeing her look this way again gave Taylor a jolt of elation. He spied an empty food tray in the corner of her room and flashed a knowing smile at her. She winked and seemed happy he'd noticed her efforts.

"Dr. Grey was in this afternoon and gave us an update on her condition." Jess said. Everyone waited for him to continue. "What?" he teased.

"Out with it, Grandpa," Jesse ordered.

Jess laughed at their impatient expressions. "Okay, okay. It was good news. He thought there might have been permanent damage to some of her tissue from exposure, but there isn't, and the cracked bone and muscle strain in her right arm are mending well. There was no physical damage to her head for him to treat, and now it seems the mental trauma is resolved. So, he's taken her off the medication." He gave his daughter a loving smile.

There was an audible sigh as all three of the new arrivals let out their breath simultaneously. This caught Jess' funny bone anew. It was so good to laugh again. Taylor saw tears of joy come to Lisa's eyes as she looked around at those she loved.

They stayed together in this healing cocoon of stories and laughter until the nurses kicked them out. Asia had been staying at Lisa's apartment, so Jesse took her back to Tangle Grove. Jess glanced at Taylor and asked him where he was staying.

"I haven't had a chance to check in anywhere yet."

"Why don't you stay at my house tonight?"

"Thanks, I'd appreciate that." He followed Jess' car up a winding road through the hills of Bella Vista. A recent rain had emptied the satiated clouds and the lights of the city lay glistening in the valley below. As Taylor swung into the driveway, Jess motioned for him to park alongside the garage.

"You're traveling light," Jess commented when Taylor pulled out one suitcase and his carry-on that held his laptop.

"My company shipped the rest of my things. They should be arriving in a day or two."

"Are you planning to stay around for a while then?"

Grinning at Jess' line of questioning, Taylor decided to give him a straight answer. "I hope so. The truth is, I care a great deal about Lisa. About your whole family. I hope I can be a part of rebuilding her life."

Jess' face relaxed at Taylor's transparency. "Of course, that's Lisa's business, but you're welcome in my home. You've given invaluable help to my family."

He studied the older man's weary eyes and the residual strain tugging at his face. "I appreciate your hospitality, and your friendship." Jess had watched his daughter go through hell because of a man, yet he was willing to give Taylor a chance to prove himself. His trust and vulnerability crumbled Taylor's defensive wall. Trust was something Taylor hadn't felt in a long while.

Chapter 20

After a regenerating sleep, unhindered by dreams or worry, Taylor awoke at first light, anxious to see Lisa again. Although he tried to be quiet, his movements woke Jess, who came out with half-opened eyes and offered to fix breakfast. At the dining table, Taylor's hands encircled a hot cup of coffee while he listened with interest when the topic turned to Fire Mountain.

"Lisa thinks she has an idea of where to hunt for the stones, but I'm not sure that isn't just wishful thinking," Jess said. "She's been under quite a strain and may be grasping at straws."

Considering that possibility, he thought back over the strange, yet deliberate markings on the tombstone. "That could be, but I'd still like to take a crack at deciphering the meaning."

Jess' mouth turned up at the corners.

He chuckled, "You think I have treasure fever?"

"I *know* it," Jess teased. "There have been very few people I've known who didn't react that way, once they heard about the mine." He grinned. "I have to admit, I was pretty excited when they pulled out the stones in '46. But after a few months of digging in our spare time and finding nothing, the luster wore off."

"I think knocking out a few rocks would give me a suitable opponent to discharge some of this anxiety," he said. "Jesse and I were making plans to drive up there on his days off. Would you be interested?"

Jess sighed. "I'd like to go along for moral support, but I'm afraid my shoveling and picking days are long gone." Regret tinged his voice, tempered by acceptance.

He felt glad Lisa's father would be joining them. He liked Jess and could see where Lisa and Jesse got their sense of humor. "Good, then, we'll make our plans and go."

Jess' eyebrows knit together. "This nightmare shattered Jesse's life too. It may be too soon for him to face it."

"I wondered about that," he agreed, "but he keeps bringing it up. Maybe the goal of saving Fire Mountain will help him face his dragons and be done with it. He was hoping it would work that way for Lisa."

"Could be," Jess replied, starting to clear the dishes. Taylor arose to help, but Jess insisted this was something he could still do. "What plans do you have for the day?"

He poured a second cup of coffee. "After I visit with Lisa, I'm tending to some business in town and then meeting Asia for lunch. If Dr. Grey still thinks Lisa can come home this afternoon, we'll pick her up and all meet for dinner. Jesse wants to go over the plans for the dig." He paused and chuckled. "You should join us. After all, you're the most experienced treasure hunter among us."

"Never thought about it, but you're probably right," Jess grinned back. "I watched the professionals in the family dig for months before they all left. That could be of some use." He finished drying the pan and put it away. "Hey, why don't all of you come back up here tonight and I'll have dinner ready?"

"Great. I'll let the others know we have a chef, and a guide."

***

The day was drier, but still cloudy when Taylor left Jess' house. He heard there was a chance for sunshine, but the sky didn't support that forecast. The drive coming back down the road afforded amazing glimpses through the clouds of the valley below and the mountains beyond. Again, wonder struck that this area created such a draw on him. His body relaxed as he drove to the hospital, his thumbs keeping time to the rhythm pulsating from the radio.

Lisa was sitting upright in bed when he walked in. She gave him a radiant smile. Irresistible, actually.

"You are lovely." He stood next to her and stroked the back of her hand with his thumb until she turned her hand over and threaded her fingers through his, pulling him downward. Not needing to be asked twice, he leaned over and kissed her mouth for the first time. Soft, ready lips met his and he deepened the pressure, sending exquisite surges through him. Reluctantly, he stood up again, bringing her wrist to his lips. That had to be enough for now.

Breathless, she searched for something to say. "Did you get some rest last night?"

"Yes," he murmured, but his mind and eyes were not focused on small talk.

She blushed under his gaze.

"I see you've got your color back," he laughed and released her hand.

They spent an enjoyable time talking about his trip to Spain and about Asia and Jesse, then she raised her eyebrows in excitement. "Dr. Grey said I can check out this afternoon. Could someone come and get me?"

"It's already taken care of. I'll be back at 4:00 and then we're all meeting at your father's to eat dinner, *and* plan our treasure hunt."

No sooner had her eyes reflected her enthusiasm, then fear overshadowed them. "You aren't planning to go back there, are you? They haven't found that cougar—Taylor, it's not safe for you or Jesse."

He watched her concern turn to dread and sought to dispel her fears with a confident attitude. "When we go, we'll have rifles and there will be three of us. I've never heard of an attack on a group of men before, so you don't have to worry."

Nevertheless, deep worry lines creased her forehead "I should really go with you, but I don't think I'm ready to face that yet."

He squeezed her trembling hand. "You don't have to do anything that scares you. In fact, we can forget the mine altogether if you'd like."

At those words, she swallowed hard and labored to bring her fears under control. "No, we need to move ahead."

He sensed her turmoil. "The biggest thing we could use your help on is working out the clues."

Her look warned that he might be treading on sacred ground.

"You can decide what you feel comfortable revealing and we'll do our best from there. There's no need for you to even go back."

She fought to resolve the conflicting emotions and replied with a tentative voice. "Perhaps if we all go together and keep a lookout..." She looked to him for reassurance.

"Absolutely. We'll do whatever it takes to keep us all safe—and unlock the Dutchman's secret," he added with a gleam in his eye. But it failed to get the response he wanted. Sensing what a huge effort she was making, he decided to change to a happier subject and allow her to get used to the idea before approaching it again. "Asia informed me her firm has hired a contractor to start on the new courthouse." He grinned as he watched her face explode with exhilaration. *Bull's-eye.*

Sitting up straighter in bed, her eyes danced with questions. "When do they break ground?"

"You'll have to wait and ask Asia. It was really her surprise, but I thought you could use the good news now."

"I can't wait to get out of this hospital. My head is fine, no more fog or dizziness. Isn't there any chance I can get out of here early?"

Laughing, Taylor leaned over and kissed her again. "You'll have to mind your doctor. Besides, I have business to attend to in town." She asked for an explanation, but he just gave her a mischievous grin.

***

That evening at Jess' home, Taylor felt more alive than he had in a long time. Jess cooked a big pot of Rose's Sicilian Spaghetti, using a sauce recipe that came from *her* grandmother. Taylor and Asia chopped the salad and prepared the garlic bread and Jesse opened a special bottle of wine he'd purchased to celebrate Lisa's homecoming.

As they stood around the table, Lisa bowed her head to give thanks and they followed. "Heavenly Father, thank you for watching over us and bringing us together tonight."

Taylor stole a glance when her voice faltered, but she continued.

"Thank you for helping Thomas see You, and for turning him around at the last. You are so faithful. Please bring healing to all our hearts and guard us with your strong hand. Amen." They raised their heads. She let out a long breath, conveying that with it went the past pain and trauma. It was time to begin again.

They sat and Lisa held her father's eyes. "I'm so thankful to have you near me." In turn, her gaze fell on each person that surrounded her at the table.

Jesse proposed a toast. "To family. And to love," he said as he looked from his mother and grandfather to Taylor and Asia.

Taylor felt honored Jesse had included him and Asia. His chest tightened with emotion. It had been too long since he was part of a family circle. They spent the rest of the meal in pleasant conversation, saving the talk concerning the mine until after dinner.

***

"So," Lisa broke the ice, "it's obvious you guys want me to spill the beans."

Jesse looked to Jess, who answered for them. "Well, we wouldn't want you to do anything against your word, but what good are the clues if we lose Fire Mountain? It seems it's either now or never."

It was understandable that they had discussed this and come to this conclusion. She pondered their argument and had to agree. "You're right, Dad," she said, and made the turn in her mind. Looking at those gathered in the kitchen, she opened up the doors to their family heritage.

"Each Guardian, beginning with the Dutchman, passed down the knowledge they had received regarding the Van Buren Trust and family secrets. I swore to Mom that as the Guardian, I would protect the location of the opals. They're only to be used in an emergency for the protection of the family property." She paused, remembering the difficult encounter with her mother. She'd been adamant about this, almost accusatory that Lisa wouldn't follow through. Yet here she was, about to divulge the secrets. But what other choice did she have?

Shaking off the rest of her doubts, she continued. "There's a poem that is the key to unlock the clues on Elke's gravestone. Dad and I were trying to use the clues but didn't come up with anything. Maybe with all of us working together we can make more progress."

She smiled for the first time since her decision to include them. "Dad, I think it would be helpful for each of us to have some paper and a pen." Jess found the supplies and handed them out as Lisa continued.

"The poem goes like this:

"Kneel on the side of honor

Lift up your eyes at the cross

And take in heaven's portal

That serves dear Lowie's ghost.

At noon the glint o'er the ivy

Will help her mark her way

What better gift on her birthday

Then to find that brilliant way."

"What's that supposed to mean?" Jess asked, frowning.

Without a pause, Jesse was on it. "*Kneel on the side of honor*, would be Elke's grave—she's the *honorable* one."

"I thought so too," Lisa said. "When Dad and I were there, I looked across the tombstone, past the cross on the headstone, and sighted an area by a large tree on the mountain. I combed that whole place but found nothing."

"What were you looking for?" Taylor asked.

"Some kind of hole or cave door, I suppose," she said. "What do you get?"

Taylor pulled out his cell phone and brought up the photos he took at the grave. He showed them the shot of the etching with light rays coming out from the edges of the door. "It could be light that glints off of a metal door," he suggested.

"Yes, but that could just represent the main door, illustrating the brilliance of the opals inside," Jess reasoned.

"That sounds right about the brilliance of the opals, Grandpa," Jesse agreed, "but the main door is rectangular, and this photo shows a rounded top."

Asia commented on the next line. "*Take in heaven's portal.* A portal is a door, and heaven can speak of the sky. So, *a door in the sky*? That doesn't make sense." She withdrew her idea.

Jesse's face lit up and he hugged her. "No, that's good thinking. If we were at the grave, lifting up our eyes to the cross that is carved on the headstone, we would be looking toward the sky. That means there *is* a door up there!" His comment heightened the already eager expressions.

"*That serves dear Lowie's ghost*," Lisa read. "I wonder if Jochem discovered another opening that caused the *ghostly* chill in the cave. And in finding it, found a stash of opals. He could've let the legend of Lowie's ghost continue for the mine's protection."

"Or even made it up," Jesse laughed.

"Why wouldn't he have created a map for finding it from inside the cave?" Jess asked.

"Maybe it's too easy to get disoriented," Asia suggested, "Remember our experience there in the dark?"

Taylor said, "It sounds like he found an air passage and closed it up with a door, the *portal*. Then he situated the markings on Elke's grave to point to where it is."

"It also says that at noon, light will be reflecting above the ivy," Jesse stated. "Mom, what do you get for *ivy*?"

Lisa pondered the question. "Ivy is a vine. Maybe he planted it to cover the area. It would create a thick mat to keep it undetected. Perhaps he then placed something reflective on the mountain above it. The other possibility is that the *ivy* is on the tomb. The *glint* will show above it. I suggest we search for anything related to *ivy* engraved in the etchings." Everyone agreed and she jotted it down.

Asia had been contemplative throughout the conversation, studying the words. "Are they still talking about Elke when they say, *Will help her mark her way*?"

"I can't think of anyone else it would apply to," Lisa answered. "*Her birthday* refers to Elke's birthday, which is October twenty-first, but I don't see what the rest of this would have to do with her. The only others who would be looking for the *way* are those Guardians looking for the opals. It seems to be suggesting that Elke was a Guardian. That fits the legend about her *guarding* people around the creek."

"That's awesome," Jesse exclaimed, beaming at her.

"The only references to time are *noon* and *her birthday*," Jess pointed out.

"Okay," Jesse summarized. "It sounds like it says there's something shining above ivy that shows the way *she* is supposed to go. *She* must represent Elke because it's her birthday—or a future Guardian. Then she hikes through the earth on her birthday, October twenty-first and finds the *brilliant way*, the place of the treasure." His brow furrowed. "Does that tell us anything?"

Lisa watched a thoughtful expression envelop Taylor's face. He rubbed the back of his neck and said, "We're looking for a certain reflection off the mountain at a certain time, which explains why we need the date—her birthday. It lets us know when the sun would be in that exact position."

"That's good," Lisa said. "October twenty-first is in a week. If it's a sunny day..."

"…at noon," Jess cut in.

"...then maybe we'd see it if we're there." Lisa finished the crescendo.

The group was silent for a moment, then all started talking at once. Lisa felt satisfied with the consensus that they would go to Elke's grave first thing in the morning and see if what they had deciphered gave them anything to work with. It was vital to be ready before the twenty-first, so they didn't miss the noonday chance.

In bed that night, Lisa tossed in a restless state. The excitement of finding the treasure and the fear of facing the place of Thomas' tragic death, twisted her insides. She knew the others were worried how she and Jesse would do the next day. In the end, fatigue won out. She managed a moderate amount of sleep mixed with dreams of brilliant rays illuminating the fire in thousands of fabulous opals.

***

This was a new day, and Taylor was full of anticipation. He wolfed down the hearty breakfast of pancakes and sausage that Jess cooked for them. Lisa grabbed a large thermos of coffee before they stepped into the cool morning air. Outside, the clouds were high and looked like they might break later.

Asia and Jesse were waiting for them at Sweet Elke Café when they drove up. Taylor followed Lisa upstairs to her apartment to get some hiking clothes and boots, noting she seemed stronger than she'd been, but still shaky. Once inside, she disappeared down a hall.

Taking in the details, his mouth dropped open. "This is beautiful," he called toward her room. She came back out and sat on the sofa to put on her boots.

"I'm glad you like it." She winced as she tried to fasten her boot with her injured right arm.

"Let me," he offered and bent down to tie the bootlaces for her.

"Thanks," she smiled, but as she stood up, she swayed.

"Hold on." He grabbed her arms to steady her and realized this was the first time they'd been alone since he returned. With his arms already around her, he pulled her to him, pressing his hungry lips onto her waiting mouth.

She returned a dizzying kiss then pulled back with a breathless smile. "With everyone waiting, it would probably be better if we were punctual going back down."

He laughed. "You're probably right, this time." He kissed her again, then opened the door. They made their way back down the stairs, dropping hands just before they entered the café.

"Took you long enough," Jesse chuckled, rising to get started.

"I thought it was time you learned some patience," Lisa returned the jest. She went to the counter to say a quick hello to Lilly and Joe, then met the others outside. The cool air smelled fresh as they piled into Jesse's pickup.

Taylor watched her expression when she spied the rifles anchored across the back window. Fear worried her forehead as she took the seat next to him. He reached over and laced his fingers through hers. "Are you going to be okay with this?" he asked.

"I don't know. So far, it's just the shakes. I can deal with those."

He focused the conversation on their adventure while they rode. "It's unlikely that we'll see the exact point of the *glint* today, but at least we can try to get our line of sight from the markings on the stone. Did you two bring your notes?" he asked Jesse and Asia.

"Right here," Asia answered, holding up the notepaper from the night before.

***

The bridge lay just ahead. Lisa watched Jesse's hands tense on the steering wheel, his knuckles white. He slowed and came to a full stop before crossing. Everyone waited.

She knew what he was going through. "Jesse, I'm having a hard time too," she said gently. "Maybe we should give it more time before coming back here."

The blood was visibly pulsing in Jesse's neck. "I feel like I did when I came looking for you, then found you lying there in the darkness." Agony contorted his face.

Asia reached over to rub the tension out of his shoulders. Slowly, Jesse got control. He took a drink from his water bottle and wiped the perspiration from his upper lip. Asia patted his leg with her hand but said nothing.

As if on cue, the clouds parted and blue sky opened over them, sending the brilliance of the sun across the truck. It worked like magic and raised their courage, allowing them to continue. Jesse drove across the bridge and pulled into the parking lot, where they unloaded.

"Taylor," Jess said, "Could you hand me the guns? I've got the ammo up here."

Taylor unlatched the rifles and handed one to Jess and one to Jesse. "Nice rifles," he complimented. "Do you hunt much?"

"Used to," Jess said. "Jesse and his cousins were more the hunters than the rest of us." He smiled encouragement and cast his grandson a sideways glance.

"I haven't been out in a while," Jesse said, "but Dan still gets out every year."

Jess loaded the guns and offered one to Lisa. "Do you want to carry your gun, or should I take it?"

Taylor swung his head toward her, eyebrows raised.

She bit her cheek. "Let me see if I can carry it." She held out her left hand to her father. Trying to balance it and not use her right arm proved more than she could manage. "My arm's still weak and I'm not sure I'd be accurate if I had to shoot. You better keep it," she conceded.

With all their supplies unloaded, they focused on their purpose and marched to the gravesite. The day became brighter and more beautiful while they walked. The creek had calmed since the rain stopped and now flowed in a gentle, swirling current. Red and gold tones surrounded them as the leaves displayed their autumnal hues, contrasting starkly with the bright blue of the sky overhead.

She breathed in the scent of the woods. "This is my favorite time of year. Feel that serenity?"

Taylor lifted his head and nodded. "It still baffles me."

She glanced over at Jesse and asked, "Are you feeling it too?" He flashed his exuberant grin at them, obviously relieved he made it through his trial. Taylor's shoulders relaxed too.

She'd hoped this would be a good day of restoration, but not only that. There was a lot riding on them being able to prove this was a viable mine. The Van Buren estate had existed intact for generations. She desperately wanted to maintain her family heritage.

***

Jess led and they arrived at the grave of Elke Van Buren. Jesse held his gun at the ready, but Taylor could tell he really wanted to look for the clues. "I can keep watch for a while," he said, extending his hand toward the gun.

"Thanks," Jesse beamed and handed him his rifle, ready to test his mettle against this riddle.

Lisa looked around tentatively and Taylor caught her eye. When she saw that he was indeed watching for danger, she turned back to their task, took out the paper she had written her poem on and began reading. "*Kneel on the side of honor.*"

Jesse walked to one side of the tomb and then to the other. From the right side of the grave, he looked back over the land beyond the creek. "The Dutchman never found opals on the flat lands. We should be on Elke's left side—that gives us a view of the mountain."

"*Lift up your eyes at the cross, and take in heaven's portal,*" Lisa continued.

Kneeling on the left side of the grave, Jesse peered toward the cross engraved high into the headstone, trying to see beyond it. With the steep angle, all he could see was sky. He moved closer to the foot of the stone and got the same result. He tried several other places, frowning in frustration. From a kneeling position, he couldn't see one place where his sight and the intersection of the cross pinpointed a place on the mountain.

"How did you see a tree line when you were here, Mom," he asked.

She walked to the end of the tomb and knelt down on the raised stone positioned there. "From here, my line of vision lands on the stand of trees I climbed to. I just assumed that the foot of the tomb was also a *side*."

Studying her position, Jesse wondered aloud, "Perhaps there were other large stones on the sides like the one at the end."

Taylor had been scanning the brush around them since they had arrived. That didn't deter his mind from taking in the conversation and reasoning with what he heard. "It doesn't seem logical that the Dutchman would leave it to chance that a stone could be taken away, thus blocking the access to his family's treasure."

"You're right," Jesse agreed. "*Kneel down*," he repeated and got back on his knees. The only immoveable position for his eyes to begin a line of sight was to lower them to the top edge of the marble stone and gaze upwards at the cross. This only further increased his aim at the sky. Fully frustrated now, he suggested that they move on to another part of the riddle.

Jess offered to stand watch and let Taylor in on the action. Appreciative, Taylor leaned Jesse's gun against a tree.

Getting back on her feet, Lisa read the second stanza. "*At noon the glint o'er the ivy will help her mark her way*. Let's see if there is any *ivy* on the tomb. If not, we can eliminate that possibility and look elsewhere for it." The four of them each took a side and scoured it for any trace.

Asia was the first to exclaim that she might have found something. "This scrollwork on the smaller door looks like it could be a stylized vine." The rest of the group joined her, including Jess, though he continued to watch for the cougar.

"It could be," Taylor said, and the rest of the group agreed. Standing back, he repeated the words and looked for a place that light could *glint* over this *ivy* spot and take them to their destination. "I don't think this can be what we're looking for, unless anyone else has a theory." No one spoke up.

They went over the rest of the clues, but after an hour, felt more befuddled than ever. "Surely Jochem didn't mean for it to be this hard." Jess said, questioning the Dutchman's judgment.

His comment gave Taylor an idea. "Lisa, were there any more artifacts or photos that were specifically handed down to you as the Guardian?"

Eyes gazing off, she seemed to go over the list in her mind. "In addition to the riddle, there were all the trust documents that I had to sign to take over as the trustee. The photo albums came to me to pass on to my heirs, and, of course, the jewels." She glanced up at Taylor. "There's a stash of old papers and some memorabilia. I guess we could go through everything."

"Let's take new photos of every side of this tomb and go back," he said. "We can print them out at home." He couldn't think of anything else to do and sensed they needed a break.

Jesse seemed downcast but helped look for anything of possible interest for Taylor to photograph. He found something that they hadn't noticed earlier. Near the foot of the crypt, someone had etched a date and initials into the cement at ground level. "It reads, *P. C. 1903*. That's probably the stonemason who worked the marble."

"Then what's this on the marble headstone?" Asia asked. Engraved with precision into the marble slab were the initials *E. C. 1918*. The others crowded into the space around the head of the grave. The marble had apparently been placed fifteen years after Elke's death.

"Maybe it took a while to get the marble here and carve it," Jess offered from his lookout position.

"Even that special door he had made for the mine only took a few months to finish," Lisa said. She gasped. Everyone looked around for a sign of the cougar. She caught their expressions and apologized. "No, I didn't see anything—but I just realized Jochem Van Buren died in 1913—that's three years before this marble was placed."

"Then who would have set it here?" Jesse asked.

"I have a hunch," she said. "Let's get back to my apartment—I have my papers in a safe there."

"You have a safe in your apartment?" Jesse asked in surprise.

She nodded with a grin. "I can't just leave our family secrets lying around."

As they made their way along the path to the truck, Jesse asked, "What else don't I know about my mother?" Lisa raised her eyebrows without giving him any more clues.

Taylor watched her eyes dart back at Jess, who continued to cast watchful glances behind him. They reached the vehicle and unloaded the guns, locking them to the rack. Safely inside, relief seemed to hit everyone, dislodging the tension. The truck erupted with excitement and animated speculation while they made the short trip into Tangle Grove. To see what was inside the safe.

Chapter 21

They had trampled fear underfoot, Lisa thought happily. Now, she hoped to find some answers in her heirlooms. When they passed by the café, however, the smell of freshly baked sweets and coffee reminded them that breakfast had been a long time ago. No words needed to be spoken and they made the detour as a unit, laughing at their shared thought.

Rushing through their sandwiches, they took their coffee to go and ascended the stairs with animated chatter. Lisa stopped. Her door stood ajar with a broken lock.

Taylor dashed past her and burst into the room, ready for a confrontation. Jesse and Jess followed and swept through the entire apartment.

She peeked in after them. No one was there, but someone had intruded. Drawers had been pulled out and dumped on the floor. Her clothes lay scattered around the bedroom, hangers and all. She looked in horror at the mess and made a dash to her office. The desk drawers were also emptied of their contents and tossed on the carpet.

She crossed the room to where an antique oval photograph hung on the wall. Gently lifting the wooden frame, heavy with the weight of the convex glass, she set it upside down on the guest bed and let out her breath. It was intact. "We're okay," she said with great relief.

Asia's brows knit together. "If you say so."

Lisa called Jesse into the room and apologized to the others as she closed the door. She held the sides of the upside-down photograph and confided in him, the next Guardian. "This is a safe that was constructed decades ago for the protection of the important family heirlooms." Her fingers deftly slid sequentially around the plain oval frame, moving strong metal brackets either up or down. At the last movement, the solid back released and opened, revealing a hinge on one side and neatly stacked papers underneath.

Entranced, he moved forward for a closer look.

She started to lift the papers, then dropped them and shut the safe again.

"What're you doing?" he cried.

"We need to call the police and report this," she said. "I don't want to expose these papers until they've investigated."

He shrugged. "I know you're right, but waiting is *so* exasperating."

After making the phone call, she asked the others to wait at Sweet Elke's. She didn't want any evidence disturbed. She also wanted to survey the damage and ascertain if anything was stolen. It was easier to do without four other people walking around her.

Twenty minutes later a patrol car pulled in front of her building. "Mrs. Richards?" the officer asked as he tapped on the door and tentatively pushed it open.

"Yes, Officer," she said, and her face relaxed. She recognized Detective Madden. He'd come to the hospital once she had recovered enough to give a statement regarding the events that led to Thomas' death. He'd been very professional, yet sensitive to her emotions.

The detective glanced around Lisa's home. "What a mess." He shook his head. "There is too much happening to you and I want some answers. "When did you discover the intrusion?"

"We were here at nine o'clock this morning. When I returned half an hour ago, the door was ajar, and the room looked like this."

"Who is the *we*?"

"My dad, son, his girlfriend, and a friend of mine," she said.

"And you all came in at the same time?"

"Yes. I opened the door, and the men went in ahead of us."

"Have you discovered anything missing?"

"I spent the last few minutes looking around and haven't noticed anything. I didn't want to move things to look under them in case there might be some evidence."

"Good." He and his partner took photographs and dusted for fingerprints. "Mrs. Richards, would you mind sitting down over here?"

He cleared off the sofa after checking it out. "Do you have any idea who would have done this and what they might have been looking for?"

Her face went blank. "With Thomas gone, I can't think of anyone else who would benefit from anything I would keep in the apartment. Someone might have thought my family jewels are here, but I keep those in a safe elsewhere. I don't think that was it, however, because my other jewelry, though not valuable, was just spilled out on the bed and left."

He made a note of this. "Could you give me a list of your enemies," he asked directly, pen ready.

Her eyes darted to his face. "Why would you think I had enemies—other than Thomas?"

The detective trained his eyes on hers. "You recently won a battle in Tangle Grove for the placement of the new downtown area, is that right?"

She nodded.

"And a group of people have been working very hard to take Fire Mountain away from your family and succeeded. These could make or create enemies. Are there other areas where you are embroiled in conflicts that could cause people to harbor ill-will toward you?"

Chewing her cheek, she asked, "If I give you names of people, who end up having nothing to do with this, wouldn't that cause them undo harm?"

He shook his head. "After I have the list, I'll sort through it and only question the most logical suspects. Most of those interviews will be dead-ends and no harm will be done. If I suspect there is more behind what they are telling me, then I'll follow that lead."

She gave him a list of the people who had opposed her. Beginning with Mayor Cook, she made her way through her former employer, Verina Fields, to Angela Basso, and her previous attorney, Gary Bristol. "I suppose anyone who lost money when we were able to sustain the current plan for Tangle Grove could also go on the list."

"What about members of the group to take Fire Mountain?"

"They already took it," she fumed. "There's no reason for them to search for anything else."

"I see," he answered. "Do you happen to know who was behind the push for Fire Mountain—besides Ms. Basso and Ms. Fields?"

"There's a petition list somewhere. Our state representative would have it."

"I'll see about that." He made a note and went downstairs to talk with Lilly.

The others came back upstairs to help Lisa reorganize her house. Jess drove to the hardware store to get a new door handle and a deadbolt to install.

Asia put her arm around her shoulder. "What a shame. I sure hope the police find out who did this."

She gave a frustrated nod while she pushed through the chaos.

That evening they sat in the reorganized apartment and ate Chinese food that Jesse had run out to get. Their energy was low, even after eating. It seemed like today they went backwards instead of making headway in decoding the clues.

She excused herself and disappeared into her office. When she returned, she had the contents of the oval photograph safe. Laying the papers on the table, she invited everyone to peruse through them for anything that could help. Her expectations were low that they would find anything of significance.

While everyone else was sorting through old documents, she retrieved the family albums, one in which she'd discovered that Adriana's last name was *Montebelli*. The old photos began to raise their spirits. They laughed at the staunch expressions that the old-timers wore when they had their pictures taken.

"Somehow, they even managed to threaten the smiles off the youngest children, a feat in itself," she said. The floppy hats and *high-water* length pants on the men brought out amusing comments. Soon they had shaken off the defeat of the day.

"Look at this," Taylor almost shouted. He'd been reading each piece of paper he picked up. "This is a receipt dated 1918 for construction, delivery, and placement of a marble tombstone for Elke Van Buren." The rest of the crew strained their necks to see it.

"It's true then," she exclaimed. "Someone besides the Dutchman set that engraved tombstone in place."

"Who else was around at the time," Taylor asked. "Do you have a family tree?" All eyes were on her.

"Not as such. I mean it's not laid out in order, but the information should all be here."

Jesse grabbed a photo album and flipped back to the first page to look for names and dates. "Someone, write this down," he said. "Here's a photograph of Jochem Van Buren and Julia Rutghers Van Buren. His dates of birth and death are 1858 - 1913, and Julia only has a date of death listed as 1906. There's no mention of when they married."

Lisa pointed at the next photo, that of Lowie Van Buren. "I don't remember ever hearing of any children from Lowie."

"This is a picture of a baby, but no information," Jesse continued.

"Take it out—carefully—and look at the back," she teased.

Jesse feigned an injured look as he lifted the photograph out of its protective plastic covering. "Joren Van Buren, born 1878. Now we're getting somewhere." Photo by photo, they went through the albums, recovering dates of births and deaths, leaving behind the other miscellaneous photographs that were not useful at this time.

"Look at this little guy," Jesse said, smiling at the impish look on the child's face. "At least they couldn't keep his smile roped in." The caption at the bottom read, Joren Van Buren II, 1902 - 1906. "He only lived to be four years old," Jesse remarked. "Something about him speaks of life, not death."

Asia leaned over to get a better look at him and then looked at Jesse. She said in amazement, "He looks just like you."

"You're right," Lisa said, comparing one to the other. "Let's see, Joren was my Grandma Klara's little brother. So, he would be my great-uncle and Jesse's great-great uncle."

"It's a little uncanny," Jesse said, recognizing his face in such an old photo.

Once they'd gone through the albums, Jess asked, "Okay, who was alive in 1918?"

Lisa called off names and he wrote them down. "Grandma Klara Van Buren married Emilio Giovanni in 1918, so they both were alive. We know they lived here but were probably too young to manage something like this. Joren's brothers, Pieter and Daan, died earlier.

"Great-Grandmother Adriana, Joren's wife, was alive until 1941, and Joren Van Buren—look at this," Lisa said. "Her husband, Joren, died the year before Elke's tombstone was ordered—1917." A wall of blank faces stared back at her. She realized they hadn't caught what she was getting at. "With everyone else gone, that would make my great-grandmother, Adriana Montebelli Van Buren, the first Guardian. And she's the most likely candidate to have come up with our riddle and the clues on the gravestone."

Silence held the room as minds synchronized the information. Jesse spoke first. "That's cool, Mom, but does it give us any more information for unraveling the clues?"

She racked her brain trying to come up with any information that she had concerning Adriana.

"Her parents died in an avalanche," Taylor volunteered. All heads turned toward him.

Lisa tilted her head in surprise. "How do you know that?"

"Mrs. Varano at the restaurant in Mont Castello told me the story of Costantino Montebelli and his wife. They were leading a group of skiers when an avalanche killed them, leaving Adriana and her sister orphans."

"Then who raised her," Jesse asked.

"Honestly, I can't remember any stories about her at all," Lisa answered, frustrated at her mother's lack of interest in their ancestors.

Suddenly inspired, Taylor suggested, "Then let's take a drive up to Mont Castello tomorrow and ask Mrs. Varano. She's a wealth of knowledge."

She lit up at the idea, excited to share the trip with him. Gazing into his deep brown eyes, she saw he was thinking the same thoughts. She smiled and moved her attention back down the list of relatives.

"Asia and I both have to work tomorrow," Jesse complained. "Be sure and take good notes." They stood and stretched, done with sleuthing for the day.

She had decided to move back into her house tonight, so Asia walked Jesse downstairs where they could say goodnight in private. Jess kissed Lisa goodbye and checked the door lock one more time before he left.

As soon as Jess closed the door, Taylor pulled Lisa to him. Encircling her with his arms, he gazed into her eyes. "I've wanted to do this all day." His mouth found her willing lips and she moaned from the pleasure of feeling consumed by Steven Taylor. Breathless, she pulled her lips away.

"I'm looking forward to tomorrow," he said softly in her ear.

She mumbled a dazed response into his neck, dizzy from the effect he was having on her. Forcing herself, she relinquished his body from her hold around his waist. Asia came through the door just as they dropped their arms, leaving just their fingertips entwined.

"See you tomorrow, then," Lisa said. "I'll pick you up at Dad's, okay?"

"Sounds great." Taylor gave her a soft kiss on the cheek. "Goodnight." He kissed Asia goodbye and left the two women alone.

Asia and Lisa sighed simultaneously, then laughed at themselves behaving like co-eds with crushes.

"It's so good to have you back again," Asia said and gave Lisa an affectionate hug. "I've never seen my dad this happy, honestly."

Lisa hugged her back, sensing the same was true about Jesse.

In her room that night, Lisa prayed with fervency, "Please help us to see what Adriana meant by these clues. Show us the way through this maze."

Chapter 22

The winding road glistened from an early rain as Lisa and Taylor made their way up to Mont Castello the following morning. Energizing blues pulsed from the car speakers in time with the wipers swiping the light spray on the windshield. Taylor's hand covered hers on the center console, warming her fingers, and her emotions. Her heart sang in anticipation of what they might discover.

As they ascended the mountains, the sun peeked through breaks in the cloud cover. The trees and brush dazzled in the beams of light reflecting off their foliage. She wished the drive would take longer and willed the magic of the moment to continue forever.

They arrived early at Varano's long before the restaurant opened. The front door remained locked, but deliverymen were hauling supplies in through the rear kitchen entrance. Taylor was just about to ask for Mrs. Varano, when she flew into the kitchen, chastening one of her workers. When she saw Taylor, her tirade stopped mid-sentence and her countenance brightened into a broad smile.

"Mr. Taylor," she greeted. Then, looking beyond him, she saw Lisa and gave an approving nod. "I see you're not alone this time. This is good that you have your beautiful woman."

Lisa blushed at the inference that she was Taylor's woman yet thrilled at the sound of it.

He introduced them and explained, "We would like to ask you more questions about the Montebelli girls. If you're too busy now, we can come back." He glanced around at all the activity.

"No, no," the signora said. "You come with me in here. I'll sit with you awhile and tell you what I can." They followed Anna Varano to the front of the restaurant and sat down in a comfortable booth in a quiet section of the building. "Now, what are you wanting to know?"

Lisa beamed. "My great-grandmother was Adriana Montebelli. If you can remember anything about her at all, it would be very helpful."

Anna's eyes widened after she understood Lisa's interest. Pausing to let the memories float to the surface of her mind, she revisited her childhood. "My mother was Bella Varano. As a girl, she was like a sister to Adriana, and they stayed close until Adriana's death. Mama used to say it happened too early."

Anna retold her mother's stories of growing up on the mountain, hiking and gathering flowers in the spring, and about the boys who were always flirting with her, but especially with the beautiful Adriana. "Mama liked to talk about her pretty smile and gentle heart. The other girls were jealous, but not Mama. She loved her best friend and was happy when the rich Joren Van Buren asked Adriana to be his wife. But not everyone was happy for Adriana."

The gladness in Anna's tone fell away. "Her younger sister, Ladonna, was a conniving and jealous child. When their parents died, Mama's family took in Adriana, but they had such a large family Grandpapa didn't think he could manage both girls.

"Unfortunately for little Ladonna, another family took her in. It was no wonder she turned out the way she did, living with them. The parents were poor and perhaps too kind." Anna donned a disgusted face. "According to Mama, the Basso youngsters overran them, and oh, the complaining." She stopped her story, catching the surprise on Lisa and Taylor's faces.

"Adriana's sister was raised by the Bassos?" Lisa asked, raising her eyebrows at Taylor.

Anna nodded and resumed her story. "Anyway, Ladonna refused to come to the wedding, but showed up later at the dinner and drank wine until she was sick." At this point, Anna's voice lowered. "This is a private matter. Mama told me alone." She looked from Taylor to Lisa. "That night, when Ladonna was so drunk, Edwardio Basso *took* her." She studied them to make sure they got her meaning.

"Later, she became pregnant, and they were married shortly afterwards. But I assure you, it was no great wedding like her sister had. Adriana wanted to help her struggling sister, but Edwardio took advantage. He encouraged Ladonna to milk money out of her, which he wasted. Once word got back to Adriana, she stopped sending money, but was very sad to know Ladonna suffered in poverty."

Anna frowned. "That was why Adriana's heart broke when Ladonna died after delivering her baby, little Costa Basso. The Basso's despised the Van Burens from that moment on and swore to get even."

Lisa's breath caught. The bad blood between their families started over a century ago. Maybe they raised Angela Basso with this same bitter hatred. That would explain the venom Angela had thrown her way from the first time they met. Lisa was lost in her musings until she realized that Anna had continued with her story.

"Mama used to say Adriana had a sadness that no one could cure, except the Dutchman."

"I'm not following you," Lisa said.

"Adriana lost her father when she was only seven. But when she married Joren, God made it up to her. Joren's father, The Dutchman, loved his daughter-in-law as he had loved his little Elke. When he died, Mama said he left Adriana in charge of the family business. That didn't sit well with her husband, I can tell you, but there was nothing Joren could do except make her life miserable.

"Mama used to say Adriana had the strength of a lion, having to deal with her drunken husband and their frequent battles. Fortunately, he died only four years after his father. The other brothers had already passed, leaving Adriana in complete control of the mine."

Awed, Lisa concentrated on the details and their significance.

"Oh, here's something that could be important." Anna smiled a sly smile. "Mama once made the comment that the brothers accused Adriana of knowing where more opals were hidden and were furious that she would not tell them." Anna appraised her listeners to see if that bit of information helped them get to what they were after. Her eyes darted from Taylor to Lisa and her smile grew as she realized she had struck gold.

Leaning forward, Lisa asked, "Did Adriana ever tell your mother that it was true or where they might be hidden?"

Anna thought for a few moments and her old eyes sparkled. "It seems she was having a new tombstone made for Elke Van Buren's grave. When Mama asked why, Adriana said it contained a family secret to provide for her family."

"Was there any mention of a *portal* or secret door into the cave?" Taylor asked, getting more specific.

"Hmm, no mention of a door, but she did mention a key that was part of the secret of Elke's new tomb. Maybe the stones are in the tomb, and you need a key to get them out."

"That's a good idea, but we have other clues that conflict with that," Lisa said.

The restaurant was starting to get busy as they neared the lunch hour and Mrs. Varano indicated she needed to manage the chores that still needed to be done.

"Thank you so much for sharing with me about my family, Anna," Lisa said. They said goodbye and she and Taylor walked down the steps of the restaurant with wide grins.

"I don't know how much information we got that will help us with the clues," he said, "but what a wealth of family history."

Lisa twirled around with excitement. She had taken notes as Anna recalled the story. "I want to get home and align all of this new information with the dates we have."

He took her hand, and they walked back to the car. "It's great to see you so alive again. It reminds me of how energetic you were when Asia revealed the mockup of the downtown area. You were like a kid on a Ferris wheel."

She smiled at the memory. "Being surrounded by loving people makes all the difference—and having an appetite to help me get back into my clothes.

He stoked the skin under her eye with his thumb. "There's no trace of dark circles or worry anymore." He breathed in the fresh mountain air. "Do you want to take a hike before we go back down?"

How does he know me so well? She gazed up at him. "That's just what I was thinking."

They headed for the path that made its way up the mountain. The ground was wet, but the path consisted of decomposed granite, creating a solid base. Their breathing grew harder with the increased exertion as they climbed up the slope of Mt. Thurman. Between the large fir trees, the road curved around a bend where they came upon the marker listing the names of the early climbers.

They stopped and she read the names, nearly dancing off the mountain. "These are *my* relatives," she shouted. "I've lived in the valley all these years and never knew this was here. When did you find it?" She wanted to know everything he had discovered. He described the story Anna told him about the climbers and the disaster that befell them, and what he learned from the museum in Bella Vista. She wanted to go there at once.

"Not so fast," he grinned and spun her around so she could take in the view that had greeted him on his first climb up here.

Her breath caught at the magnificence of the panorama that surrounded her. "Oh Taylor," she said, and fell silent. Standing behind her, he held her in his arms. She laid her head back against his chest and felt his heart quicken.

"I love you," he whispered in her ear.

A thrill filled her soul. Linking her hands in his, she said, "And I love you." She turned around and tipped her face up to meet his eyes. His mouth met hers as he gathered her close for a long moment. When they drew apart, it felt as though they had always been together.

Holding hands and laughing, they bounded down the mountain. Hunger pangs let them know it was past lunchtime, so they ordered lunch before going back down to the valley. Across from her, his gleaming eyes filled with adoration, drenching her parched heart.

"Lisa, we know how we feel about each other and we're old enough to know the difference between love and infatuation."

She nodded, smiling at what she hoped he was getting to.

His expression thoughtful, he said, "I know this is soon, but I want you to be my wife and partner in this life. We don't have to set a date right now, but I want to know we are going in that direction."

She knew she could count on his commitment. She also knew her heart had already committed itself. "On the drive up, I thought maybe it was too soon to consider a new relationship. But when my first thought went to what people will think, it clued me in I was falling back into my old pattern. I don't want to waste any more years alone and miserable. Yes, I want to marry you, more than anything else in the world."

At ease now, and with great elation, Taylor called for the waitress and ordered two glasses of champagne. He lifted his glass. "To the woman I love today and will love until the day I die." Their eyes linked, flooding her with joy.

On the drive back, he asked, "When do you want to tell the kids?"

She was wondering the same thing, thinking she should explain to Jesse first. "I think..." Her cell phone interrupted her reply. She shrugged her shoulders at him and answered the call. It was Jesse, so she put it on speaker.

"Hi Mom. Did you guys learn anything that will help us find the opals?"

"We got a lot of great information that may help, but tonight we need to sit down with the family tree and piece it together. Can you come to my house after work?"

"I can get off early if I really push it, but that still won't get me there until about seven-thirty." He sounded dejected. "You guys will have it all worked out by then."

"We'll wait for you. We have other plans that will keep us busy until then." Jesse was quiet on the other end. "Jesse?"

"What plans?" Jesse's voice sounded strained.

Taylor and Lisa looked at each other. "We're on our way to the museum to check out a couple of leads that Mrs. Varano gave us, then we're going to call Dad and see if he wants to get some dinner."

Relief lifted Jesse's tone. "That's a great idea. If you get back to your apartment before me, tell Grandpa to save me some clues." He hung up and Lisa glanced at Taylor.

"It's too fast for him," he beat her to the point. He shrugged, looking disappointed.

"I'm sorry," she said, bringing the back of his hand to her lips. "Let's give him more time to get used to the idea. I know he likes you."

He took her chin between his thumb and forefinger and gave it a squeeze. "There's no rush. We have a lifetime."

***

Taylor swung his car into a parking place in front of the museum and opened the door for her. She drank in the love from his breathtaking eyes as she took his hand. They entered the building, and he stuffed some folded bills into the box.

Stan Harding nodded, then took a closer look at her. He must have recognized her from the newspaper photos. "Hello, Mrs. Richards," he said as she neared his desk. His eyes moved to Taylor, then back to her. He seemed to be forming an opinion. "You were in here a while ago," he stated to Taylor.

"Yes, I was," Taylor said. "You were very knowledgeable, and we were hoping you could be of assistance again."

Stan eyed Lisa. "Frank Harding is my son. I was real proud of him helping to oust that crooked mayor in Tangle Grove." He paused and smiled. "He speaks very highly of you. I'd be happy to help in whatever way I can."

"Thank you, Mr. Harding." Lisa liked Stan's earnest face. "Would the museum have any record of two stonemasons, one with the initials P.C. who lived around 1903, and one with E.C. in 1918?"

"I recognize the second one, Emilio Costini. He carved many of the headstones and some of the more impressive crypts in the Southpark Cemetery. No recollection offhand of the other fella, though." He scratched the stubble on his chin. "Now let's see, where could I find that?"

He led them across the uneven wooden planks that served as the floor in the antiquated building and stopped in front of a file cabinet that held copies of birth records. "Let's see," he said as he looked through the *Cs*. "Good, *Costini*. Emilio Costini, born 1898, died 1943. Parents were...Pablo Costini and Gabriella Lombardi. Looks like they could be father and son," he declared with a smug expression.

"That makes sense," she said. "It's likely that Pablo would have taught his trade to Emilio. Are there old papers stored here, like receipts, letters, that sort of thing?"

"Well, let's go look at the photo albums," Stan said. He made his way to another corner of the building where he and Taylor had searched through the Van Buren family photos. Taking down a leather album, he laid it with care on the large wooden table. After examining the list of family names, he turned to a section near the end and stuck his finger on a photo of the Costini family. With great relish, he looked up at them. "There they are."

They wedged closer together to see the large family of Pablo Costini. A typed name identified Emilio. Lisa noted he was built like his father, short in stature and brawny, with massive forearms. The casual picture showed the boys in their undershirts, muscled and olive-skinned, smiling widely. *Unusual for those days.* Flipping the pages, they studied the rest of the photos and names.

Stan turned to the back of the leather album. "There are miscellaneous letters and such in the backs of these." Sure enough, at the end of the photos, someone had preserved old memorabilia under the plastic sleeves. Stan left them to browse and went back to his perch to finish his crossword puzzle.

They sat down on old, hard stools and continued to search for anything that might provide useful information. Passing up the sentimental pages of collected letters and cards, they came to handwritten bills and receipts. Among them were orders for headstones and plaques for the Costini men.

"This is it," Taylor pointed. Her eyes swept over the paper. It was the order for Elke's marble tombstone but was barely legible. He wasted no time asking Stan, "Do you have a magnifying glass?"

Stan lifted his head. "You'll find one there in that drawer in front of you."

Taylor pulled out a large, yellowed glass and buffed it. When he positioned it over the order, they could read the date, November 16, 1917. The dimensions were listed, along with a note that the engraving must be done *exactly* as the attached drawing represented. Lisa scrutinized the page. There it was. The original hand drawing for Elke's gravestone.

"Can we make a copy of a couple of these pages?" Taylor asked.

Stan held a self-satisfied look as he pointed to the newer-model copy machine that seemed to clash with the surrounding paraphernalia. "Let me take it out," he instructed Taylor, who set the leather album down at the front desk. With extreme care, Stan took out the order and the drawing and lifted his eyebrows in surprise. "Hadn't seen that before." When he finished, he returned the pages to their homes and handed the copies to Lisa.

Not finding anything else that added to the information they needed, they thanked Stan and left. "Let's grab a cup of coffee and look these over," she suggested, and they headed for a café close by.

As Taylor opened the coffee shop door, Angela Basso stepped out, looking back over her shoulder into the cafe´. "Call me tomorrow, Ernesta," she commanded to someone inside. Angela shifted her focus forward and caught sight of Lisa with Taylor. A cryptic glare took possession of her face and hatred spit from her eyes. It was obvious she wanted to rail against Lisa, but Taylor's presence seemed to dissuade her. Instead, she took a quick, uncomfortable glance back into the café, then pushed past them without speaking.

"That was strange," Lisa said, glad there hadn't been a confrontation. Inside, they placed their order and sat down. The server brought their coffee, and they began to discuss the pieces of information they'd gathered.

Feeling an odd sensation, she stole a glance across the room. She encountered two eyes peering from small slits housed in a wrinkle-worn face of an old woman. They glared at her before darting away, but the vicious look that accompanied the stare remained etched on the crone's face.

Lisa shuddered and Taylor followed her nervous eyes across the room. He grabbed her icy hands. "Do you know her?"

"I've never seen her before, but she looks like the embodiment of evil." She shivered.

The old woman got up to leave and shuffled with a jerking motion toward the door. What could have been an old tapestry tablecloth with a hole for her head, draped over her heavy rolls. It hung at an angle, partially obscuring the faded and wrinkled skirt that covered the remainder of her bulk. Her white hair had thinned to baldness in spots and the rest tangled out of a bun that looked as if it had been put in place years ago. As she passed closer to their table, a stench reached their noses. She paused and glowered at them, sending chills down Lisa's spine, then pushed through the door.

Taylor studied Lisa with a quizzical expression. "I'd certainly like to know what that was all about."

"Not me," she answered. "I hope I never see that person again." They finished their coffee in silence. Once outside, she shook off the encounter. "I'm really looking forward to tonight," she said, hoping for a breakthrough when they met with the others.

***

When they assembled at Lisa's apartment that evening, the five of them sat at the dining room table and sifted through the documents in front of them.

"You guys uncovered some interesting stuff," Jesse said to Lisa and Taylor, while adding each ancestor to the family tree.

She nodded while examining the papers she'd retrieved from her safe with Taylor.

"Interesting," Taylor said. "These are instructions for the engraver to create a place where an instrument of some kind could be fitted into the slab of marble. It is dated 1917. Does anyone remember anything about an object that sticks out of Elke's gravestone?"

They all shook their heads. He took out the copy they made at the museum and placed it in the center of the table. Next to it, he placed the enlarged copies of the gravestone that Asia made of Taylor's cell phone photos. They were a perfect match, even revealing the small hole recessed into the top right-hand side of the marble slab.

Scouring the photograph, Jesse pointed to the small notch. "We always assumed that was for flowers." He chewed his lip. "Why is it there?"

Taylor took a guess. "If everything on this tomb was a tool to help the Guardian find the opals, then let's assume the hole is necessary to solve this puzzle." He stood a paperclip upright on the drawing of the top of Elke's gravestone where the hole was indicated. Then he took a pen and laid one end on top of the paper clip. He set the other end of the pen down on the drawing at the bottom edge of the gravestone. Following the angle of the pen, they could tell the line of sight would appear much lower on the horizon at the actual grave.

Taylor re-examined the drawing of the compass. "Look at this. The only place on the engraved compass where the radiating lines actually *cross* are at this one intersection. All the other engraved lines stop before they cross and pick up again on the other side of the line." He moved the lower end of the pen and aligned it with that one radiating line of the compass.

"Lift up your eyes *at* the cross." Lisa repeated the rhyme with more accuracy. "Not *to* the cross, like I'd supposed. Taylor's pen represents the exact position we need to be in to see the *glint* above the ivy." She grabbed his face in her hands. "You are brilliant."

"But that only gives us one point to determine the angle," Jess corrected. "How tall is the object represented by the paperclip?"

A determined frown knit Jesse's brows together as he drew imaginary lines at several possible angles. "There's no telling which is the correct angle. We need to find what went into that hole to get the exact line to follow." The others agreed but were stumped.

Lisa remembered something Anna Varano told her. She read the notes from the morning and ran across the reference to a *key* that Adriana told Anna's mother was a clue for unlocking the secret. At the time, Lisa thought that meant the rhyme—the rhyme was the key—but now she was not so sure. "Would your key to the mine fit into that hole, Jesse?"

Jesse's head swung back to the hole in the photo. "The size would certainly be close. I'll be right back," he shouted, and headed back to his apartment to retrieve the key. The others stood and stretched, taking a break from sitting and thinking. Asia suggested they go for a walk and the rest of the crew took her up on it.

The evening was cool but dry as they turned up toward the courthouse. A bulldozer waited its turn on the job and Lisa envisioned the new building with great satisfaction. This project was safe, but what about her cherished mountain? Would the cave become a place for the public to vandalize and litter? She'd looked forward to taking her grandchildren exploring one day and explaining their inheritance.

She bit her lip. The days were counting down. Soon, she would be required to hand over the keys, eliminating her family's private access to the Dutchman's mine. Her stomach knotted at the thought. This happened on her watch. Her lips pressed together with her increased determination to break this code.

They had turned around and were coming down the far side of the street, when Jesse's truck sped toward them and screeched to a halt. He swung the door open and jumped out. "Someone stole my key! They ransacked my apartment and found it," he sputtered in complete frustration.

Lisa's mouth hung open. Taylor ran to Jesse's truck. "Did you call the police yet?"

"They should be here in a few minutes. I couldn't get hold of you guys, so I drove over, but I need to get back."

Fully frustrated, Lisa said, "Taylor, why don't you and Asia go in the truck with him. Dad and I will get my purse and keys."

***

Jesse Richard's apartment, the young man sat waiting in his truck when Detective Madden's squad car arrived.

"Hi Jesse. I intercepted your call and requested the assignment. This is my partner, Hank Reynolds. This additional crime is compiling into quite a case that's gone on too long.

"Way too long," Jesse fumed.

Madden and Reynolds searched Jesse's room and the yard for evidence. This time they got lucky. "Over here," Reynolds called out. Clear footprints showed below a window on the back side of the house. Muddy scuffs revealed the struggle it took to scale up and over the high window ledge. The lock looked like it had been of no use for decades. "This is how they got in," Reynolds said.

"Good work, get the prints," Madden said, sounding encouraged.

Jesse joined his mom and everyone in front of the house under the porch light.

Madden walked around the building and addressed them. "If you could guess what this is all about, what would you tell me?" He looked from one to another.

Lisa answered, "It's apparent now, that they were looking for the key to the mine. Fire Mountain is due to be absorbed into the city limits, but—and please keep this confidential—there is a stipulation. If we can prove that it's still producing, we can keep it as an open mining claim. If not, the mountain becomes public property. Apparently, someone wanted Jesse's key to get into the mine before either happens."

Jesse growled. "We should go up there and see who tries to open the door with my key."

"That's a good idea, but I think it would be wiser for *us* to post someone there." Madden turned to Hank who came back with the footprint and set it in the police car. Continuing his line of questioning, Madden asked, "Who would you think is the most likely person or people to want to get into the mine?"

"Angela Basso," they said in unison.

"I guess that's a logical place to start then," he said and flipped back to the names Lisa gave him during the first investigation. The footprint they'd found could belong to a small man or a woman. Is this the only key you have?" he asked.

Jesse watched a curious expression flick across his mother's face. A glance at Taylor revealed he'd also seen it. He answered Madden, "My two cousins have keys too. In fact, I better call them right now." He dialed Dan's number. After listening for a moment, he said, "I can't understand you." Whatever Dan said made Jessie's eyebrows raised in surprise. He set his phone on speaker.

Madden listened closely as a man huffed to catch his breath and said, "...caught two guys...trying to steal my...key."

Jesse's eyes widened, as did the rest. "Do you have them? Have you called the police? Do you know who they are?" Jesse was throwing questions at him faster than he could answer.

Dan gasped in spurts, "Yeah, I've got 'em right here. No, I haven't had time, and yes, they're a couple of the Basso guys."

"The police are here," Jesse said. "I'll send them right over. Are you sure you can hold them?"

"Oh, yeah," Dan assured. "Two of my friends are here so they're not going anywhere."

The detectives took Jesse with them in the patrol car and sped to Dan's home with lights and sirens blazing.

***

"Looks like we'll have an end to this part of the mystery very soon," Taylor said.

Lisa gritted her teeth, looking miserable. "I wanted to have Jesse's key to fit in the marble tomorrow. If the police need to keep it as evidence, it will be long after October twenty-first before we get it back."

"Perhaps Dan will still have his key and you can use *it*," he suggested.

She rubbed her furrowed eyebrows. "He'll want to know why and then everyone will know what we're up to. The mine will be open to the whole family, and they'll exhaust the emergency cache." Her voice trailed off.

"What is it, Lisa?" Taylor asked, seeing the conflict on her face.

"I'm not ready to say more right now."

He flinched.

"I'm sorry," her eyes pleaded for understanding. "It has to do with my duties as the Guardian and I think I've given away too much knowledge already." He looked away and shook his head.

They left Jesse's apartment, opting not to drive to Dan's house. Asia and Lisa were already at the car, while Taylor paced his stride to match Jess' slower gait. He glanced sideways at the older man and confessed, "I think I know some of what Thomas felt like when he was left out in the cold on issues dealing with Lisa's family." He wondered if Jess had any of the same frustration when his wife was the Guardian.

Catching Taylor's eye, Jess answered, "It's really not an issue if you choose not to make it one. Heck, you know more about the family business than I did in fifty-nine years of marriage." He grinned.

Releasing his breath, Taylor knew he was right. Lisa was bound by her sworn agreement to the family and had already revealed much more than she was comfortable with. It wouldn't do to push her to go against her own integrity. He clapped Jess on the shoulder. "Thanks. It does help to keep things in perspective."

Lisa relayed Jesse's message as Taylor approached the car. "Detective Madden has the two Basso brothers in custody. Jesse's going to hang out with Dan for a while and will see us in the morning."

Back at Lisa's, Taylor left Jess in the SUV while he went upstairs to say goodnight. Asia closed the door to the guest room to get ready for bed.

"Come here," Taylor said and opened his arms.

Lisa moved next to him, laying her head on his chest. "I'm so tired of all this drama."

He rubbed her neck. "I know, but it's almost over. The police will put a stop to the attacks on you and they'll probably be able to trace them back to Angela." Pushing her hair back from her face, he checked to see if she would respond to that happy thought.

She offered a wicked smile. "Imagine how good that will feel, seeing Angela get what is coming to her." But frustration instantly replaced the sense of indignation. "When you figure how much of this grudge was passed down through the generations, it makes it a pretty sad situation. Look at all the damage that's been done because of the wealth of the mountain and the jealousies surrounding it." She caught his eyes. "If it wasn't for the need to prove the mine was still active, I would rather keep the opals where they are forever."

He nodded. "There's a good chance you're a lot like Adriana. She saw all the damage the wealth and waste had caused and hoped to limit it in the future. Maybe that's why she made it so difficult to get to the stash of opals. It would take perseverance as well as the key."

At the word *key*, Lisa started. "I believe Adriana was talking about a real key, not the rhyme as a key. We've got to get Jesse to bring Dan's back." She called Jesse but only succeeded in leaving a message for him.

"It will still be there tomorrow," he kissed her forehead. With her eyes, she asked for more. He moved warm kisses down her face, connecting with her eager lips. Too soon, he had to bring their closeness to an end. Her father was waiting for a ride home. They both sighed, causing a spontaneous chuckle.

"Good night," she said, still holding his hands.

"See you tomorrow, Sweetheart," he answered, and pushed out the door.

Chapter 23

Would today be the day? The morning was bright, and Lisa chatted with Asia while they headed down the stairs to meet the rest of the group. Jesse had reported that Dan gave him his key without a question. She couldn't hold back her smile at the eagerness she sensed.

Everyone jumped into Jesse's truck and headed off to Sweet Elke Park. Sitting comfortably next to Taylor, she felt grateful that neither she nor Jesse had any misgivings about going to the park now. They had faced that demon and were anxious to conquer the next—the secret that Adriana Montebelli hid on Elke's grave.

They loaded the rifles and all but ran to the site. Jesse went to the far side of the crypt, and she tried to set the key into the hole on top of the marble. Disappointment was tangible when there was no way the large key would fit.

"Just hold it there for a moment, Mom," Jesse instructed while he looked down the line that *crossed* on the engraved compass. Looking past the key, the line of sight brought him closer to their mark. "It points to a rocky outcrop, but it's a large area. We could look for months over that pile of rocks and never find it. It's got to be more exact than this," he grumbled.

"Are all the keys the same size?" Asia asked.

"Yes," Jesse answered.

Lisa hid her furtive eyes and said, "There must be more clues in the documents at home." Heaving a huge sigh of disappointment, Jesse picked up his jacket and they began the trek back to the car. A war raged in Lisa's mind. Almost to herself, she said, "Even if the key fit, we still don't know what the *ivy* is, so it wouldn't do us any good to have it."

"But maybe we would have noticed something else if the key had fit," Jesse argued. "You know, one clue leading to another."

She shrugged heavy shoulders, her mind running over all the possibilities. Deep in thought, she meandered down the grassy path along the stream.

Without warning, the ground pounded under her feet. The hair on her arms stood up. She turned. *The cougar!* Her heart stopped.

A gunshot blasted. She screamed and grabbed her ears, dropping to her knees. To her right, her father stood stock still, rifle raised and braced against his shoulder, his attention focused on the huge cougar that lay close to the place they had been standing only moments ago.

Asia had also shrieked and now rushed to Lisa, her face filled with terror. Lisa held the frightened girl and tried to recover from the shock.

Jesse, Taylor, and Jess ran to the animal, guns at the ready. Jesse called back after examining the cat. "He's dead." He hugged his grandfather, "Great shot!" The older man filled his chest with the air he'd forgotten to breathe. Taylor also congratulated him.

"I heard something and looked behind us," Jess said. "He was bounding—I'm telling you—bounding after us. I had no time to think, just swung my gun around, caught him in my scope, and pulled the trigger. Lucky shot, that's all I can think of." Jess' hands trembled as he recounted the moment. It could have gone in another direction.

Lisa ran the distance to her father, sobbing with fear and relief, reliving the danger she had faced. "Thank you, Daddy," she said, throwing her arms around his stocky shoulders and allowing him to comfort her in his protective embrace. She held his hand as they walked with an unsteady pace back to the truck.

Jesse called in the shooting to the police department to let them know the cougar was dead. "They're sending someone to pick up the animal." He swallowed and caught Lisa's eyes. "Forensics testing will show if this was the one that killed Dad."

They drove back to Lisa's apartment for a somber lunch and rifled through the family photos again. Picking up a formal photo of Adriana as an older woman, Jesse remarked that he hadn't noticed she held a key in her hands, along with the small bouquet of flowers. "It looks similar to ours but has a more intricate design."

Lisa's head jerked around from the kitchen. "Let me see," she demanded. Her abruptness brought surprised stares. She caught herself and offered a quick apology.

Getting out the magnifying glass, Jesse tried to read the engraving on the key. "It looks like numbers. I can make out a six and a four but can't quite get all the numbers." He stopped and squinted.

Taylor caught Lisa's eye and waited. Giving up, she relaxed the tension in her shoulders and let out a sigh. "It's the Dutchman's birthday, 6-4-1858."

Jesse looked at her, awestruck. "How do you know that?"

"Because I have the key. I was hoping it wouldn't be necessary to reveal *everything* I know as the Guardian, but it's obvious we need that key as well." She disappeared into her room and came out carrying the Dutchman's own brass key.

Jesse's hands were reverent as he examined the century-old relic that had belonged to his great-great-great-grandfather. "It's just a bit smaller than mine. I bet it'll fit perfectly in the niche in Elke's tomb."

Taylor peeked at it. "Look at the intricate hole cut through the key over the numbers of Jochem's birth date. It looks like it was drilled after the original key was fashioned."

"But even with the key," Lisa complained, "we don't know what the *ivy* is, so we still don't know where to look. It could be anywhere on that rocky outcrop."

Asia was absently drawing on her notes while the rest struggled to make sense out of the clues. Taylor watched her as she accented and stylized the lines in the word *ivy*.

"It can't be," he exclaimed. All heads jerked to attention. "The *ivy* isn't the plant—it's the number *four* in Roman numerals—IV."

They looked at the detail of the key. The hole sat precisely over the *four* in the birth date. Jesse let out a whoop. He grabbed Asia and they danced around the room like crazies. Giving each other high-fives, Jesse was ready to be out the door, but Lisa stopped him.

"Let's wait until we're sure the police have been and gone with the cat. I don't want them watching us at Elke's grave. Jesse pulled at his hair in mock frustration.

"Besides, the time isn't right until the day of Elke's birthday," Jess added.

Jesse threw himself on the sofa and heaved a great sigh. Asia sat down next to him, picking up his hand and kissing it. "You're almost there."

Lisa smiled as she watched them. Jesse pulled Asia over and kissed her lightly on the lips. "Thank you. You make the waiting tolerable."

While delayed in their search, Lisa sorted through the papers strewn over her dining room table. "Look at this. Here's a handwritten copy of the poem and the initials *A.V.* That has to be *Adriana Van Buren.* The Dutchman was already dead, so she has to be the one who created the clues. Adriana's getting more interesting all the time."

Taylor came over to look at it. "I can see why you would think that," he laughed. "You're both very creative."

She kissed him on the cheek. "Thank you for the compliment." Then, catching the deepening fire in his eyes, she allowed her gaze to linger, letting the excitement of their longing invade her with delight. While the rest were engaged in a conversation about the thieves, Taylor tilted his head and Lisa followed him through the dining room and into the kitchen.

Quietly, they embraced. He nuzzled her ear and she chuckled silently and pulled away. "I knew you were trouble," she said. He lifted a rogue eyebrow and reached for a glass to get some water.

"Do you want some ice," she asked, turning to the frig.

"Sure," he said and kissed the back of the neck, sending chills down her spine that had nothing to do with the ice filling the glass.

"How long do you think we have to wait here?" Jesse called from the living room.

She shrugged at Taylor and answered. "Why don't you call Detective Madden and ask him if they've got the cougar," she suggested. "Does anyone want something to eat or drink?"

"Not unless you have some cookies," Jess said. She got out a plate and arranged some packaged cookies on it. Taylor sat back down at the dining room table and focused on the photos lying there.

"We're good to go," Jesse yelled, sticking his phone in his pocket. He made for the door, eliciting a round of laughter. They drove to the park where he rushed to the gravesite, taking a rifle just in case the cat had a family member nearby. She followed, carrying her key. "Come on, Mom," he shouted.

Breathless from running after her son, she tried the key. It slid with precision into the notch on the top of the grave. Jesse stood on the far side of the crypt. He aligned his sight with the *cross* of the two lines on the engraved compass, then looked up through the hole in the key above the *4* of the Dutchman's birthday. It pinpointed a spot on the distant outcrop. "We've got it!" he shouted. The rest of them lined up to see it. "Let's mark it and get up there."

Taylor looked through binoculars to see if anything was visible, but nothing was obvious. "It won't do any good to scramble up there today. If it's as simple as looking through the hole, then we didn't need the part of the rhyme about the *glint*, the time of day, or Elke's birthday."

Shading his eyes, he checked the position of the sun. "I think that at a precise moment, the sun will hit something up there. It will cause a reflection that can be seen by looking through the key at a certain angle." He held his hands and demonstrated the process.

Jess came around to see what he was talking about. "We might not have to wait until her birthday if we could use astronomical charts to tell us where the sun's going to be in eight days."

Excited, Lisa nodded. "That's easy to check. All we have to know is how many degrees the sun is going to move and wait a little past noon until it simulates its position on October twenty-first. We can at least get close."

"I'm taking off work next week," Jesse stated. "This is too important, and I can't keep my mind on my job anyway."

The sun sat low as they made their way back to the truck. A feeling of hopefulness floated between them. Very soon, they hoped to solve the mystery and find the location of a very rich vein of opals.

Chapter 24

An indecent amount of activity occupied each member of the quest the next day. Lisa blew out an impatient huff. Things seemed stuck in molasses.

Jesse telephoned his frustration to her. "I've spent hours waiting at the sheriff's office to identify my stolen key. Then Dan had to identify the thieves in a line up. It was Adam and Stephen Basso who broke into Dan's house and the police think they can link them to the break-in at your house too."

She had already spoken with Detective Madden, who'd finished his report regarding his interview with Angela Basso and her brothers. He indicated it was obvious to him that she had instigated her brothers to steal the key and was leaving them on their own. He felt it was just a matter of time before they broke down and accused her.

After breakfast, Asia left to meet with the construction engineers and oversee the foundation layout of the new courthouse.

Putting away the last of the morning dishes, she sighed her impatience. Taylor was busy consulting with a professor at the local university regarding the sun's movement over the next week. He mentioned he had other business to handle and wouldn't be available until evening. She couldn't think what would occupy him for hours at a time and was disconcerted at his evasion when she tried to pin him down.

The only thing left for her to do was go back through the information they had collected to make sure they hadn't missed anything before their trek back to Elke's grave tomorrow.

***

Coming together for another attempt the following morning, Lisa asked Taylor to keep his rifle close by. They arrived at the gravesite, armed with the key, the poem, and an adjusted timetable. Jess and Asia stayed behind with binoculars and a walkie-talkie, while Lisa led Taylor and Jesse up the trail and along a ledge. Thirty minutes later, Lisa said, "Okay, we're here."

"Jess says to go back a few feet," Asia relayed.

"Are you certain about that?" Taylor called back to Asia.

"Yes. He says Jesse is standing right in front of the exact spot."

Jesse searched the rock behind him. "I don't see anything."

"We're still early," Taylor said.

Lisa shaded her eyes with her hand and looked up at the sky. They had another fifteen minutes until the sun would simulate where it would be at noon on Elke's birthday. She said into the speaker, "We don't see anything unusual here, so we're waiting to see what happens at the right time. Keep your eyes out for anything that might be the *glint*." She laughed at the sound of it. They were so hopeful today. It seemed like nothing could get in their way again.

Checking his watch, Taylor said, "Okay, here it comes." He counted down from ten. They scanned the face of the outcrop, hoping to find a reflection that would give them the clue to where they were supposed to look.

Horrified, Jesse shouted, "There's no way the sun can bounce off of this ledge—it's behind it." Sure enough, the face of the ledge was in the shadow. "Now what?" he slammed his palm on the rock face.

"We may have to wait until Elke's birthday to find out," Lisa said, also frustrated.

Taylor followed the angle of the sun's rays that shown back toward Jess and Asia. "Look!" The sun hit a small, embedded piece of metal on a large uneven rock that rose up below them and five feet back toward the grave. It reflected a strong ray of light.

"We've got a glint!" Asia's voice shouted over the speaker. "It's amazing—look below you, about three feet."

Jesse and Taylor hung over the ledge they were standing on. "It's here!"

"We found it!" Lisa screamed into her speaker. She laid down and stared at a second small metal plate. Shaped like the one on Elke's grave, it had been fixed into the rock wall under the ledge.

Taylor examined the area. "This wouldn't be invisible from below because of that sharp rock that shoots up in front of it. That low point between two of the *teeth* of the rock would only allow the sunlight to reflect off of the metal at exactly noon on Elke's birthday."

The ledge on which the threesome stood hung out and over the metal plate, obscuring it from above. They let themselves down over the edge and discovered a flat area to stand on between the mountain and the jagged rock. Before them was a small door with a rounded top—just like the one engraved on the tomb. Jesse didn't hesitate. He inserted the Dutchman's key into the lock. It clicked, and the door opened.

Lisa kept Jess and Asia informed of their progress. "Jesse just shimmied through the opening. Taylor's holding the rope, but it doesn't look like it's necessary. I can see Jesse. He's climbed down about eight feet and is standing on solid ground." She and Taylor craned their heads into the hole and gasped at the large cavern.

"He's shining his flashlight around. Oh Daddy, wait till you see this!" She felt ecstatic. "The deposit is HUGE. Many of the opals are already exposed. They're the most beautiful reds and oranges and a rainbow of other colors. It must go for twelve feet—no, Jesse says it's farther than that. What are we going to do with all of these?"

She and Taylor followed the illumination of Jesse's flashlight. Fantastic colored lights infused the scene and danced within the cavern, disappearing into the blackness at the back of the cave.

For a split second, a familiar shudder jolted her. "Lowie's ghost—just like in the main cave." She pulled her head outside into the light and the dread left. Taylor followed her movements and acknowledged the same sensation. She set her jaw, unwilling to give in to fear. Instantly, she was back down on her belly, craning to see inside again.

Jesse took out the rock pick he carried with him and broke off a good-sized chunk of the brilliant rock. He climbed out of the hole, and they sat down together, gaping at the fire coming off the exposed sections of the opal egg.

Lisa was the first to speak. "Here's what needs to be done and I'll need all of you in on it." She looked at the two men. "Jesse, as the

Guardian, I have to ask you to keep this a solemn secret from the rest of the family. I know it's not fair, but it's necessary to protect this cache from being depleted."

"How do you plan to do that when we have to bring this back to town to prove we are still mining opals?" he asked.

"The location where we found the stones doesn't matter, as long as they were in Fire Mountain. We're going to take enough of these raw rocks down and plant them where you and I were digging the other day so family members can find some on their own. It's obvious that these are freshly mined, so the authorities won't have any qualms about this being a viable mine, and we can keep control of the mountain." Her voice was even and calculating.

"Are you sure it's okay for all of us to take some of these, Mom? What about the *emergency* clause?"

"I thought about that, but in this circumstance, I think allowing a few stones to be found will fit the criteria of my commitment. Besides," she looked back into the hole, "there's enough down there for many generations to come."

Standing on the mountain, she lifted her head skyward and shouted, "Thank you." They'd found the vibrant gems that would allow them to keep the real treasure—the mountain her ancestors had purchased, worked, and passed on to them for safekeeping.

Jesse scurried back down, chipped off more of the opal-bearing rocks and stuffed them into his backpack. He handed it up to Taylor who exchanged packs with him. He filled the second backpack and Lisa stuffed more into Taylor and Jesse's jackets. Then they trudged back down the mountain with their heavy loads.

Jesse was overjoyed to show Asia his stash, promising her the most beautiful stone of his find.

Searching the faces around her, Lisa delighted in the exuberance that had replaced what seemed like ages of grief. They packed up their tools and drove the short distance to the mine. She opened the door with her key and took them to the tunnel where she and Jesse had been digging. Jess helped Jesse and Taylor carry in the load. They placed the raw opals far back in a good-sized hole they had chipped out, stuffing rocks and clay in front of them. "Okay, it's done," she said.

Outside, Jesse held up several chunks of opals to the light. "I'll keep the best specimens to present as proof."

"Good. Get them back to town," Lisa said. "Then I'll call the newspaper and give them the story. In the meantime, Jesse, I'd like you to call your cousins to let them know they might want to do some treasure hunting." She grinned. "After they've dug for a while, you might point them in the right direction."

Jesse laughed with her. Her Grandma Klara had talked about this game the family played whenever anyone found a new vein, sending one-another on wild goose chases. However, this was the first time Lisa and Jesse's generations would be able to play.

***

After Lisa had called the newspaper, she called her attorney, who was happy to handle his side of the issue. When questioned by the reporter later, she was able to confirm that Fire Mountain was safely back in the hands of its guardians, the Van Burens.

The story appeared on the front page. She smiled and pushed back her leather chair. It had all worked out. Jesse and his cousins were in town today, displaying the fine opals they *found* to the curious onlookers in Bella Vista.

Jesse phoned and said, "Angela Basso passed by and just smiled. I thought she'd be incensed."

A few days later, Lisa learned why. She opened a letter from an attorney working for Angela and Ernesta Basso. He stated that Ernesta was Adriana Montebelli Van Buren's great-niece. She was claiming a right to mine opals as a legitimate blood relative of Adriana's sister, Ladonna Montebelli Basso.

"What's this?" she fumed. She stomped into the dining room where she'd stacked the notes they'd compiled while researching their family history. Moving to the interview with Anna Varano, she read her notations. Ladonna Montebelli had a son, Costa Basso. The attorney's letter was saying that Costa had a daughter, Ernesta Basso, born in 1927 in Mont Castello, where she still lived.

Lisa's mouth dropped open. *Ernesta was the old lady in the coffee shop.* She thought about calling her attorney but was tired of the hassles. She had the spiteful thought of just opening the cave to the eighty-year-old woman and Angela and letting them claw around with picks in the dirt, knowing that the opals had all been extracted. She almost called Jesse to get his opinion but called Angela's attorney instead.

"This is Lisa Richards. I understand you are representing Ernesta Basso in her attempt to mine opals in the Dutchman mine. As the Trustee of the Van Buren Family Trust, I can assure you that, outside of blood relatives of the Dutchman himself, I am within my legal rights to prohibit anyone from entering the mine."

"I'm sorry to have bothered you, Mrs. Richards," the attorney said. "It's a moot point at this time. Ernesta died the day after I sent the letter to you. It's my understanding that Angela Basso is not in the same Basso bloodline as Ernesta, and I have counseled her that she has no legal right to Ernesta's property."

***

The following week, Lisa invited everyone to dinner at her apartment. Jesse and Jess were the first to arrive. Their faces were alive with enthusiasm as they recapped the adventure they had been through.

"So," Jess said, "Angela finally found a way she could get into the mine, through Ernesta, and then the old gal dies. That's gotta smart."

"Not only that," Jesse filled in, "Angela's brothers have testified that she paid them to steal the keys to the mine. When Detective Madden pressed them, they said she wanted to get into the mine before it became public property, which makes no sense. If we haven't been able to find opals for half a century, there's no way she's going to waltz in there and pick them up off the floor."

"There's never been any logic with Angela," Lisa said. "She's blinded by the anger and envy her family has kept stirred up for generations. Now, she's facing a jail sentence. What a waste."

Taylor and Asia came bounding through Lisa's front door. "Guess what we have?" Asia laughed with excitement. Lisa saw the same enthusiasm in Taylor's face.

"Okay, what's up?" She had no idea where they had been all day, or for a number of unexplained hours on other days for that matter.

Unrolling a set of plans on the dining room table, Taylor and Asia each stood to one side so she could see. "That's Jim Cook's old accounting office on the corner," she said. The plans showed an upgrade from Jim's frugal ideas. "These are great new designs. Who are you working with, Asia?"

Asia gazed with pride at Taylor and introduced him as the newest addition to the Tangle Grove renovation team.

Lisa's mouth dropped open as she saw the truth in Taylor's eyes. Still stunned, she asked, "So you're behind the corporation that bought Jim's place?"

"Not only Jim's, but also the two properties that Verina Fields sold off," Asia answered. She turned to the rest of the pages, revealing the new designs for the other buildings as well. "Dad's going to put in a bike shop, and he's already found a skilled mechanic to run it."

"This is a natural area for biking. The terrain offers everything a cyclist could ask for," Taylor said, grinning. "Besides, I need to have something to do if I'm going to retire here."

She ran into his arms. He held her, rubbing his cheek against her hair. She glanced up at his face, then followed his eyes and caught Jesse's concerned expression. Still unable to discern what was bothering her son, she felt apprehensive and let go of Taylor.

Jesse stood abruptly and moved to Asia's side. He took her hands and smiled into her eyes. Speaking loud enough for everyone to hear, he said, "Asia, I love you more than I thought possible. Will you be my wife?" There was an intake of breath as everyone except Jesse gasped.

Looking into his anxious face, Asia answered, "Yes, Jesse. Yes." Beaming, he pulled an extraordinary ring out of his pocket and slipped it onto her finger. It was the gift he had promised, the most stunning of the fire opals from the cave.

"It's gorgeous," Asia shrieked.

"It's a six-carat black opal," he explained. "I had it cut into a cabochon oval. See, the rounded sides allow the brilliant colors to be visible from any angle."

Asia tilted the ring for all to see. The exquisite stone not only exhibited the fire shades of red, orange, and amber, but was also flecked with green, electric blue, and aqua. And a diamond. The freeform gold setting fit smoothly on her finger.

"I added the diamond to make it an engagement ring," he said and kissed her.

Lisa knew the value of the opal could have purchased a small house, but she also knew Jesse had others saved. She and Taylor gazed with happy surprise at their children.

Jesse turned to them. "I was going to do this later, but you two were moving so fast, I needed to pop the question sooner." Seeing no comprehension in their faces, he spelled it out. "If you guys got married before we did, I'd be asking my step-sister to marry me."

Laughter burst from Lisa and Taylor as they understood the reason for Jesse's resistance to their relationship.

Jesse reached out his hand to Taylor, "I know it's a little late, but may I have your blessing on our marriage?"

Tears misted Taylor's eyes as he looked at his daughter's radiant face and then to Jesse. "I'd be honored to have you as my son-in-law," he said, shaking his hand.

Lisa hugged Asia and stepped to Taylor's side. Gazing at him, they shared a silent agreement to put off their own announcement until later and let the young couple bask in the glory of this moment.

Jess made his way over to congratulate his grandson and kiss his soon-to-be granddaughter. "I only wish Rose was here to see this," he said, still missing his lifelong love.

"I guess this has turned into an engagement dinner," Lisa laughed.

Standing behind her, Taylor wrapped her in his arms. While they watched Jesse and Asia show off her ring to Jess, Taylor whispered into her ear, "Thank you for allowing me to be a part of your amazing family."

Until that moment, she hadn't been aware of how much she'd lived without. Now she had a good man who loved her—and her family. Someone who wanted to share her vision.

One of the bible promises her grandma Klara use to say came to mind. She whispered, "I will pour out on you a blessing that is too big for you to hold." Her eyes brimmed and flowed over with gratitude.

THE END

Epilogue

Jesse and Asia planned their wedding for early spring. Asia invited her mother to participate, but she declined, stating that Taylor's presence was too stressful for her to tolerate. In addition, she had plans to be in France at that time. The situation had the potential to be emotionally disastrous for Asia, but it turned out to be a blessing.

Reveling in the fact that Asia would be her daughter-in-law, Lisa felt honored to help with all the shopping and details that needed handling.

Taylor and Lisa decided to wait until summer to marry so they could have the ceremony at the site of her largest undertaking, the Montebelli Inn. With one construction crew working on the courthouse, Lisa decided to hire a second company to build the inn. The contractor was certain he could finish by their August date, one year from the day they met.

One afternoon, Lisa sat in her new office on Main Street in Tangle Grove and placed the order for an extraordinary fountain from Italy. It would be the focal point in the courtyard of the inn. When she hung up the phone, a delivery truck pulled up and a young man brought in a small box and sat it on her desk. The package was from Anna Varano in Mont Castello.

"Curious," Lisa said and sliced through the tape. A leather box was enclosed. When she lifted out the timeworn object, a note fell out, addressed to her.

My dear Lisa,

This belonged to my mother, Bella. She was Adriana's best friend throughout her whole life. I have taken out the things I wanted to keep, but I thought you would like to read the letters Adriana sent to Mama. You should maybe go through the box when you have a lot of time, and a tissue.

I am glad to hear you will be marrying that handsome Mr. Taylor, he is a good catch!

All my love,

Anna Varano

Lisa started to open the box, but remembered Anna's words to save this treasure until she could devote her whole attention to it. She unlocked the bottom drawer of her desk, set the gift toward the back, and locked it again. She smiled. In time, she would open the box and learn the rest of the secrets of the Montebellis.

FIND OUT WHERE IT ALL BEGAN IN THE PREQUEL:

Adriana's Secrets

The betrayal alone would have crushed a lesser woman.

"If you enjoy romance, action, adventure and mystery, you'll love this book!" -Dana Rongioni, Author

"Absolutely powerful and so well written." - J. Savurbks, Book Reviewer

Visit the author at www.cherylcolwell.com

Made in United States
Troutdale, OR
05/29/2024